S0-ADZ-529

A Novel

CHERYL DELLA PIETRA

TOUCHSTONE
New York London Toronto Sydney New Delhi

Touchstone
An Imprint of Simon & Schuster, Inc.
1230 Avenue of the Americas
New York, NY 10020

First Touchstone hardcover edition July 2015

Interior design by Akasha Archer

Manufactured in the United States of America

10 9 8 7 6 5 4 3 2 1

Library of Congress Control Number: 2014032642

ISBN 978-1-5011-0014-7
ISBN 978-1-5011-0015-4 (ebook)

For Ty

CHAPTER 1

Everybody is laughing except for me. I'm scanning the faces, trying to remember names, as they listen to Walker Reade recite from his novel in progress. To my right sits Devaney Peltier—that's how she introduced herself to me, first and last name, like she's kind of a big deal. She's Walker's full-time girlfriend, and she's braying like a donkey, the act made more absurd by the rings of white powder encircling her nostrils like two tiny powdered doughnuts. Claudia Reynolds, the aging assistant, is curled up across from me, gazing at Walker in adoration, laughing the hardest. To my left sits Rene Wang—or *enfant terrible artist Rene Wang*, as he's been described, without fail, in the New York City media since the day in 1983 when he famously set dozens of roosters loose in Times Square in a performance-art piece he called *Koch's Cocks Can*. He's chuckling lightly, his lips pursed, eyebrows up—his "hysterical" look, I will later learn—as he taps a long ash from his Davidoff cigarette into the mermaid-shaped tray on the table before him. I don't have to work to recall the names of the other two people here. They're undeniably famous. Crushed up beside Rene, almost sitting in his lap, is former vice-presidential candidate George Stains, his head thrown back, lips glossed with scotch, a small drop of blood dried at the bottom of one nostril. And next to Claudia is Larry Lucas, former teenage heartthrob, now Oscar-winning actor, doubled over like a man passing a kidney stone. Everyone is in hysterics. The only problem is, I'm not sure what they're laughing at.

Devaney passes a large tray of cocaine to me—if it were flour, it would be enough to bake a small cake—and I smile and nod, as if she were handing me a plate full of mini-quiche. I have, to this point in my life, done exactly two lines of coke, with an ex–college boyfriend. He was filthy rich, and coke is what the filthy-rich college boys did when it was time to do drugs. I did those lines to try to fit in with his crowd—the same conundrum I'm weighing right now. To stall, I daintily perch the tray on my knee and listen politely. A notebook sits on the table in front of me. I brought it here to Colorado from New York City. It's a reporter's notebook, the kind I sometimes use for my own writing. I think it will be good for taking notes. I think it will show I am serious about wanting this job.

"That is so . . . *fucking* . . . *funny*, Walker," says Larry, as I try to keep my face from flushing. Larry Lucas, it's worth noting, played the leading man in several of the teen comedies of my adolescence and, suffice to say, played a leading role in more than a few of my teenage NC-17 fantasies. Under other, less overwhelming circumstances, I might be breathless about the fact that I can reach out and touch him.

"Y'all're'funny, Walker, baby," says Devaney, threatening to turn an entire sentence into a contraction.

When, after several more seconds of collective howling, my gaze drifts back to Claudia, I notice something: her eyes are open wide, unblinking, pleading. I can be a little dense in moments like these—too caught up in processing my surroundings—but I sense that she might be signaling me to do something. She's smiling at me wide and crazy, like some kind of insane puppet. Then it occurs to me a second too late.

I'm supposed to be laughing, too.

"Hey, *new girl.*" My head snaps toward Walker, and I reach for my notebook, still balancing the enormous tray I've yet to partake from.

Rene, sensing opportunity, reaches for the coke. "Let me help you out with that, honey," he says, his face entirely too close to mine. He snorts two quick lines and passes the tray to George, barely looking at him. The room is eerily quiet as I scan the faces once more. We're in Walker's living-room-cum-kitchen, the six of us arranged on his perfectly circular couch like numbers on a leather clockface. A round coffee table is at the center of the couch, and it holds the group's detritus: George's scotch glass and bottle of Dewar's, Rene's pack of Davidoffs, Claudia's Dunhill blues, Devaney's Newports, Larry's Heineken, an enormous unsmoked joint, the aforementioned mermaid ashtray, a matching dolphin ashtray, my highball of Wild Turkey, Claudia's glass of red wine, Rene's Metaxa sidecar, which I helped him mix in an effort at chumminess, and Devaney's vodka and cranberry. The tray of coke never really settles on the table. It just keeps getting passed around like it's crowd-surfing at a Hole concert.

The only way to get on and off the couch is by climbing over the back. The only person not on the couch is Walker, who is perched behind us on a barstool tucked into a long counter. There's little doubt about the message the seating arrangement sends: he's the captain on this ship of fools.

"*Hello?* Is she *alive*?"

"Yes, Walker, sorry," I say.

"What are you sorry about?"

I look around the room for another cue. Claudia is now focused on rolling a piece of lint between her thumb and forefinger.

"Go easy on her, Walker. She's just getting the lay of the land," Larry says.

Walker ignores Larry completely and fixes his aviator sunglasses on me. "*Speak, for Christ's sake!*"

My heart begins pounding so hard I can feel it in my ears. The strangers here probably wouldn't offer me more than mildly detached concern under normal circumstances. But now that everyone is coked up and drunk, I am little more than a buzzkill. I knew this outburst was coming one way or another. I knew from the books, the articles, the interviews. I have done my homework. Walker Reade does not suffer fools, and no one—not presidents, CEOs, law enforcement—gets a pass. I also know from said research that caving is worse. I square my shoulders to him and try to remain calm. "I was just listening, Walker. If I'm going to be your assistant, I need to know the story."

Walker stares at me now from over his sunglasses. His eyes are a pale steel blue. "That doesn't mean you can't enjoy it, too."

"But I *was* enjoying it. Very much." Walker worries his Zippo around in his hand. I can make out the skull and crossbones on the front of it every other turn. He grabs a Dunhill red from the pack in front of him; the room is so quiet that the *schk* of the lighter visibly startles Rene, who appears to run at two speeds: aggressively engaged or disconcertingly spaced-out.

"Then crack a smile, dumbhead."

George clears his throat and passes the tray of coke to Claudia, who immediately passes it to Larry. Everyone is quiet, waiting to see what's going to happen next, including me.

"I'm not dumb," I stammer back, sounding far less convincing than I had hoped.

"Oh, that's right," Walker says. "Alessandra here went to an *Ivy League* school." Devaney shifts uncomfortably on the couch. I can actually hear her teeth grinding. "It says so right here, on her thin résumé."

Walker pulls a piece of paper from a folder on the counter in front of him, and I visibly recoil. I'm a year out of college. The last thing I want is a staged reading of my résumé in front of this crowd.

"I thought it was great," I say.

"Which part?" He blows a cloud of smoke directly in front of him, seemingly unaware that it wafts directly onto Devaney's head.

In truth I cannot recall a single coherent passage from what has just been read to me, and I briefly wonder what superman at Burch Press is tasked with making this book readable. "All of it, Walker. It's really funny."

"All right. What does it remind you of? Which of my works does it remind you of?" He takes off his Tilley hat and sunglasses and downs the rest of his Chivas and water. Without his signature armor—aviators and hat—he's suddenly transformed from iconic writer/drug-addled playboy to unexpectedly sexy middle-school math teacher. He's only in his early fifties; I didn't expect him to be almost completely bald.

I can feel the clock ticking. What *does* it remind me of? I've read all of Walker's books many times over, except the last two—the penultimate one a collection of political essays regurgitated from various magazines, and the most recent one so poorly reviewed that I couldn't justify allocating even a fraction of my meager financial resources toward it. The previous five were so fluid and tight that nothing about what he's just read reminds me of any of them.

I glance back at Claudia. She's trying—and failing—to subtly mouth something to me. I look to Larry, who simply scrunches up his face and runs his hand through his thick, dark hair, winking, a gesture that I assume is intended to convey that this drill is somehow par for the course. Larry passes the tray of coke to Walker, trying to distract him.

"Here you go, big guy. Let's have some fun. When does the game start?" The crowd is ostensibly here for an NBA play-off game.

"Half an hour," Walker says shortly, passing the tray to Devaney while still staring at me. Rene lights up the joint, choking mightily on the first drag.

"Am I in a time warp here? Is time standing still for anyone else? I asked a *goddamn question*. What does it remind you of?"

"The second half of *The Wake*?" I say halfheartedly, referring to Walker's fourth novel.

Walker actually ponders this for a moment—surprised, I think, that I've answered him. After a long pause, he says, in overly dramatic fashion, "Why, oh *why*, can't I find someone with half a brain in her head to fucking help me? It's not like I'm trying to find a *neurosurgeon* with a pretty face. . . . You would think I was looking for someone to take notes in Mandarin . . . or separate water into its hydrogen and oxygen atoms. But I don't need any of that, do I?" Although this seems a rhetorical question, several people are, in fact, shaking their heads. "I just need someone who knows my books and has working index fingers to press a few buttons on my fax machine. Why on earth is this so hard . . . ?" He trails off before barking, "*Try again!*"

"I'm sorry, Walker. I don't know."

"What in the fuck do you mean you don't know?"

"It's very . . . *unique*." My mouth goes dry.

Rene cringes when I say the word. He passes the joint George's way.

"Well, looks like I have another moron on my hands. Where does Hans find these people?"

"Excuse me?" I say.

George pours himself another three fingers of scotch and takes the joint from Rene. It's jarring to watch George consume drugs like a cracked-out nickel whore. I mean, the man was once the state of Ohio and a heartbeat away from running the free world.

"Have you even read anything I've ever written, missy? You and your stupid notebook."

"Of course I have." Not only have I read all of Walker's early work, I have studied it extensively. You don't come of age in the 1980s as an aspiring writer without at least a passing familiarity with the oeuvre of Walker Reade. There had been a time, not long ago, when Walker Reade was not just a writer—Walker Reade was a Writer Who Mattered. Regardless, I sense that this is perhaps the wrong moment to tell him *Liar's Dice* is what made me want to write, or that his radical social commentary altered my worldview. I tuck the notebook behind my back and try to casually hold my drink. Every move I make now feels conspicuous.

"You hate it," says Walker.

"I don't."

"If you're going to be out here, you have to tell me the truth. That's what you're getting paid to do!"

I briefly consider reminding him that I'm not getting paid anything until he officially hires me. This is my three-day trial period. Even if I survive this, I won't get paid until he delivers some real pages. That is what I've been told the deal is.

"Walker, go easy. It's her first day," Claudia says.

"Walker, baby, let's go do something *fun*," says Devaney,

popping up from the couch like a character in a musical. She passes the tray of coke to me.

Walker ignores her, goes into the other room, and emerges with his seven books, every one a hardcover. He stacks them on the counter. *Biker* . . . bam! *Liar's Dice* . . . bam! *Ship of Fools* . . . bam! *The Wake* . . . bam! *Crossroad* . . . bam! *Rabbit Hole* . . . bam! *Traffic* . . . bam!

"To the cabin," he demands, pointing my way out the door. "And don't come back over here till you've read these—no, *memorized* these. . . . *And are you going to do that fucking line or what?*" I stare down at the tray of coke I've been holding entirely too long for this crowd. I've been a bartender for three years. I'm a drinks girl, not a drugs girl. I'm horribly ambivalent about the tray in front of me. Too ambivalent, I think, for this place. I pass the tray to Rene and attempt to scuttle over the back of the couch, thinking I've just fucked this whole thing up in less than an hour. My shot. I grab the books, feeling hot down my neck, as I hold my head high—as if my literary hero hasn't just called me an idiot—and retire to my quarters.

CHAPTER 2

It's hard to believe that Claudia is the same age as my mother—fifty-two. If I could conjure split-screen, time-lapse films of their lives, here's how it would look. On the left side of the screen would be Claudia's sun-dappled San Diego upbringing; on the right, my mother's grim childhood in Naples, Italy. While Claudia is building sandcastles and drawing sideways looks from surfers, my mother is scrubbing floors by hand and learning to wring chicken necks. . . . While Claudia is rushing headlong into a brief, restless marriage to a Ginsberg-quoting grad student, my mother is entering the enduring, passionless bond with my father that would beget me and my three older brothers. . . . And while Claudia today bears the sex- and drug-weathered beauty of Joni Mitchell, my mother remains steadfastly committed to her lifelong performance art: a wash-and-set homage to Anita Bryant in her orange-juice-loving, gay-hating days.

Claudia has been Walker's personal assistant for more than twenty years and, as I am learning, plays an unenviable host of roles. In just my first hour, she has seamlessly morphed from mother to confidante to punching bag to secretary to drinking buddy. She's taken each gear at top speed—a marvel, if exhausting to watch—yet never once appeared in danger of crashing. My one-day take on their relationship: it's an amplified version of most bad marriages.

"Don't worry about it. He likes you," Claudia says to me when she comes back to the cabin. It's ten minutes since I've been banished from the party, and I'm lying on the couch reading Walker's most recent book, *Traffic*—the one I hadn't read.

"Yeah, right."

"Trust me, he does. That excerpt *was* like the second half of *The Wake*. Wildly mediocre. You were spot-on. He just couldn't lose face in front of those guys."

"This last book I really hadn't read. It's not that bad."

She ignores the comment and lights a Dunhill blue. I notice her fingernails are unpolished and cut to the quick. "More to the point, *I* like you." Many things about Claudia put me at ease, not the least of which is her voice. It has the timbre of a gentle, distant foghorn, the product of apparent decades of chain-smoking. It looks like her last haircut was several years ago; her dirty-blond mane hangs almost to her waist. In short, I like her, too. But I'm also not fooled by her whole white-poet-top-and-blue-jeans hippie act. She's clearly the anchor on this listing ship, and if I want to stay out here, her approval could mean everything.

"Any advice on how to not get eaten alive?"

"Why do you think I'm over here? First, tell me honestly: Are you scared?"

"No," I lie.

"Honestly?"

"Okay. A little." It seems better to couch this as minor nerves rather than the teeth-rattling terror it actually is.

"Don't be. Or, at least don't show it. You actually did pretty well back there, standing up to him. He doesn't like a pushover. Do you like steak?"

"I love everything about steak."

"Well, good, because we don't eat much else around here. There's a ranch up the street, and Walker buys a whole cow from George and freezes it. Come sit with me in the kitchen. And bring that notebook."

I follow Claudia into the kitchen and watch as she turns on two cast-iron skillets, then sprinkles salt in the bottom of one. She slices a bunch of wild mushrooms—which, I will later learn, she foraged herself—and grabs a stick of butter, a lemon, and some Worcestershire from the fridge. From the pantry she pulls down a black-pepper grinder and a bottle of scotch.

"This is Walker's favorite. It'll be done in a minute."

Once the pans are screaming hot, she grinds the pepper onto two rib-eye steaks and throws them in a pan, chucks a tablespoon of butter into the other pan, and throws the mushrooms in. When the steaks have seared, she flips them, puts a pat of butter, lemon juice, and a few shakes of Worcestershire on each, along with two turns of scotch in the pan, dips the pan into the gas flame and takes a half step back as the whole thing ignites. She pours two glasses of cabernet and spoons the mushrooms and steak and its juice onto our plates. Not a motion is wasted. Nary a thought is devoted to the acts. The entire production takes maybe fifteen minutes.

Before I even start eating, Claudia takes a Dunhill blue from its pack and lights up. She never asks me if I smoke or if I mind. She just shakes another up from the pack and points it toward me.

"No thanks, Claudia."

"Okay, take out that notebook. Rule number one: stop saying no."

"But I don't smoke."

"You were smoking at Walker's."

"Well, I only smoke when I drink."

"Start drinking then." She pushes the wineglass toward me.

"Okay, okay." I take the cigarette and lean into the Bic lighter Claudia is cupping in front of my face. She retrieves a starfish-shaped ashtray from the dish drain and sets it down between us.

"Walker does not like to party alone. It's a deal-breaker if you're not going to partake. That's as plain as I can put it."

"Wait. He's going to force me to do drugs?"

"Of course not. No one's forcing you to do anything. He just won't ask you to stay. As plain as I can put it."

"Got it." The idea of "partaking" with Walker Reade is not undaunting. Walker's drug abuse is legendary, the very backbone of his most famous works. I have no idea, aside from The Tray, what else might be coming my way.

"Rule number two: don't get caught up with the celebrities. Walker is famous people for famous people. Everyone wants to say they did a line with him or shot a gun with him. It's Rome out here. There's a lot of 'When in Rome . . .' People misjudge sometimes . . ."

"Okay."

". . . what they can handle. What they're doing."

"Okay . . ."

"Just try to stay focused."

I am writing furiously in my notebook about guns and Rome, but I have no idea what Claudia really means. I can't yet. "You're saying this because of Larry?"

Claudia gives a quick nod. Apparently it wasn't all my imagination—Larry Lucas was kind of checking me out. "Larry's a nice guy, but it's just better to not be involved with anyone while you're out here. If you stay, you'll get enmeshed with Walker—you have to in order to do it right. With him, with his book." Claudia starts to continue but stops, once and then twice, rolling the end of her ash around in the bottom of the tray. "The book . . ."

"Yeah, the book."

Claudia takes a long drag and tamps out the remaining half of her cigarette. She takes a bite of steak and a sip of wine, then leans back in her chair. "It's awful. You know that. But all of a sudden, there are a lot of mouths to feed out here, mine included. At this point, we just need pages. Lionel will fix it." Lionel Gray is Walker's longtime editor at Burch Press. "You're the first person out here who I really think might be able to do this."

"What on earth makes you think that? You don't even know me." I put my cigarette out, too, and finally start eating. The steak is one of the greatest things I have ever tasted.

"I know people." She dips a piece of steak into the scotch sauce. "We've had two kinds out here: smart people who were no fun, and fun people who were not smart. Walker needs someone who can be everything he needs when he needs it. Plus, you strike me as a little more grounded than some of the characters we've had. Walker teased you about your schooling because the last Ivy Leaguer we had out, princess needed her beauty rest. She couldn't do a single toke without spiraling into paranoia, for God's sake."

"Well, my father is the only person who ever called me princess, and that was with a healthy dose of sarcasm, so I think we're safe."

Claudia lights up another cigarette midchew and picks up her wineglass. "Do you have a boyfriend back home?"

"Sort of. Sort of not." Claudia nods firmly, as if she intuitively understands the pathetic nature of my current love life. As if she knows everything there is to know about Tom—the rich kid from Long Island who has been booty-calling me for two years. All of this seems loose enough to Claudia's satisfaction. I am effectively free of distractions. No fiancé is going to show up at the doorstep wondering about anyone's intentions out here—though I'm not sure I can say the same about my brothers.

"What's the deal with Devaney?"

"Don't worry about her." Claudia waves her hand in front of her face. "Walker's already bored and it's only been three weeks. But he made her quit her hostessing job to stay up here full-time, so that's one more mouth to feed. If she gets in your way, you tell me. My guess? She'll be gone in about a month."

"Okay."

"Your job: keep him writing. Hours: in general, I'm the day shift and you're the night shift. We'll overlap some of the day, but I won't get in your way, and you won't get in mine. It's just easier that way."

"Define day and night." Something tells me this is not as obvious as it seems.

"I take care of Walker's affairs from eight to eight, then I retire to the cabin. You come over when he asks for you—usually sometime around three in the afternoon—and work all night with him. The general rule is hands on the typewriter by two a.m."

"So, wait. What happens between three p.m. and two a.m.?"

Claudia lets out a sharp laugh. "Let's put it this way: anything *can* happen. You'll see." I'm trying to make sense of the math but can't—eleven hours before any work potentially starts?

Claudia pours me more wine. "Okay. Now put the notebook down. You'll see. Don't worry."

"Hold on. One last thing: He still uses a typewriter? It's the nineties for crying out loud."

"Yes. And he hunts-and-pecks, too, so it takes long enough even when he's on his game."

"Does he even own a computer?"

"There's a Mac Classic and a printer in the den. I don't think he even knows how to turn them on. You're welcome to them."

"Okay . . ."

"Look, he's not a total dinosaur—he just fell in love with the fax a few decades ago—and, you know, old habits. . . . Nothing's going to change, so you have to adapt. I presume you know how to use a fax machine?"

"I've been an intern at *Beat* for almost a year. My index fingers work."

"Good."

I take another cigarette from Claudia's pack and light it. "About tonight . . ."

"Here's rule number three: keep your skin thick. Walker gets mean, but it's just from 'the drug.' He's not dangerous. He won't hurt you in any way. And he will apologize. Trust me, he's going to ask for you tomorrow when he gets up. So be ready."

I ponder the meaning of the phrase *be ready*. I have no idea what that means out here. For a normal job I would do as I've always done—keep my eyes open and try to act right. But I have a feeling that in this job it might feel better to close those eyes, like I would on a roller coaster or a plane that's going down. And I have even less of an idea of what "acting right" means out here. Maybe it's simple, like Claudia said: Relax. Drink more. Smoke up. Say yes. If The Tray comes my way, a few lines won't kill me. If that's what it takes to ensure that I never again have to put ice in a shaker while some guy from Jersey watches the pour on his Long Island Iced Tea, well, that's a price I'm willing to pay.

I finish helping Claudia wash the dishes and retire to my

spartan bedroom—little more than a full-size bed, a small card table that I suspect is to serve as my desk, and two shelves of books built into the wall. I pull out a picture of my family, one taken at a party they threw a year ago, before I left for New York—my mother looking every bit like the caterer. Her brow is furrowed. She has one hand on a tray of eggplant, another on a bottle of Frangelico. She's pouring cordials for my dad and uncles, who are playing boccie on our front lawn, but she's clearly not happy about something—most likely that I'm leaving. I pull out another photo from the same night of me with my three older brothers: Mike, Stefano, and John Dante. We're on one of the West Haven, Connecticut, beaches, wading in Long Island Sound. I remember how shortly after the photo was taken I was unceremoniously thrown into the water. The overriding emotion registering on my face in the picture: a visceral restlessness that even my smile can't mask.

I take out a third photo, of Tom and me at a graduation party at his parents' estate on Long Island. Tom has never called himself my boyfriend nor I his girlfriend, though we have mutually violated each other regularly since our senior year in college. Ours is a deeply confusing bond, charged by our both knowing that Tom is slumming it with me. In college I served food to him and his frat brothers at the dining hall. Now that we're both in New York, little has changed. A year out he's already making gazillions of dollars doing something boring and morally sketchy in finance—a job Daddy was glad to hand him. Meanwhile, I'm working for free at a magazine, slinging drinks to amateur alcoholics on Bleecker Street, sharing a mouse-infested studio with my old college roommate. Tom's nothing that I have to actively deal with right now, which is nice. Still, I'm glad I have this picture, just in case I need it.

I place the photos on the shelves drilled into the wall next to my bed and peruse the book spines: P. J. O'Rourke, Ken Kesey, Timothy Leary, F. Scott Fitzgerald, Jane Austen, Ernest Hemingway. The younger of these are Walker's contemporaries, although Walker's literary niche—the blurring of the line between fiction and truth, coupled with scathing political discourse and an almost mythical ingestion of drugs—is his and his alone.

Then I take out my own manuscript—a book I have been working on since college. Working title: *Pegasus.* Perhaps the notion of a horse with wings who carries Zeus's thunderbolts might seem an inappropriate metaphor for a book based on the life of a twenty-two-year-old recent college grad. But getting this book published is mostly the reason I've decided to come out here, and I'm desperate to conjure whatever lightning strike I can.

I only have one duffel for this, my three-day trial period, after which I will either be asked to go home to pack and return—or go home for good. I rummage in the bag for my pj's, make myself comfortable, and curl up in bed with Walker's book. My lids grow heavy around midnight, and even though I'm tired, I find that sleep does not come easily. Claudia's words keep coming back to me. *Be ready.* Months later, when I recall this moment—me, having smoked just two cigarettes; me, with trouble falling asleep; me, with my little notebook at the ready—it will all seem so unbearably quaint, so ridiculously naive, I'll think I've remembered it wrong.

CHAPTER 3

"Good morning, Sunshine." Walker says this without a trace of venom as I step into the breezeway, the screen door squeaking, and I'm flooded with something like relief. I've lived to "audition" another day.

"Good morning," I say cheerily, turning into the living area, although I gather the term *morning* is used loosely around here. It's 3:15 in the afternoon, and Walker is sitting on the barstool where he was yesterday, only now a Selectric typewriter is on the raised counter in front of him. To his right is a window that looks out onto the front of the property. Next to the window is a cabinet, and underneath that is a CD player. Behind him is a stove and a microwave; in front of the long counter is the circular couch and coffee table. On the far wall, past the couch, is the largest television I've ever seen—easily four feet wide. It must weigh two hundred pounds. CNN is on with the volume off, and a Lyle Lovett CD plays quietly in the background. From this position in the room, Walker can basically cook, work, play music, watch TV, socialize, and monitor the front yard, all without moving an inch. He is in a light blue cotton bathrobe, like one you'd find at a luxury summer resort, smoking a Dunhill red cigarette with a filter on the end. He's sipping a black coffee that Claudia prepared for him before I was asked to come over. Next to the coffee is a large glass of scotch and water.

"How'd you sleep in our oxygen-deprived mountain air?" Walker's compound is a mile and a half above sea level, which I will find annoying later when it takes me three tries to bake a respectable cake.

"It's not any worse than New York. Pollution-choked versus oxygen-deprived. Kind of a wash."

I see the edges of Walker's mouth turn up ever so slightly, and I start rummaging through the cabinets and the pantry on the other side of the room. Between Claudia's admonishments and my own intuition, I decide I must do two things: act like I can take charge of a situation, and do something fun. I also need something to calm my nerves. Drinks seem an obvious way to accomplish all three.

The pantry contains an inordinate number of canned goods, enough to survive on for a few months if you weren't afraid to ingest that much sodium—although if last night's cokefest is any indication, any actual sodium probably gets snorted around here. There is a veritable Warhol installation of Campbell's soup—about two hundred cans—plus green beans, baked beans, black beans, tuna fish, crabmeat, baby shrimp, chickpeas, carrots, tomato sauce, baby corn, mushrooms, canned salmon, hearts of palm, beets, white potatoes, artichoke hearts, chili, green peas, pineapple chunks, mandarin oranges, sauerkraut—even a few cans of SPAM.

"Did you raid some school's hunger drive or what?"

"What are you, from the ATF? What are you looking for?" I had seen in the news that the Bureau of Alcohol, Tobacco, and Firearms had actually paid Walker a visit recently, so this joke is not without an edge.

"A pitcher."

"Behind the bar, for Christ's sake."

I glance around the room, taking it all in, in a way I was incapable of doing last night during my initial "interview." The decor is best described as deer hunter meets sports bar meets quilting bee meets *Architectural Digest.* Walker, I will later learn, likes to tell people that he lives in a "crude log cabin," but it's the outskirts of Aspen in 1992, not Abe Lincoln's boyhood home. For all of the debauchery that apparently goes on here, there are still smart leather coasters, handmade quilts, hand-carved African masks, and vintage guns—comforting touchstones for someone like me who expected bong water in her coffee cup, not the Maxwell House Walker pours for me now. I poke back behind the bar in the living room and find a two-quart, cut-crystal pitcher.

"Jeez, you could kill a man with this." I grab the handle and curl it like a dumbbell. The thing must weigh ten pounds.

"You can kill a man a lot of ways," Walker says offhandedly.

"Is that supposed to creep me out?" I grab a cigarette. Walker has three packs in front of him. His Dunhill reds, the English cigarette that he smokes through a short filter, along with a random pack of Marlboros and a tin of colored Nat Sherman party smokes, presumably leftovers from yesterday's gathering. This seems as good a time as any to start saying yes, so I take a Marlboro red. "May I?"

Walker cups a Bic lighter in front of my face and hands me the mermaid ashtray. He motions for me to sit on the stool to his left, leans over with his left arm, and starts rubbing my right shoulder; his eyes are clear and soft, like a panda's.

"Sorry about last night, sweetheart. I don't know what gets into me sometimes."

"It's okay. You're right. I wasn't as prepared as I should have been. I'm actually glad I got the opportunity to read *Traffic.*" Here I decide to lie: "I thought it was pretty fantastic."

"You did, huh?"

"Yes. Come to think of it, that's what last night's reading reminded me of. Chapter six. You know, the way the whole thing is paced, the tension between them, the audacity of the crime spree, the whole Bonnie-and-Clyde subtext, the humor . . ."

Walker doesn't say anything but continues to knead my shoulder, staring directly at me. This goes on for so long that the point of sizing me up comes and goes. He's so close I can smell him. Walker Reade smells like Irish Spring, tobacco, and whiskey. He smells like men used to smell. After a few more minutes I can't tell what the point of this staredown massage is if not, in fact, to simply release some tension in my neck. His hands are large and strong. The man can give a massage. Then it just becomes awkward. I finally break eye contact, reach for my cigarette in the tray, and take a long drag.

"Marlboro reds, huh? That's a real cigarette," I say finally.

Walker stops kneading but leaves his hand on my shoulder. He's closer to my face than I'm usually comfortable with, but it's not menacing in any way. "Who do you think you're dealing with, sweetheart?"

I place my left hand on Walker's right shoulder so we are now face-to-face. "Don't worry," I say, now looking at him straight on. "I'm well aware you're a real cowboy." I take another drag and blow the smoke out of the side of my mouth—either succeeding in looking cool or failing miserably by trying too hard. My radar out here is jammed.

"Hmph," he says, releasing his hand and reaching for his own cigarette. "What's the pitcher for?"

"Bloodies, of course. Where *is* your spice rack?" I ask, getting up.

"Hot dog! Now we're talking."

He points to a cabinet and I rummage through, taking out black pepper, celery salt, regular salt, Tabasco sauce, and Worcestershire. I pull a can of tomato juice from the floor of the pantry—one of about a dozen—and find an opener and a wooden spoon in the drawer next to the sink. Walker looks at his watch and pulls out a yellow envelope from the cabinet.

"Can I presume that you have cowboy boots?" I ask. "Don't they make you buy them when you enter this town?" The cowboy boots, as I noted upon landing, did not discriminate in the Aspen airport: they were worn with equal contrivance by anorexic plastic ladies with black leggings, midlife-crisis fat-guy wannabes, gay guys, Hollywood types, and actual real cowboys.

"None that I wear. Larry gave me a pair of snakeskin boots, but it's not really my speed." Indeed, if Walker parties like a rock star, he doesn't appear to dress like one. Yesterday he had on a polo shirt with khakis and Converse Chuck Taylors, looking more Mister Rogers than Keith Richards.

"I didn't realize there was a speed you couldn't handle," I say, opening all of the spices and pouring the tomato juice into the pitcher. Having worked the brunch shift at a midtown-Manhattan hotel bar, I know from Bloody Marys. I add all the spices, stir the whole thing, and give Walker a taste from the wooden spoon. His eyebrows go up.

"You're overlooking the difference between not being able to and not wanting to," he says.

"You take horseradish?"

"Nah, it's perfect."

I find a bottle of Stoli in the freezer—three actually—so I fill two glasses with ice and pour a shot and a half of the vodka into each one. I top it with the bloody mix and pour each glass into an empty cocktail shaker and back again. I cut two lemon wedges and hang one over the side of each glass.

"Thank you," Walker says. "Cheers." We clink glasses as Arkansas governor Bill Clinton appears on the TV. He's running for president, pressing the flesh at a California rally. The ladies seem to love him.

"This fucking scuzzball," says Walker, shaking his head. In addition to his semiautobiographical novels, Walker traffics in political commentary (often brilliant) and sportswriting (often on drugs).

"What's wrong with him?"

"Fuck. Look . . . if Clinton is elected, you're going to get someone who really believes his own bullshit. And that's dangerous."

"As opposed to?"

"I don't know . . . Nixon."

"Nixon?!"

"He lied with a straight face. So what. They all lie. Don't get me wrong: I never loved Nixon. He was a filthy sow of a human being. As depraved as they come. But at least he never *believed* his own lies. He was just a straight-up crook." Walker turns to me quickly, as if he's just remembered something. "Speaking of scuzzballs, stay away from Larry."

"Excuse me?"

"I saw you two last night."

"Cripe, Walker, I said maybe four words to Larry."

Walker takes a plastic bag from the yellow envelope and dumps about a half cup of cocaine onto a plate; far more than that remains in the envelope.

"You were having eye sex. Everybody could see that. Trust me, you're too smart for him."

I know from Claudia that Larry spends about half of his time off set at Walker's. "If you think he's so dumb, why do you have him out here so much?"

"Because he knows how to have fun." This is Walker's shorthand for *he can ingest truckloads of drugs.* "Plus, he's accomplished. You forget that Larry's got an Oscar. He's not even thirty." Larry Lucas is well-known—and frequently mocked—for his unnecessarily immersive approach to the craft of acting. Five years ago, in an attempt to shed the teen-heartthrob label and be taken seriously as an actor, he traded in his famously gelled mane for an unkempt shag, a prosthetically enhanced brow, and oversize glasses in an effort to portray a mentally challenged man who wanted nothing more than to marry a mentally challenged woman in a weepy treaclefest called *To Be Happy*. The movie was a shameless rip-off of the Shaun Cassidy vehicle *Like Normal People*, except it wasn't made for TV, and it won Larry the Academy Award for Best Actor in a thin field that year.

"Then he must be pretty smart."

"Trust me, he's not. That dumbass couldn't find snow in Alaska." Walker starts cutting lines with a Visa card. When he puts the card down, I notice the expiration date.

"You know that's a good card, right?"

He takes a look at it, as if considering for the first time that it could be used to purchase actual goods and services.

"Well, look at that. This expires in 1994. Fuck me. I've got to talk to Claudia about that."

Devaney emerges from the back bedroom in a pair of Walker's boxer shorts folded over at the waist and an oversize, yellow T-shirt that's slipping casually off her left shoulder, no bra strap in sight. She does a line and pours herself a cup of coffee. Walker playfully reaches over to grab her ass, and she swats him away and flops down on the circular sofa, facing the TV. She grabs the remote, flicking around until she settles on a talk show. There is something about Devaney I envy—how she fits in here so casually, doing drugs, looking sexy. More than that, I'm hoping she'll satisfy Walker's desire for someone to do lines with him right now.

"You want a Bloody, Devaney?"

"No," she says shortly.

"Turn that crap off," Walker says. "I'm watching something."

"News, news, and more news. It's boring. It's the same dang stories over and over."

"Give me the remote," Walker says evenly.

Devaney takes the plate of coke and does one more line, then slams the remote down on Walker's typewriter. She grabs her coffee and retreats back to the bedroom.

"Don't worry about that," Walker says, waving his hand, as if I might for some reason be concerned with the complexities of Walker's go-to tail, which doesn't appear all that complex: He's fifty-two years old. She's half his age, talks like Scarlett O'Hara, and looks like a young Debbie Harry. End of story.

"I'm not worried," I say. "And don't worry about Larry. What are we doing today anyhow?"

"Well, we have to start by getting you some clothes first." He says this as if it were the most obvious thing in the world, as if I've lost all of my clothes in some unfortunate natural disaster. He does a line and hands me the plate.

"What's wrong with my clothes?" I'm wearing a black, long-sleeved shirt, black jeans, and black leather shoes.

"You look, I don't know, *Amish*, for Christ's sake. Like an Amish funeral director. It's almost impossible, your look. Terrible. Depressing. A waste."

"Thanks, Walker. You really know how to make a girl feel good." We both stare down at the plate. I'm thinking of all of the ways I've compromised my dignity for a job—the basic drudgery of what I've done up until now. The dining hall, the bar, the unpaid internship. These jobs were all supposed to lead somewhere—to some job like this one. If I have to compromise for this one, too, at least it will get me someplace I actually want to go. I lean in and do my first line with surprising gusto, tasting the bitterness of the postnasal drip.

"It's a compliment, missy. I'm saying you have potential." He takes another sip of his drink. "Plus, you make a damn good Bloody."

"I know my look's a little drab, but it's not exactly tragic."

"Trust me, it's tragic. Then we have to go harass that jackass Henley."

"Who's Henley?"

Walker just rolls his eyes. "Then we need to get some flowers. Then we have some dinner. Then we shoot some guns. Then we have some fun."

"When do we write?"

"Later."

We're quiet for a moment, sipping the drinks, when I begin to feel the cocaine. Then suddenly I am keenly aware that I am most definitely, *wow*, feeling the cocaine. The two lines I did with Tom had barely done a thing for me, but this . . . this is Walker Reade's drugs. They're good. If I had to describe the feeling, it would be "reset." I am ready. For what I'm not sure, but whatever the hell it is, I'm in. "I looked over your pages last night," I say.

"You did, huh?"

Walker changes the channel back to *Crossfire* and puts another CD into the player—Dire Straits.

I'm about to open my mouth when Walker declares, with no room for argument, "Fuck the pages. Go put some makeup on, for Christ's sake. You're going out with me."

CHAPTER 4

"I'm not coming out."

"Come on, let's see."

"Um . . . no."

"Don't make me come in there," Walker says.

"Actually, I don't mind if you come in. I just don't want anyone else seeing me in this getup. It's absurd." We're at a trendy boutique in downtown Aspen, and Walker has picked out six outfits for me to try on. This, the first one, makes me look like I'm in the evening-gown competition for Miss Puerto Rico. I open the door a few inches, and Walker's eyes pop wide. "I'm letting you in here on one condition."

"What *now*?"

"One page. Later tonight—whenever. But one page before I go to bed."

"Fine. Just let me see."

I open the door and catch the saleslady eyeing me in the mirror as Walker comes in, slamming the door behind him. It's obviously not the first time he's been here with a young lady.

"Hot dog! See, I knew you had potential." I am wearing a fuchsia minidress.

"Walker, this is not me."

"Exactly. Remember, your clothes are hideous."

"Okay. I get it. Is there no happy medium here?"

"Do you really think I've gotten to my place in life by searching for happy mediums?"

"Fine. But do we have to inject your philosophy of life into my wardrobe?"

"I'm the one who's going to have to look at you all day and try to be inspired to write something. Plus, I'm paying. So technically it's my wardrobe."

"What does that make me, then?"

"Right now? A very underpaid and mouthy mannequin."

"Ouch. Can I not maintain some dignity here?"

"Overrated. You look great. *Sold!* What's next?"

"Turn please."

As I'm changing, Walker turns away and pulls what looks like a small cigarette case out of his pocket. He takes a small spoon from its side, opens the case, and does a quick hit of coke.

"Okay, really, this is too much." It's a fishnet shirt with a built-in bra. Walker has chosen a miniskirt to go with it. "This is, I don't know, stripper on her day off."

"And who doesn't love a stripper going to Home Depot? You look great. Here." He hands me the cigarette case. The earlier line has worn off without incident. I do another hit.

"Does this not reek of the worst kind of objectification?"

"Oh my *God.* When was I teleported to a women's studies seminar at Vassar?"

"That's your answer?"

"Yes. C'mon, this is fun. Loosen up, girl. Number three."

"Around."

Walker turns and does another quick hit. I can hear the saleslady pacing outside.

"Everything okay in there, Mr. Reade?" she says, a thinly veiled hysteria rising in her voice.

"Good God, woman. Leave us alone!" he barks.

"Walker, that's rude."

"What, I'm fucking spending money in here. Lots of money."

The next outfit is a surprisingly conservative tennis dress with spaghetti straps and built-in shorts.

"Cripe. What fantasy is this fulfilling?"

"The Tracy Austin one. Here."

I eye the cigarette case and recall Claudia's words. I sure as hell can't analyze each line put in front of me. I shove the spoon up my nose again, and suddenly, again, everything kicks in. I am *awake*. Twenty cups of coffee awake. We both start talking a little too quickly over each other.

"I look like jailbait."

"You are jailbait."

"I'm twenty-two."

"I repeat—"

"The official definition of *jailbait*—"

"You think I don't know the official definition of *jailbait*?"

"I'm old enough—"

"It's more a state of mind, sweetheart."

"What about Devaney?"

"Not as close as you'd think."

"Mr. Reade, may I help your friend find any sizes?" The saleslady is speaking slowly and deliberately now, loudly, like she's asking for directions in a third-world country full of deaf people.

"How many different ways would you like me to tell you to go away?!"

I can tell this woman is seriously torn between wanting to rid her establishment of two questionable coke fiends and minding her monthly commission.

Now I'm just trying to get us out of there. "What are we doing next?"

"We're fucking with Henley."

"Who's Henley again?"

"Just shut up."

"You shut up."

"*Mr. Reade . . . ?!?*"

"Christ almighty! Just take everything. We'll get everything. Let's just get the hell out of here."

The other three outfits are a red cocktail dress, a cowgirl skirt and ruffle top, and a pink tracksuit.

"Leave that one on," he says, waving his hand up and down at the tennis dress. In the name of expediency, I do.

We head out to the counter, where the saleslady is standing nervously, lips pursed. She eyes me disapprovingly, as if this were all my idea.

"You'd think we weren't spending thousands of dollars in here," Walker says, twitching for a fight. "You'd think we were about to suffocate a kitten in here or something."

"Or something." She looks at me and quickly brushes her nose.

I do the same and a shocking quantity of white powder falls from my finger.

"Is this how you treat all your customers?"

"No," she says pointedly. "All of this?"

"Yes, no thanks to you." As she's ringing, Walker goes to the back of the store where the shoes are. "What're you, a seven, Alley?"

"Yes . . . exactly."

Walker comes back with two pairs of sky-high heels—black, open-toed sandals and shiny red pumps.

"These, too."

"That's 1,256 dollars." The saleslady softens her tone slightly. "How are you paying?"

"Cash, sweetheart. That's how." Walker pulls a giant wad of hundred-dollar bills from his front pocket and peels off thirteen of them.

"Thank you, Mr. Reade."

"It's about time I got some fucking thanks around here."

The saleslady puts the clothing and the shoes into four bags and hands them to me with two judgmental fingers on the rope straps. Outside, we spill back into Walker's red convertible, a 1973 Chevy Caprice Classic. Some version of this car has played prominently in many of his books; I almost can't believe I'm sitting in it. Walker tucks my bags into the floor of the backseat and starts rummaging around.

"What are you doing back there?"

"Prep" is all he says.

I turn around, and Walker is wrestling a large contraption from underneath a blanket and mounting it onto the back of the Caprice with what appears to be a giant suction cup. Magnets might also be involved. This homemade machine appears to be the love child of a bullhorn and a battery-operated double-cassette player and looks like it was made in someone's garage after that someone smoked a huge amount of pot. Either that or it was stolen from a seventh-grade science fair. He puts two tapes into the machine.

"What the hell is that?"

"Buckle up. We're off to Henley's."

We make our way back up the mountain near where Walker lives but take a sharp left before his house, winding farther up the road until we reach a neighborhood of what appear to be newly built mansions. I had always imagined one bought a mansion for privacy, but these seem to be inhabited by people who either couldn't afford the privacy or had some misguided fantasy that they would be a part of a "community." In front of me, about ten mansions are huddled close together in a development, like a parking lot full of mastodons. Several cars are parked in their respective driveways, but not a single person is in sight.

Regardless, it's time for Walker to start the show. He pulls the car to the curb, reaches in the back, turns the machine on, and resumes driving. Suddenly, simultaneously, two sound tracks overlap at an earsplitting volume. One is "The End of the Innocence," and the other is of a woman engaged in a strenuous bout of hog calling. It sounds something like this—"Offer . . . *Sooey* . . . up your . . . *piggypiggypiggy!* . . . best defense . . . *Sooey!*"—and the effect is several things at once: mesmerizing, horrifying, and hilarious. Every so often, as we drive slowly around the neighborhood, a window opens or someone comes out on their porch to see Walker, cheering him on. A few folks snap photos. And then I see him: Henley. Henley is *Don* Henley, and he has the look of a man who has been long tortured by Walker's nonsense. He eyes us coolly from the top window of his house, his precious Top 10 hit getting the shit beaten out of it by a wild hog. I am doubled over laughing—the coke making it easy to laugh wildly, hysterically, at Don Henley's angst—as Walker puts the car in park, stands up, and shoots Don Henley the double bird. Henley just shakes his head and retreats into the shadows.

Walker makes his way back to the main road and pulls over. He pulls a bottle of Tanqueray from underneath the seat and hands it to me.

"Ugh. Italians can't drink gin." I'm not just saying this because I hate gin. I could kill a man after a single martini. Walker fishes under the seat and pulls out a bottle of Gentleman Jack.

"You got cocktail nuts under there, too?"

"This is for courage. Drink."

I take a long swig from the bottle. "What do I need courage for?"

Walker fiddles in his pocket and pulls out what look like two small postage stamps with purple pyramids on them.

I stare at them and mentally chronicle the litany of clichés that will justify taking one. *When in Rome . . . Seize the day . . . You only live once . . .* Then I remember something my brother John Dante used to say: "You want to hang with the guys? Then grow a pair."

"Want one?"

Normally I might be more cautious. But now, here, in the front seat of the Chevy, slightly coked up, wearing a tennis dress, whiskey on my breath, Walker's other hand on my knee, I realize that this question is merely rhetorical. I'm in now. More important, Walker is inviting me in. I pick up one tab of the acid and place it on my tongue, Walker starts chewing on the other, and the car lurches forward.

Von Gundy's Garden Center is a retailer that has applied the expansiveness of a big-box store to something more intimate—flowers. When you are tripping on the finest acid in the universe, the place is nothing short of a miracle. Walker and I are holding hands, smiling wide, and walking through the aisles like two children in a Stevie Nicks song—while rainbows aren't exactly present, or unicorns manning the aisles, the glorious *feeling* of them is, as we go from the purple-peony aisle to the red-impatiens aisle to the yellow-daisy aisle. Endless aisles of greenery are here as well—ferns, potted plants, small trees. Walker grabs a large flatbed dolly and I climb aboard. He steers through the aisles, stopping here and there so I can pick up flats of golden marigolds, pink pansies, red begonias, white geraniums, and purple petunias. We head to the checkout, and I am lying on the dolly, surrounded by the flowers. Walker is looking down on me, smiling a devilish grin, his filtered cigarette hanging out of his mouth, unlit.

"You look amazing," he says.

"I feel fucking amazing."

"Here." He hands me a stick of peppermint chewing gum. "You're going to hurt your jaw." I am aware that I am grinding my teeth—a vague sort of awareness, like being aware of global warming but unable to do a thing about it—but I don't feel a thing. It takes me about five minutes to unwrap the stick of gum as I lock in on the folds of the wrapper and the noise it makes through my fingers. I roll the gum up and pop it in my mouth.

I look at Walker quizzically, as if the meaning of the universe has just been opened to me, as if I've just discovered antimatter. "*God . . . damnit*, peppermint is so good. *Why* have I never noticed this before?"

Walker chuckles as his jaw works the filter of his cigarette—the affectation, I realize later, built expressly for this purpose. The woman at the checkout is all business, and she works around me, using the handheld scanner to ring out the flats. She doesn't even notice Walker, though when they finally make eye contact,

I can tell she recognizes him as the crazy man who comes here often with drugged-out girls in bright dresses, but she clearly doesn't know *who* he is. I sit up on the flatbed as she continues to scan. She is beautiful and detached, with caramel skin that glows. I have no idea what she's doing working checkout here. It seems to me she should be a swimsuit model or the multi-culti candidate in some beauty pageant. She looks so lonely. She only speaks once to announce the total: $1,123 and change. Walker again takes out his wad of hundreds and peels off twelve bills.

"Keep the change, sweetie. And lighten up, already."

Her expression barely changes. "Thank you, sir."

We head back into town and pull into Poppies restaurant—a local fine-dining institution. Walker grabs a gun from beneath the blanket in the backseat, along with a backpack, and hauls out a large potted plant that we got at Von Gundy's and puts it on the ground.

"Holy shit. What in the hell is that?"

"A backpack."

"No. The other."

"A fern."

"No . . . the *other*."

He considers the gun for a moment. "A telephone . . . What the hell does it look like?"

"A gun."

"A Taser gun, actually."

"I thought we were going to dinner."

"We are." He says this like it's the most obvious thing in the world that we'd be bringing a weapon to a quiet candlelit dinner. I'm already teetering mentally—the acid making me feel exposed and jumpy—but I'm trying to remain casual, together. Or at least some approximation of what casual and together might be, were I not whacked out of my skull. There is the added layer of my wanting to impress Walker. I want him to know that I can handle whatever he throws at me. I'm hoping this is the peak of the trip.

"Why do you need a Taser gun?"

"You just never know."

"You usually only bring a gun to a gunfight."

"See, that's where you city folk have it wrong. Shut up. Stop worrying. And get the fern."

It's seven, and a fair number of tables are full. For a split second when we walk in, the restaurant goes completely silent as everyone processes Walker's presence—then the opposite occurs, with everyone speaking a little louder than normal. Or at least that's how it seems to me. Walker and I are still flying high as we approach the host, who greets Walker warmly.

"Ron. How's it going?"

"Just fine, Walker. What can we do for you tonight, sir? Can I check any of that for you?" Ron gestures toward the gun, backpack, and potted plant with no evident sign of alarm, which instantly puts me at ease. Maybe this is what they do in the Great American West—they bring weapons into fine-dining establishments because they can. Check them, even. Because they can. Just in case. Walker palms Ron a hundred-dollar bill and asks for a table.

"Of course. Right this way." We are led to a large six-top in the back of the room. Walker takes the plant from me and puts it in front of us.

"What is this for, again?"

"Hiding, you moron." By now every patron is staring at us.

"I know you are trying to hide, but this is really drawing *more* attention to us, don't you think?" I will later on try to make the same argument to Walker about his aviator glasses and Tilley hat—the signature trademarks that he thinks lend him anonymity but, in fact, broadcast his presence like a sixty-foot neon sign.

"Nonsense." He smiles broadly at me. He hasn't stopped smiling for an hour. I open the menu, and the words start shifting around. A third of the menu appears to be in French, a third in English, and a third in some language I can't begin to comprehend. Urdu? Esperanto? Regardless, my eyes can't seem to focus on two distinct words that would convey a foodstuff, and my heart begins to palpitate wildly.

"You have to order," I say, fingering a leaf of the fern, trying to calm myself.

"No problem." Walker signals to one of the waiters. "Garçon!"

A small man with wire-rimmed glasses comes over. He's wearing a black vest with a red tie. "Are you ready to order, Mr. Reade?"

"I like your tie," I say to the waiter. "It's awfully dark in here, Walker."

He ignores me and starts ordering. "Yes, uh, let's have five of the porterhouse steaks . . ."

The waiter looks puzzled. "Each steak is for two people."

"Right. I guess you're new here. So, five of the porterhouse steaks. Very rare, please. Then we'll have three orders of the double-cut pork chop. Two of the fettuccine dishes. Two grilled salmons. Four Caesar salads. Two iceberg wedges. One clams casino. One clams oreganata. The raw-bar tower. A side of creamed spinach. A side of potatoes Anna. A side of french-fried potatoes. And, for dessert, a key lime pie."

The waiter is writing furiously. ". . . a piece of key lime pie."

"No, *the whole pie*. Actually, *three* whole pies."

"The walls, Walker," I mutter, trying hard to sound as blasé as possible about how the whole restaurant suddenly seems to be breathing. Or maybe it's just me. Maybe my breath has gotten really loud. I'm holding on tight to the menu. Although I have that sinking feeling that people who are having a heart attack probably have—that something is new and not right inside their own body—I have suddenly lost the ability to convey what, exactly, is happening to me. So instead I just sit, mutely clutching the menu, trying to appear normal.

"Something to drink?"

"Two shots of Wild Turkey, and a bottle of the Lafite."

"The Lafite?"

"Of course, the Lafite. Get on that, son."

"Right away, Mr. Reade."

The waiter scurries back to the kitchen, and we are soon awash in service. The movement is comforting. Someone is decanting wine. Someone else is pouring water. The two shots of Wild Turkey appear, as if by magic. Walker nods toward me, and we down the Turkey in one gulp.

"I don't know if I'm being normal, Walker. Do you know what I mean?"

"Of course I do. We're not. Trust me, we're not. Let the Turkey settle in."

"Are all of these people staring at us because we're tripping—not acting normal—or because you're Walker Reade?"

"Both."

"Either way, it's starting to freak me out."

"Stay cool, sweetheart. You're okay. You'll get used to it. Just ride it. Don't let it ride you."

When our order begins to arrive, it's like a UN food drop—if

UN food drops were delivered to acid-trippers with little to no appetite. The appetizers come, which we barely touch. Then the salads, which also remain untouched. Then the steaks and chops and pasta. It seems as if all of the food is here for some reason—to look at or play with or think about, as if we are in some fancy-food museum. I'm not quite sure what to do with it, but eating it never crosses my mind. We just keep lighting up cigarette after cigarette and drinking the wine. Then I make the grave error of gazing too long at the pasta.

"The fettuccine. Walker . . ."

Walker looks over and starts laughing. He's chomping on his cigarette filter. It keeps going up and down. Up and down.

"It's not terribly funny. This shouldn't be happening."

"Why not?"

"Are you seeing this?" My stomach lurches. "Are you getting this? Please say you're getting this."

"Calm down. Calm down. But, yeah . . . Sure . . . Of course . . ."

The fettuccine is making its way across the table from the far end, seemingly multiplying on its way toward us. It wouldn't make sense that Walker would be seeing the exact same thing. But whatever he's seeing is apparently pretty strange, too.

"Hmm," he chuckles. "I think it's time to go. Garçon!"

Three waiters appear. "We need all this to go . . . ASAP!" Walker grabs the bottle of wine. "And the check."

I spy the bill as Walker removes the last of the cash and a credit card from his wallet. The $3,000 in cash we'd started the day with is all gone. With the wine and a 30 percent tip, the whole thing comes to about $1,500. The waiters accompany us to the car, where, among the flowers, they attempt to fit the eleven bags of food and three pies. I am carrying the fern.

"We should have done this at a less expensive restaurant."

"Why?"

"I don't know. You just spent on this meal what I live on in a month."

"That's no way to live, sweetheart. You're going to learn that out here if nothing else."

Once we are outside, away from the darkness of the restaurant, I suddenly, shockingly, immediately feel better. Great, actually. My heart stops palpitating. My stomach ceases lurching. We go for a drive, fast on the highway, and it's exactly what I need: the wind through my hair, my head thrown back, and my eyes closed. Walker's hand gently smooths my hair, and I smile.

CHAPTER 5

The grounds at Walker's property comprise his house and the cabin, a large garden area with a peacock coop next to it, and a vast expanse of land behind the main house that serves as both an oasis of privacy and a de facto shooting range. The peacock coop houses four actual peacocks, who spend most of their time roaming the grounds like a cocky group of land surveyors. As for the shooting range, I know Walker's collection of firearms numbers in the hundreds. The compound is surrounded by a barbed-wire fence and a large locked gate at the end of the driveway. Walker has a devoted following that ranges from Ed Bradley to the drugged-out kook who was recently arrested here, loitering at the edges of the property. The pilgrims travel from far and wide to catch a glimpse of Walker, leaving manuscripts (which go unread), bongs (which are completely redundant), and booze (which is only consumed if unopened) in their wake. They deposit these offerings at a makeshift shrine outside the gate composed of a menagerie of several carved, wooden animals—coyotes, owls, a panther, a llama—a scrap-metal windmill, an inappropriately sexy Gorgon, and one large brass pig. As we pull up to the gate, Walker gets out of the car and quickly, almost furtively, walks behind the pig. He glances over both shoulders, kneels behind the sow, and unlatches what appears to be a small trap door in its ass. He pulls out a large, yellow envelope and goes to open the gate.

As Walker slides back into the car, I see Claudia and Devaney sipping red wine out on the front porch, admiring the sunset. They're sitting at opposite ends of the single long table that takes up most of the space—Claudia poring over a checkbook and Devaney reading *The Firm.* As Claudia eyes the car coming up the driveway, her face is a crossroads of emotion. Her smile is wide, but her eyes scream worry. There is no mistaking the look on Devaney's face. She's pissed.

"Well, what have we here?" Claudia says, walking up to where we've parked.

"We brought dinner. And flowers. Some clothes." I can see Claudia mentally tallying the respective tabs. With one quick look into my eyes she knows we're tripping.

"You two having fun?" Claudia starts taking the bags of food out of the car. Devaney is pretending to read as she drains the last of her wine.

"Devaney, get the hell over here and help Claudia," Walker says. "You, too," he says to me. The three of us snap to attention. Claudia hands the bags to Devaney and begins hauling the plants and flowers over to the garden area. Through the clarity of my trip I see Claudia in a different way—the selflessness she wears like a halo, the love for Walker in every move she makes, even as she's stepping in peacock crap.

"Hey!" Walker is snapping his fingers in front of my face. He shoves the bags of clothes into my hands. "Everyone inside!"

Inside, however, as I rediscover, is the last place I want to be. We're still tripping pretty hard, and once we enter the kitchen, the whole room-breathing thing starts happening again. I have the distinct sensation of being an air molecule trapped inside a set of asthmatic lungs, and I'm having a hard time getting comfortable. As we unpack the bags, Devaney opens one of the porterhouses and the potatoes and grabs a fork and knife from the dish drain. She looks both hot and menacing with the steak knife poised above the porterhouse—like a porn star in a horror movie—but she's seriously freaking me out.

"You guys are doing the pyramids without me?"

I would love to know how exactly Devaney is aware that we're tripping, but I suppose it's made obvious by the way Walker and I pace nervously around the kitchen, our pupils dilated to Keanian proportions. Walker's still carrying the bottle of red wine from Poppies, and he offers it to Devaney like a penance. She eyes the bottle and a grin breaks over her face.

"The Lafite." She takes a wineglass from the cupboard and pours it to the rim. "You're forgiven. Now get out of here. This one looks like a caged animal," she says, pointing at me. I do not, at this point, know Devaney's exact age, but she and I are probably only a few years apart—still, she talks and acts like she's at least a decade older. I'll find out later that she's been living on her own since she was sixteen.

Walker takes my hand and leads me down a hallway opposite his bedroom. At the end of the hall is a room with a hot tub, a TV, and a minifridge. Another full, stocked bar is to the right of the hot tub. To the left is another door—at first I think it's a wine room of sorts, but when Walker flicks on the lights, we are completely surrounded by guns. He takes down a rifle and hands it to me.

"Holy shit."

"This is a .22, a lady's gun. So act like a lady when you use it." I nod, having no idea what this means. Am I supposed to curtsy? Not pick stuff out of my teeth? I hold the gun gingerly, as if it's going to explode all on its own. Not only have I never handled a gun, I've never even seen one up close.

"For Christ's sake. It's not going to grab your tit."

I grip it more firmly, completely convinced it'll go off at any second, as Walker takes a huge gun off the wall.

"And this is a .44. A man's gun."

"It's all a little phallic, isn't it?"

"A *lot*. Follow me."

We head through the sliding glass doors of the hot-tub room outside to Walker's shooting range. A variety of targets are set up—life-size figures of Ronald Reagan and Marilyn Monroe among them—and stick-on exploding targets with bull's-eyes on them. Walker sets a target on a large piece of mounted plywood and walks back about twenty yards. He motions me over to where he stands—I'm both spacing out on how the wind looks through the trees and stroking the cool handle of the rifle like it's a baby anaconda I'm trying to soothe.

"Come here."

I don't have to tell him I've never held a gun. It's obvious. He stands behind me and we aim the rifle at the target. Since I've never held a firearm, I have no idea what's going to happen. I am also still tripping, so any ideas I have are probably wrong. I decide to just trust Walker. I can feel his breath in my ear; he smells like expensive red wine; his body is solid and still around me, tamping down my fear. He puts my index finger over the trigger and we pull, the gun kicking back slightly. We miss the target. I only hear the *ziiing* of the ammo going through the air. That wasn't so terrible.

"Shit. Fuck it . . . you won't miss with this." Walker pulls the Magnum out and wraps his arms around us. He's holding me close, telling me where to look. He's warm against me, making the gun feel even cooler. The .22 made me feel like a pioneer woman shooting squab for supper. The Magnum gives me a penis—a really big penis.

"Pull it."

I do. Three things happen simultaneously: The .44 kicks back, throwing me to the ground. The exploding target explodes. And I realize I'm almost totally deaf. Walker is laughing like a madman.

"Oh my God," I say, staring at the sky, unable to move. "Can you hear anything?"

"What?" It sounds like Walker is a half mile away.

"Fuck." My ears are hot and ringing. I'm sure this is permanent.

"*What?*"

"Jesus, Walker." I can now only hear these words inside my own head; I could be whispering them.

"You hit it! You're a pretty good shot!" Walker screams.

I can barely make out what Walker is saying. I look over and see the plywood smoking. "I can't fucking hear anything."

"What do you need to hear?" Thankfully, when he says this—with the conviction that only a man on drugs can muster—it sounds slightly louder. "Come on, get up."

He grabs both of my hands in his and lifts me up. Our faces are about an inch apart, and with the sun coming down, the steam of our breath mingles together, even though it's on the verge of summertime. Walker looks directly into my eyes; his are sparkling in the setting sun.

"You're a real cowboy, too, you know?"

I'm fairly jaded for twenty-two. I don't remember the last time I felt "thrilled." But hearing these words from Walker—from his mouth—sends a hot, little spark through me.

He takes me over to a bench on the outskirts of the range and lights up two cigarettes, handing me one. We sit there for a long time, guns on the ground, chain-smoking. A breeze cuts through the tall grass and the trees, as darkness falls over the range. The air smells like smoke and juniper. Walker's arm is around me as we stare toward the sky. My ears are still ringing, but less so now. I am relieved to hear the sweep of the wind.

"I'm just about tapped out. You?"

"Yeah," I say, something like disappointment registering in my voice.

Walker picks up my rifle and hands it to me; he picks up the .44 and takes my hand. "Let's go eat. We have work to do."

Back at the house, Walker puts the guns away while I begin reassembling a nice supper for us. According to Claudia, this will be part of my job—to make things "nice," give Walker a happy place in which to write. I take out one of the sizable porterhouses and pop it in the oven along with the creamed spinach. I rebuild the seafood tower as best I can and put two of the Caesar salads in a serving bowl. Walker comes into the kitchen, a bottle of red wine under his arm, and grabs a corkscrew. I pour us two glasses of water and put two wineglasses on the counter next to Walker's typewriter. I notice a handful of index cards on the counter to the right of the typewriter, arranged neatly in two rows. On them are curiously self-helpish creeds, such as *Do it now* and *Problems are opportunities in work clothes.* While Walker doesn't exactly strike me as the "artist's way" kind of writer, I'm not about to make fun of the cards. The guy has a National Book Award and a Pulitzer. He must be doing something right.

Even though I have only been here for two days, Walker and I settle into a comfortable rhythm as we putter about the kitchen.

Walker sits to the left of his typewriter and I sit next to him, just as we were this afternoon when he was rubbing my shoulder and apologizing, which feels like it happened several days ago as opposed to only seven hours. I carve the porterhouse, place a half dozen slices on each of our plates, and spoon salad and creamed spinach on the side. Walker pours the wine and the two of us sit, watching a basketball game, largely in silence. Walker stops halfway through the meal and pours the other half of the cocaine from this afternoon on a tray. He cuts two lines, does them both, then passes the tray to me. I place the tray to the side, figuring I've earned a break, and finish my supper while Walker lights a cigarette. Every once in a while he yells at the TV.

"Fucking Clyde Drexler. He has all the intensity of a fucking deer in the woods."

"What exactly does that mean?"

"He just . . . lets it happen to him . . ." Walker trails off and reaches across me for the tray. He cuts two more lines and does them, then cuts another and passes the tray to me. This seems like a more pointed invitation, and I do the line, even though between the acid trip, the coke at the clothing store, and the alcohol I've consumed today—and continue to consume—it seems utterly redundant. Still, I'm exhausted both physically and psychically, so the by-now-expected pick-me-up, the moment it kicks in, is welcome. I clear the plates with manic vigor and wash them as Walker puts a piece of paper in the typewriter and starts hunting-and-pecking away.

"I'm glad to see you're keeping up your end of the bargain," I say.

"Meaning what?"

I look down at the ridiculous tennis dress I'm still wearing. "You know, you said you'd write a page if I wore these silly clothes."

"You do look silly." Walker leaves this hanging out there. He could have said it conspiratorially, as if it were all in good fun, but it comes out mean. It doesn't take Betty Ford to figure out that once the coke comes out, the gloves come off. "All day you've been in that stupid outfit making a fool out of yourself."

I say nothing and take a sip of wine.

"What are you writing?"

The last word is barely out of my mouth before Walker jumps in. "What the fuck do you mean, 'What are you writing?' *Great Fucking Expectations*. What do you think?"

I look at Walker evenly, searching for a clue. He's not budging. "Maybe I should head back to the cabin for a bit?"

"*Leave?* You can't *leave*. I'm going to have an assistant who *leaves* every time things get a little rough? Maybe you're not cut out for this, sweetheart."

"I am, Walker. What do you need?"

"Hint hint: *this is the job interview.* Any moron can shoot a gun with me and snort my coke. So here's a clue: I need you to stop asking me what I need. That's what I need you to figure out." He goes back to typing, and I figure that perhaps he has some inspiration. To lighten the mood, I head over to the wall of movies next to the TV, where a quick glance confirms that Walker's taste runs from the classics (*Scarface*, *The Godfather*), to vintage porn (*Caligula*, *Deep Throat*), to that genre of eighties road movie built on the thinnest of premises (*The Great American Traffic Jam*, *Cannonball Run II*). I put in *Dog Day Afternoon*, do another line for solidarity—maybe one of the stupider things I've done tonight as an involuntary twitch settles into my right cheek and my palms start to sweat—and make my way to the fridge. I find an entire bag of limes and then head to the bar and grab a bottle of Cuervo and some triple sec. From the dish drain I take the pitcher I used for the Bloodies this afternoon and a hand juicer that Claudia uses for Walker's orange juice. I cut the limes in half and start juicing them right into the pitcher, squeezing them with a cocaine-fueled aggression that would be hilarious to me were I sober and watching myself with some degree of remove.

"Good call," says Walker, though I'm not sure if he's referring to the film or the pitcher of margaritas I'm mixing. "Call over to the cabin and see if Devaney wants to come over."

"Okay." I go into the back room that serves as an office and dial the cabin. Claudia picks up. I can hear Walker typing away in the kitchen. "Hey, Claudia."

"Alley. You okay?"

"Yes."

"For the record, when I said, 'Stop saying no,' I didn't mean for you to never say no. Only about three people who've ever come out here could really keep up with Walker."

"I'm good," I say, even though my facial twitch won't let up and my palms are excreting stigmata-like buckets of sweat. "He's typing."

"He is? Hot dog! Good."

"He wants to know if Devaney wants to come over. I'm mixing margaritas."

"Oh, great. Great. Yeah. Whatever he needs. I'll send her over."

"She's coming," I say as I walk back into the kitchen. "Rocks or salt?"

"Both." I take three highball glasses and two plates from the cupboard. On one plate I pour a thin film of the triple sec; on the other I shake some coarse salt. I dip the rims of the glasses into the triple sec, then coat them with the salt. I take ice from a tray in the freezer and fill the glasses, then pour the margaritas, garnishing each with a wedge of lime. Devaney comes in looking spruced up in a white, eyelet top and a pink jersey miniskirt straight out of the Walker Reade collection. Even though she saw me before, this is the first time she registers the tennis dress.

"How's your serve?" she asks, grabbing a margarita.

"Apparently not as good as yours," I say, eyeing her up and down.

"Well, I know how to play the game."

"At least I'm keeping it inside the lines."

"You don't serve aces though, sweetie."

"Are we, like, done with this extended metaphor?"

"With what?"

"Girls," says Walker. "Come on. I'm working over here."

"What're you fixin' to work on, baby?" Devaney slinks behind Walker and starts massaging his shoulders. The word *girls* rings out too true right now. No matter how professional I'm trying to be, it's hard not to feel like one more coked-out, drunk "girl" tending bar in a tennis dress around here.

"The book," I say.

"A letter," Walker says.

"What letter?" I ask.

"To Hans."

"Bauer?"

"Yes. Be quiet."

Hans Bauer is the editor in chief of *Beat.* He and Walker have been friends for more than twenty years—friends . . . or associates . . . or mutually beneficial parasites. It is, as Claudia has already hinted, a complicated relationship. Devaney and I sip on our margaritas and pretend to watch the movie.

About fifteen minutes later, Walker pulls the letter from the typewriter and hands it to me. "Okay, prospective assistant. Read it." I start scanning the page. "Out loud, for Christ's sake."

"Dear Hans: You are nothing but a sell-out corporate greedhead trying to take advantage of your writers. How am I supposed to survive on a measly $10 per word? If you want your ski lodge to remain standing and free from immolation, I would cough up double. I have mouths to feed."

"You want more money for the excerpt?" I ask. *Beat* is publishing chapter 1 of the book—the chapter that was read aloud the first day I was here—as the September cover story, a gesture by Hans that has taken on the gloss of a favor—or compensation for his having canceled Walker's regular political column last year after almost two decades.

"Gosh, you're quick. Fax it."

I head over to the fax machine and see *Hans Bauer* on the programmed phone numbers. I press 2 and the pound sign, sending the sheet through. When the confirmation sheet prints, I place it with the others in a box next to the machine. Devaney goes and sits on Walker's lap.

"There. Your first editorial task. Well done."

"Now what?" I ask.

"Now you get the hell out of here." Devaney turns around, and Walker's hand falls to her ass. "Good night."

"Good night." I grab my drink and head over to the cabin. Claudia is still awake, scrutinizing a datebook, with a glass of red wine. A cigarette is burning in an ashtray.

She nearly jumps when she sees me. "Well?"

"Well what?"

"Are there pages?"

"Not exactly."

She visibly deflates, and a cringe crosses her face. "A letter then."

"Yeah. To Hans."

Claudia lets out a long sigh. "Please tell me he didn't ask for more money?"

"Kind of."

"Please tell me you didn't fax it?"

"Hmmm. I didn't know I wasn't supposed to. Why?"

Claudia's head drops.

"I'm sorry, Claudia. I've been here two days. I don't know what I'm supposed to do and not do. Walker asked me to."

"We need to save Walker from himself right now. It's the fourth letter he's sent this week to Hans. No reply."

"I didn't know."

"I know. It's okay. Look, I'm heading off to bed. You should get some rest, too. You've had quite a day."

"Yeah, okay. Claudia . . . ?"

"Yes?"

"What exactly is my job description here? I don't know what I'm supposed to be doing."

"You're doing it. Atmosphere. Fun. Inspiration. The clothes, the drinks, the guns. Just make it fun. But pace yourself. The pages will come."

"That's it?"

"Yes, and hands on the typewriter by two a.m. No matter what."

"Thanks."

"Get some sleep."

Claudia heads off to bed and I sit in the living room, wondering what tomorrow will bring—if Walker wants me to stay or go. I consider what it took for me to accomplish what I did, which wasn't much—the sheer quantity of liquor and drugs, not to mention the adrenaline still coursing through my veins, keeping me up now despite my exhaustion. I go into my bedroom and take out my own manuscript—the novel I've been working on since college—and stay up for another hour, editing and rewriting, but mostly taking myself back to baseline. I am lulled by the scratch of pencil on paper, the comfort of my own thoughts. I know I'm pinning too much on this book, but I sense I'm holding in my hands the one thing I can cling to out here—if I'm asked to stay.

I nod off somewhere around two in the morning. About an hour or so later, I hear the cabin door open, and something is shoved under my bedroom door. When I wake up at 9:00 a.m., a screaming hangover locked on my brain, I see that it's not one page, but two, for Walker's novel. At the top of the first page, in Walker's signature scrawl, is *A promise is a promise.* On the second page at the top Walker has written, *Go get your stuff tomorrow and get back out here. Hurry.*

CHAPTER 6

Lionel Gray is a New York City book editor as such a creature might appear in a movie. He wears an ascot and wing tips with no visible irony. His graying hair is slicked back just so. His office boasts a mahogany desk. Leatherbound compilations of the complete works of Shakespeare line the wall—as if he makes his way through act 2 of *As You Like It* over his '21' burger, ordered in. Pictures of two children are on his desk, a boy and a girl, who might be twins. They look like they have been raised by a team of well-paid staff, and I wouldn't be surprised to learn that they are currently ensconced in some outrageously expensive boarding school—even though they appear to be about ten years old. It's just that contrived.

As I sink into the red-leather chair opposite Lionel's desk, I keep waiting for tea service from a willowy assistant—or whatever else it is that happens in a movie about a book editor. Instead I get Lionel Gray's steady, withering stare. Lionel has been Walker's editor for decades, and he's seen many versions of me before in recent years—the one who is going to be different from all the others.

"Mr. Gray."

"You're Alley."

"Right."

I'm trying hard not to feel self-conscious in this cheap suit—trying hard to sell it. But Lionel is the kind of person with an eye for bad stitching and poly blends. He could probably sniff his way to the exact rack at Strawberry where I bought this brown pantsuit for $30. I'm completely broke; it's as simple as that. My only other new clothes are the ones I got in Aspen, and the pink tracksuit isn't exactly screaming *reliable*.

"Not *totally* what I expected," he says.

"Is that a good thing?" My voice comes out casual and old and chummy.

"We've had quite a parade of assistants out at Walker's."

"I've heard, from Claudia."

He pulls my résumé from out of a folder, as if looking at it for the first time. "Hmmm. *Playboy* college fiction-contest winner? *Beat* internship I knew. *Harper's* internship. Penn grad. Okay, you're smart. But Walker needs more than smart. Sometimes those cocktail waitresses get more out of him."

"Well, it's funny. Rose hooked me up with Walker mostly because she knew I was also a bartender." Rose is Hans Bauer's longtime assistant at *Beat*. I was one of the few interns who didn't treat her like the help, and she rewarded me with the lead for this position when it came across her desk.

"Well, that's a start. Here are the facts, between you and me: Walker's blown through most of his advance, but his books still sell. Shit, that one two years ago was a compilation of old crap, and it sold almost a million copies. People buy what Walker puts out. It's that simple. But Walker spends. He took almost a million-dollar advance for two books. Deadlines have come and gone on just this first one. We need pages."

"I understand that, Mr. Gray. I think I can deliver this."

"Well, everyone thinks they can . . . at first." This line probably comes out more ominously than intended, but I don't flinch. "We both know you're too young to really be qualified as his editor. So you leave that up to me. I need pages I can work with. Just get him to write. That's it. Whatever you get out of him should be faxed to me as soon as humanly possible. Understood?"

"I get it."

"Those two pages you sent were very good. So you must be doing something right. Plus, they were actually legible." He laughs a little at this. "Don't tell me Walker is finally getting computer savvy?"

"Actually, that was me."

Lionel is evidently used to receiving Walker's pages straight out of the typewriter, complete with Walker's handwritten edits in a scrawl normally reserved for prescription writers. But after Walker slipped the two pages under my door, I typed them into the Mac Classic, which I had moved into my room at the cabin, and . . . well . . . I guess one could say that I tweaked a few things myself. Nothing big, but there had just been so many missed opportunities, it had seemed senseless to let them pass. I knew enough to know that Walker's prose, at its best, has a certain volume, and on those pages, the volume was way too low. After I made my edits, I printed the two pages out fresh and faxed them to Lionel. Only later, after a good night's sleep, did I question the wisdom of this move.

"Just keep them coming."

"I'm on it."

"I'm sure you are." He rests his hand on his chin. His wedding band looks huge. "So here's the deal. Eight assistants have come and gone in a year and a half, and I have a mere fifty pages to show for it. I've paid good money for these eight assistants, but no more. It's too hard to tell who's just out for the party. So this job is now one hundred percent incentivized. I need the rest of this manuscript in decent shape in six months. You deliver, you get twenty-five thousand dollars. You don't, you get a pretty interesting line on your résumé. This isn't negotiable. So, are we clear?"

"Got it."

Lionel leans back in his chair and puts his hands behind his head. "You'll have to give me that *Playboy* piece. You working on something bigger?"

"Yes, sir. Nearly finished." My novel is based on the *Playboy* piece—my Ivy League tell-all. I've been working on it for almost two years. I can't even imagine what it could become in Lionel Gray's hands. I don't want it to appear as if I'm angling for my own business, but I figure if I don't do it now, I might not have the chance again; I'm front and center with Lionel Gray.

"It'll be ready about the time I turn in Walker's manuscript," I blurt out.

Lionel smirks. "There'll be time later to talk about that. Just get back out there and get to work."

After my meeting with Lionel, I take the Metro-North train to New Haven, Connecticut. My parents live in West Haven with two of my three brothers, John Dante and Stefano, twenty-four and twenty-six, respectively. My oldest brother, Mike, twenty-eight, is married and lives less than a mile away. My three brothers work with my father at his plumbing business—and have long tried to get me to do the same.

In truth, it was not *me* that the Russo men wanted at Russo Plumbing. What they wanted was a *version* of me who would answer phones and clean up the basement. A version of me in jean shorts and a Russo Plumbing T-shirt with a double process and full manicure. A version of me who would happily fetch Italian subs from Harry's Deli at lunchtime and be sweet-yet-firm to the customers on the other end of the phone. A version of me who would fry chicken cutlets with my mother, even in the dead of August, wash dishes, get married—provide grandchildren. The problem, for them, is that that version of me never materialized, leaving everyone deeply confused about what I'm really up to—and why. No one understands my ambition. When I got into college, the conversation with my father went something like this:

"College? Good for you, Cat. You'll be the second. Talk to J.D. You doing business like him?"

"No. I want to be a writer."

"A writer? Like newspapers?"

"Like novels."

"Oh, good."

"I already got in."

"To what?"

"College?"

"I know. You just said. Southern, right?"

"The University of Pennsylvania."

"Where the heck is that?"

"Philadelphia."

"Are you trying to kill your mother?"

"No . . . It's an Ivy League school, Dad."

My dad paused. "I'm proud of you, Cat. But why you gotta go there just to write? Go to Southern, like J.D. It's cheap and good enough. Who's gonna pay? You've gotta tell me if I'm gonna have to pay."

"I'm not asking you to. I got a partial scholarship."

"Let me know what you need."

"I'm good."

"Door's always open. When you come back. Door's open."

Of the whole exchange, it was that last thing he said, the reflexive notion that I would fail—the "when"—that set me on fire. It was all I needed to get me through.

My brother John Dante picks me up from the train station in the twenty-year-old Cadillac he restored himself. When I lean in to kiss him, he smells like Drakkar Noir and motor oil.

"So . . . ," he says.

"So what? Does this thing even have seat belts?"

"Stefano says you were out in Utah or something." His hands grip the steering wheel a little too tightly, and I notice his fingernails now look like my dad's—cracked and filthy.

"Colorado."

"What the hell were you doing out there?"

For the first time I process the plush, red seats. "Did you reupholster this?"

"Yeah, last summer."

"I feel like I'm in a mobile Turkish brothel."

"I wish. What were you doing out West?"

"Interviewing to be a writer's assistant."

John Dante nods, his faraway look betraying the slightest jealousy. "Anybody I'd know?"

"His name is Walker Reade."

J.D.'s eyebrows shoot up. "Walker Reade?"

"You heard of him?"

"I'm not an idiot, Alley. I went to college, too, you know. Of course I've heard of him." J.D. got his degree in business administration from Southern Connecticut three years ago. In addition to solving basic plumbing issues, he keeps the books for my father's business. "I'm just not sure that what I know about him would suggest that he's all that good for you."

"What?"

"The drugs? The drinking? The young chicks . . . like you? You must think I'm some kind of idiot. I know things about him, Alley. I read *Liar's Dice.*"

"Calm down, J.D. First, I don't think you're an idiot, so stop saying that. Second, I'm smart enough to know a good opportunity when it comes my way. He's actually pretty normal. Do you really think I'd put myself in danger?"

"No, but why can't you just get a real job? You paid all that money for that school and you can't even get a real job?"

"In case you hadn't noticed, there's a recession. And what I apparently didn't realize when I plunged myself into debt for my diploma was that the degree doesn't get you the job. The connections do. And I don't have any. So maybe *I'm* the idiot. And second of all, it's Walker Reade. *Walker Fucking Reade*, J.D."

"Hmmm." He stops at a light and looks at me squarely. Apparently he's on assignment. "Dad asked me to see if you'd come home for the summer and help out."

"What?! Huh . . . help with what?"

"Stuff for the business. We're expanding."

"Yeah, that's not happening."

"Just for the summer. We all know you're on your way to becoming a famous novelist," he says in a smart-ass way that makes me want to slap him in the face.

"Look, J.D., you have to admit this opportunity could put me on the right track."

"Yeah, if you survive . . . maybe."

I roll my eyes not so subtly. "Right, J.D. I just busted my ass putting myself through an Ivy League school. I've done two of the most prestigious magazine internships in New York. I won the *Playboy* college-fiction contest. I'm broke and up to my eyeballs in debt. And I'm going to sit on my ass all day and, what, order parts? Answer phones about shit-clogged toilets and schedule drain snakes while Walker Reade moves on to the next? Maybe you *are* an idiot."

"Fuck you, Alley. I was just asking."

"Well, what did you think I was going to say?"

He lets out a snort through his nose. "You're a snob."

"Why? Because I have ambition that no one around here seems to understand? I'm sorry that I don't think I'm going to find fulfillment bringing Dad and the boys sambuca and coffee every night while you watch baseball in the breezeway and Mommy does the dishes. Because we all know that's how this would turn out." I'm speaking a little louder than I probably mean to, but my family brings it out in me—a frustrated shrillness that's never otherwise on display. We are a block from my parents' house.

"Fuck you." He pauses, softening his tone. "What are you going to tell Mommy?"

"What do you mean? I'm telling her I got a job and I'm moving. I'm a grown-up. This is what grown-ups do." I dial my voice down a few notches, too. "Look, J.D., don't tell her about Walker. She'll just get all worked up. The fact that I'm leaving will be hard enough." My mother never even liked me being in Philadelphia or New York, which were reasonable train rides away. Colorado might as well be Thailand.

"What's up with your New York place?"

"Cara's sister is taking my room. She graduates next week." Cara is my roommate from college. I thank God that I only have to cover two weeks' rent; after that, I'll have about forty-seven dollars in the bank. "Just don't tell Mom anything, okay?"

"What about your job at the bar?"

"Trust me, there is nothing in this world that is easier to do than quit a bartending job."

John Dante pulls into the driveway, which is currently housing three other cars: Stefano's Ford pickup, my mother's Lincoln Continental, and my dad's van. The men run the family business out of our basement and garage, so all of the cars remain in the driveway year-round. I can smell the all-day sauce from outside.

"She doesn't even know who he is, Alley." He's right. My mom reads cozy mysteries that involve muffin recipes. My dad reads two sections of the *New Haven Register*.

When I walk into my parents' house, Mike, Stefano, and my dad are out on a call. My mother is setting the table for supper with my sister-in-law, Lisa, who's five months pregnant. My mother drops a handful of forks on the table when she sees me and runs to the front door, hugging me aggressively, almost violently, effectively voiding me of my next breath. When I come up for air, I am overcome by the smell of garlic and fried meat.

"My Alessandra." She goes back in, this time for a humid kiss on the cheek. Even though my mother has been in the United States for most of her life, she still speaks slightly accented English.

"Hi, Ma." I kiss her back.

"Where have you been?" she says in an accusing manner. "Stefano says you were out West somewhere. Nevada or something. Why didn't you tell me?"

"Stefano has a big mouth." I move in to give Lisa a kiss. "I didn't want you to worry about me."

"What do you mean? I'm your mother. I always worry about you."

"I know, Ma. I'm fine."

"Someday you'll understand. God willing." I'm only twenty-two and my mother is already gunning for me to breed.

Lisa, thankfully, is buying me time. "John Dante, take your sister's bag back to her room."

My mother hands me the forks and starts taking wineglasses out of the credenza. She and Lisa and I finish setting the table.

"How're you feeling, Lee?"

"Fat." She puts a French-manicured hand on her belly. "Just really fat." I have a feeling "just really fat" might be a direct quote from my brother Mike.

"Stop. You look great."

"How's New York?" she asks. My mother looks at me out of the corner of her eye.

"Good. Good. Working a lot . . . I actually got a job."

"I thought you *had* a job," my mother says, picking at a dried sauce spatter on the tablecloth.

"That was an internship. This one pays money. Well, *will* pay money."

"What's that supposed to mean?" she asks.

"I'm assisting a writer with his next novel." My mother makes a face. "Out in Colorado."

My mother stops arranging glasses and sits down. "What are you saying?"

"That I'm moving temporarily to Colorado for this job and that I'll be back in about six months when he's done with the book." I try to say this as matter-of-factly as possible, but she's not buying it.

"You're going thousands of miles away to live with some man you don't know?"

"No, Mom. I'll be living in a guesthouse on his property, with his female assistant."

"How many assistants does this man need?" I consider Devaney, too, and think to myself that my mother is not without a point.

"She takes care of his business affairs. I'll be helping with his book."

"Mmmmhmmm." My mother is endlessly suspicious of men and their intentions with me.

"It's a lot of money if I help him finish the book."

"How much?"

"Twenty-five grand." My mother continues to look unimpressed as John Dante enters the room.

"Twenty-five grand, what?" J.D. asks.

"Dollars," I say. "I'll make that much if I help this writer finish the book."

"Who is this person?" my mother asks. "John Grisham?"

"His name is Walker Reade. He wrote mostly in the seventies and eighties. He has a lot of awards—a Pulitzer, a National Book Award."

My mother shrugs and throws both hands up. "I never heard of him."

This is a relief, of course. Lisa is quiet as she sets the spoons down with a little too much intent. When she catches my eye, one eyebrow goes up.

"That's a lot of money," J.D. says. "What would you do with it?"

"What else? Student loans."

"I told you, you shouldn't have gone to that place. You have to be *pazza* to spend that kind of money with perfectly good schools around here."

"Yale's not any less expensive, Mom."

"*Southern* is. And UConn. You're too good for UConn?"

"No, Ma. But it's done, okay? I'm graduated. Now I've got to make some money. And it's not just that. I'd be working with one of the best editors of all time—someone who might someday want to publish *my* book. I can accomplish three big things for six months' work."

I watch as J.D. counts in his head the number of rationales I've mentioned, then asks, "What else, besides your book and the money?"

"It'll probably get me a job back here. I'm coming back, okay?"

"Hmmmm . . ." is all my mother can say.

Just then my father walks in with Stefano and Mike trailing behind him. The three of them together look like that evolution-of-ape-to-man T-shirt—the exact same humanoid at three different stages. They're even dressed alike in khakis and blue T-shirts with RUSSO PLUMBING across the back. They all wear identical pagers; a wrench is sticking out of Mike's front pocket.

When my mother heads back into the kitchen and my dad heads for the bathroom, Lisa tilts her head toward Mike's crotch and says coyly, "You happy to see me, baby?"

Stefano laughs. "It's only his tool. No big deal."

"Why you breakin' 'em off on me?" Mike says, leaning in for a kiss as he pats Lisa's belly.

"Hey, guys. *Hello*?"

"What's up, Alley Cat? I see you there." Mike comes over and kisses me on the cheek. Stefano waits behind him.

"Stef, what's up?" I take his hand and lean in for a kiss. He also smells like cologne—slightly more expensive cologne.

"Where you been, Cat?"

"You know where I've been. Everyone knows where I've been thanks to your big mouth."

"What, you said Nevada or some shit."

"Jesus . . . Colorado. You know, the American West isn't just an interchangeable collection of states. I was in Colorado."

"Yes, it is," J.D. says. "Cows, corn, horses, cheese."

"That's Wisconsin," I say.

"Whatever. They have cheese in Colorado."

"Yes, but they're not *known* for cheese in Colorado. That's Wisconsin." I am perhaps arguing a bit too passionately about the exact location of the Cheese Belt.

"Who cares? It's not here," J.D. says.

My dad walks into the room and plants a kiss on my forehead. "What's not here?"

"Alley."

"You can hang here for the summer. Rent-free. You can work on your writing. Your mother hasn't touched your room."

"Really, Dad. I'm good. I'm taking this job."

"Really?"

I look at him evenly.

"Don't give me that look. You know how many kids would like to have a paying job and live rent-free? You make it sound like I want to pull your fingernails out."

"Thanks, Daddy. I'm good though."

My mother enters from the kitchen and starts putting food on the table: a giant platter of meatballs, sausage, braciole, and pork ribs from her all-day sauce. A huge bowl of steaming cavatelli, a platter of baked chicken, a salad, and a bowl of freshly grated Parmesan cheese.

As we eat, the scene plays out in slow motion, the way great athletes say it happens when they're in the zone—the plumbing jokes, the semicrude banter, the casual sexism—with me, taking it all in like a moderator at a focus group. There's my dad, who actually, sincerely wants me to come help him this summer, even though I have one of the greatest writers of all time offering me a once-in-a-lifetime opportunity. *Really.* There's John Dante, smart but destined to never rise above what has been carved out for him here—the basement expectations and daily grind just enough to keep him going. There's my mother, who wants nothing more than for me to be married and pregnant and frying meatballs all day for someone who would, in an ideal world, work for my father. There's Mike, clearly in love with Lisa, but barreling toward an inevitable affair about three years after that baby comes. And then there's Stefano, who might be gay. In Italian families, there are some things you'll never know. I barely understand how I can love these people so much yet not be able to wait to get out of here, as if the contentment, the lack of ambition, and the conforming notions might be contagious.

"So you gonna do it, Cat?" Stefano asks.

"What?"

"Leave us," my mother says, her lips pursed.

"Yeah, it's done." I look down at my plate, astonished that I actually have to say what I say next. "Someone around here could congratulate me, you know."

Everyone looks around, wondering whose role that is.

J.D. finally speaks up. "Give 'em hell, Cat. You're going to do great."

"Thank you, J.D."

But there are no other takers. My mother starts pulling at threads on the tablecloth, her gaze averted and intent, and I can tell she's wondering exactly where she went wrong.

When I get on the plane the next morning, I'm happy only once we've reached our cruising altitude of thirty thousand feet, comforted by the anonymous landscape of plastic cups and pretzels, tomato juice and close quarters with strangers, the flight attendants and their carefully studied makeup. I like being in this limbo—suspended in the sky, somewhere between the place I've left behind and wherever it is I'm going.

CHAPTER 7

At first I think the guy behind the counter in the Aspen liquor store is holding a can of beer in his right hand as he rings up my order with the left. Fifteen large bottles of liquor and five cartons of cigarettes later, when he turns to put it all in a box, I realize the can is not a can at all, but a prosthetic hook.

"You need anything else?"

"Do you have any grappa?"

As he wrinkles his nose, I give him the once-over. He's your garden-variety tanned ski bum. In other words, really, really cute. His brown hair is short and combed neatly to the side.

"Your car run out of gas?" He goes to the far end of the counter and pulls out three bottles. "It'll all mess you up pretty bad. This one"—he points to a slightly sinister-looking label in Italian—"is five bucks more."

"Sold."

"How are you paying, and I need to see ID."

"Walker Reade's account," I say, pulling out my Connecticut license. This is what Claudia told me to say.

He pauses and reaches under the counter, pulling out a notebook, but his eyes never leave mine. "Devaney still up there?"

"Yeah, she is."

He starts writing in the notebook with his left hand, the hook resting on the right-hand page. "So that means, hypothetically speaking, of course, that you could go out with me."

"I suppose. Hypothetically speaking."

"Look, I shouldn't even be giving you this. Walker's account is not in good standing."

"So you'll only give me the booze if I go out with you? There's a name for girls like that, you know." I'm mesmerized by the hook, trying hard not to stare but also trying hard not to not stare.

"I'm having a party tomorrow night." He writes an address on the back of a card for the store. "Ask Devaney if she wants to come, too. She knows where I live."

"A party, huh?"

"I presume you like to party?"

"I guess one would presume that given where I'm hanging my hat these days. I'm Alley."

"Pete."

I hold out my right hand to shake. He grabs it with his left and squeezes.

I cringe. "I'm sorry, I should have offered you . . ."

"It's all right." He laughs. "I do a mean high five with the right, but I didn't know if you could handle it."

Walker lives fifteen minutes outside Aspen in a small town known mostly for its local tavern. After I drop the liquor off with Claudia, she tells me that Walker wants to meet me there, at the tavern, for an early dinner.

"Maybe, you know, throw something on," she says offhandedly, looking up and down at my jeans and T-shirt.

I can take a hint. Now that I'm here, officially hired, Claudia seems to be letting me know as subtly as possible that it's time to play ball. I go back to the bedroom, scan through the new clothes Walker bought for me, put on the least offensive getup—the fuchsia minidress and a black jacket—walk down the mountain about a half mile, and spy the Caprice in the parking lot. As I turn to head inside, I see a bus full of tourists—bikers and hikers—turn onto Walker's road.

The tavern is decorated with Christmas lights, and Tammy Wynette's "D-I-V-O-R-C-E" plays on the jukebox at the far end of the room. A postage-stamp-size dance floor is in front of the jukebox. The floor looks newly sanded. The place smells of cigarette smoke and chili powder—a by-product of its Tex-Mex menu. Walker is sitting with the newspaper at a table by himself, chewing mindlessly on the filter of his cigarette as he peers through his reading glasses. Four shots are on the table—two in front of him and two in front of the place where I'm to sit.

"Did you get the booze?" he asks abruptly, not even looking at me.

I take my jacket off and sit down. "Barely."

"What's that mean? You look nice . . ."

"Your account . . ."

"That Captain Hook bastard. My account is fine." Walker puts one of the shot glasses in front of me. It looks like a small, chocolate milk shake.

"What are we drinking?"

"Biffs."

"What's a Biff?"

"Shoot it." He hands me one of the glasses in front of him. "It tastes like Baileys and whiskey."

"Very good."

"It's pretty gross."

"Not after three of them. Then it's genius."

The waitress comes over. She has an overly large name tag with CANDACE engraved on it.

"Hi, sweetheart," Walker says.

"What can I get you, honey?" Candace starts rubbing Walker's shoulders and laughing at all of his jokes. She ignores the way his arm brushes her leg. After seeing how Walker tips, I completely understand the depth of her obsequiousness.

"Let's see, two orders of the chicken enchiladas, two orders of the cheese enchiladas, three orders of the tamales, three burgers, very rare, four sides of fries, two more Biffs, and two beers, sweetie. Coors is fine."

"You got it, baby." Candace rubs the top of Walker's head on her way into the kitchen.

"You expecting company?"

"Christ, I hope not."

"Are you capable of any kind of, I don't know, culinary restraint? How come you can't just order an entrée and then I order an entrée. We split an app. Drink a little. Done."

"It's not interesting. I have a reputation to uphold."

"A reputation for wasting food?"

"For excess, you moron."

"I get it, but are four orders of french fries really buying you street cred?"

"What do you think?"

For the first time I really look around the tavern, which is nearly full. All of the patrons are in various stages of gawking at Walker. A group of drunk college guys in the corner are out-and-out staring. Various Aspen types are catching a glimpse through dark sunglasses, and some locals in cowboy hats and boots swing by to say hello as Walker holds court.

"Today is a good day," Walker says to me. "We're celebrating."

I'm trying to figure out exactly how different a "celebration" might look from any other day out here.

"What happened?"

"Based on those two pages, Lionel is releasing some more of my advance. That rat bastard Hans finally got back; he's upping my rate. And Larry's coming out tomorrow for the weekend. Here." He hands me another Biff, which actually does taste better the second time around. I'm definitely getting buzzed.

"I bought you some grappa today."

"What the hell is that?"

"Really? The man who eats adrenal glands for breakfast doesn't know what grappa is?"

"I don't go in for those guinea drinks, sweetheart."

"I didn't realize you were so discriminating. But let me mix you a cocktail with it when we get home. Then you can tell me."

"You look nice in that dress, you know."

"Thank you."

"Anna Magnani. She wouldn't have worn that dress exactly, but you look like her."

"I don't know who that is."

"Really? The proud guinea has no knowledge of one of Italy's national cinematic treasures?"

"I don't go in for those old movies too much."

"Yeah, well, you should. She's not beautiful, but earthy. You want to rub garlic on her nipples and lick it off."

"Gross."

"You should try it sometime."

The ungodly assemblage of food starts to arrive, which I'm thankful for. The Biffs are hitting me pretty hard. Patsy Cline's "I Fall to Pieces" comes on the jukebox.

"Hey, Walker, how about a picture?" The college boys have finally drunk enough courage.

"Sure, why not?"

One of them hands me a camera and the five of them group around Walker. They all have pints of beer, and Walker poses sideways with the Biff and his filtered cigarette.

"Okay, say *beer*."

"*Beeeeeeeeer.*"

I take three snaps, and there are handshakes all around.

"Can we buy you guys a drink?" one of them says.

"Always," Walker says. "Round of Biffs. Then we've got to chow, boys."

"Thanks, Walker."

"I need to head to the head."

While Walker is in the bathroom, I notice that all eyes are now on me—me and my ridiculous dress, sort of drunk, chewing halfheartedly on a tamale. I am trying to appear serious—I am the woman out here for professional purposes, thank you very much—but this dress is not aiding the effort. I train my eyes on the bathroom door, waiting for Walker to come out. When he does, he is transformed. Not markedly—it's as subtle as a twist in the corner of his eye. But I'm fairly certain that nothing was, in fact, eliminated on this bathroom trip.

"I'm going tomorrow night to a party," I say matter-of-factly as he sits back down.

"No, you're not."

"Yes, the guy at the liquor store invited me and Devaney. I mean, I figured it was Friday . . ."

"I'm sorry. Do you think you're working at a bank? Some fucking temp job? Friday? Throw your calendar away, sweetheart. You're not going anywhere."

"Uh . . . okay."

"You think this is a vacation? You're here to help me. Get it? Nothing else. I mean nothing. And you are especially not here to work on your own writing."

"What makes you think I'm working on my own writing?"

"Claudia, that's what."

One morning at the cabin a few days ago, Claudia had offhandedly asked me what I was doing. If it wasn't crystal clear to me before where her loyalty lies, it is now. I'll have to be more subtle.

"Don't you care that I'm writing a book?"

"I care more that this beer is almost empty."

"Did it ever occur to you that I want to learn from the best? That I might like a mentor?"

"Please, sweetheart. Did it ever occur to you that I don't give two shits about you and your writing career? I have enough to worry about with my own."

I reach into my jacket and grab a cigarette. Walker holds out his Zippo lighter, cupping his hand around it.

"It's a fool's job anyway. If I had to do it all over again, I'd go to law school. All the money I've paid lawyers over the years." Walker has, thus far, lived through two divorces and several firearms violations. A wrongful-termination suit brought by a former assistant was thrown out last year. His most high-profile problem was one recent three-month legal odyssey, where an interviewer accused Walker of sexual harassment, an accusation that resulted in a search of the property, where various drugs and explosives were found (again, thrown out). Then there's the whole host of hard-to-categorize offenses that have kept Walker's lawyers busy over the years. I mean, what do you call it when you bring a leaking fifty-pound bag of lime into a crowded bar and stagger through the joint? Or set off a boatload of fireworks on a pig farm? Or douse your oversize Christmas tree in gasoline, shove it up your chimney, and set it on fire? When all has been said and done, it's amounted to a collection of disturbing-the-peace and public-drunkenness violations. Walker's cred is preserved. And the Tom-and-Jerry act with local law enforcement endures.

"You have a National Book Award and a Pulitzer and everyone here is staring at you. I think you've done all right."

"Is that what you want? Everyone staring at you? So you can't go out for a beer without the whole frat house wanting to hump you? You can't eat that, sweetheart. Awards neither. You'll go broke in this business. If you want to be famous, there are easier ways, especially for a girl."

"You've never even read anything I've written."

"And I don't plan on it. Where's our waitress?"

Walker flags down Candace and asks for two pieces of chocolate cake to go.

"Let's get out of here."

Once we're in the car, he takes a small plastic bag out of his pocket and starts jamming whatever's in it into the chocolate cake. He hands me a plastic fork. "Have a bite."

"What is it?"

"Just eat it."

"Jesus, Walker. At least tell me what it is." He puts a forkful in front of me, and I see gnarly, dried globs in the cake. Mushrooms.

"You don't trust me?" This question seems a little beside the point. Of course I trust that these are proper hallucinogenic mushrooms. The real question is if I want to do them. A few days prior I'd had something of an epiphany: I would treat my time out here like AA, but in reverse. Instead of adopting a "one day at a time" approach for *not* abusing substances, I was going to take that approach *for* abusing them. I grab the fork and chew slowly. Even buried in the chocolate the mushrooms have the consistency and smell of dried manure. Walker takes a couple of bites of his cake and starts up the Caprice. I notice the backseat has a blanket covering up something.

"Where are we going?"

"To have some fun . . ."

I pause to consider the terrifying-yet-liberating notion that anything could be under the blanket—a block of headcheese, an AK-47, a human torso, a flamethrower, five keys of coke. I light up two cigarettes and hand one to Walker as he puts the Caprice in gear and starts up the mountain. It's still light outside, and Walker puts his hand on my knee, which he's taken to doing every time we drive together, like we're some old married couple. I don't shoo his hand away, but my hand never covers his; instead I put my left hand under my armpit and smoke so I look like Bette Davis. It's not exactly a "professional distance," but it's the closest thing to one I can maintain under these circumstances.

When we get to the top of the mountain road, the tourists I had seen before are in various stages of eating and hanging out. They instantly recognize Walker, and several of them start clapping and yelling and taking pictures. Walker stops the Caprice and I can feel the drugs starting to kick in a little. They're my first-ever mushrooms, and the early reviews are good. It feels like the acid minus the edge—I'm just happy in a simple, uncomplicated way. We are both smiling widely, and when Walker reaches into the backseat, grabbing from beneath the blanket what appears to be not the Taser, but a small handgun, I'm so blindly amused that I don't even pause to consider that someone might die. The group of hikers—about fifteen in all—recoil in unison. I see one of them run to a call box. Walker grabs my hand and puts it in his, and we shoot the gun together, straight up into the air, as he lets out a pronounced "Yee-ha." The gun makes an awful screeching sound, and Walker and I fall back into the car as he guns the engine, launching us first in a big circle (as we are in a Caprice convertible, this move has all of the dramatic effect of trying to do a doughnut while riding on the back of a whale) and then down the hill. It occurs to me in a shroom-induced laughing fit that I am now a character in a Walker Reade novel. I am The Girl in the Car. It feels like we are on a great big roller coaster that only knows how to go downhill . . . fast. The Caprice winds down the mountain with a force seemingly its own. Walker and I are cracking up so hard we aren't even making any noise. A parade of lights materializes behind us, and for a few seconds I am excited because I think we've stumbled upon a carnival. They appear so festive at first—the lights of two squad cars dancing in the setting sun.

"Quadruple fuck . . . Listen to me, sweetheart," Walker says in his best Bonnie-and-Clyde voice. "You do not have to talk to the cops . . . *ever.* You get it? This is your right as an American citizen." I nod and smile, completely unable to accept that we might be in some kind of real trouble. It feels like we're on the set of a movie—a happy, happy movie.

Walker pulls into a driveway and the two cop cars stop behind us. They obviously know who Walker is and seem to process me, with my big smile and fuchsia minidress, as his flavor of the month, which might not be all that far off. There are two female cops and two male cops. The pair of women, both hefty redheads—they could be sisters—approach me.

"Can I see some ID, please?"

I'm looking at the cop sisters and their bad flame-red dye

jobs, mesmerized by the shine on their badges, their extreme red-haired-ness. I briefly wonder if they're Irish, my mind wandering to some picture of a Gaelic countryside with a hand-built stone wall where everyone wears cream-colored, cable-knit sweaters . . .

"Yoo-hoo," one of them says to me, swiping a hand in front of my smiling face. "Hello?"

"We're just here visiting our friend," Walker says. "Unless we're under arrest, we'll be seeing you."

Walker takes my hand. He seems impressed by my defiance in the face of authority, but my silence is born less from any political statement and more from the fact that I'm shrooming out of my gourd. I can't quite stop looking at the lights and all of that red hair.

"Walker, what were you doing on the mountain?" one of the male cops asks. He appears to be the kind of person with a fitness "regimen." His partner has the feigned importance and baby-soft skin of a rookie. "You're scaring the bejesus out of the tourists. Where's the gun?"

"I don't have any gun. It's a screecher for scaring away crows. Not my fault they thought it was a gun."

"Have you been drinking today?" the other cop asks. I can't stifle a laugh. Have we been breathing?

"Are we under arrest?" Walker asks.

"Not yet, big guy," Mr. Fitness says.

"Then we'll be on our way." Walker flings open the car door, pulls me across the front seat, and we start walking slowly toward the house in front of us. The cops behind us are in deep discussion. My guess is they don't know if they should try to make a big score or stop messing with the local color.

"Walker," one of the redheads calls out. "Dry out here a little before you go home. Get the girl home safe."

“Thank you very much,” Walker says as he rings the doorbell. A bearded man with long hair and glasses wearing a plaid shirt and cargo pants appears at the door and lets us in, smiling widely, shaking Walker’s hand like he’s been expecting him all morning. He waits for the door to close completely before his face dissolves into disbelief, then rage. Then he starts laying into Walker.

“Really, Walker? You’re bringing the cops directly to my house? I was about to start flushing.”

“Sorry, Jim. It was all a little bang-bang.”

“Bang-bang is what I should do to your head. What are you on anyway?”

“The fungus, sir. It’s among us.”

Jim takes a quick look at me. Walker nods as if to say I’m all right.

“You need anything else?”

“Just a few minutes to make sure they’re gone.”

“Anything else?”

“What do you have?”

“What do you want?”

“I’m a little low on the drug.”

“You know I just left an envelope in the pig about an hour ago, right?”

“Wouldn’t hurt to get a little more.”

“Come on downstairs.”

Walker points to the couch, where I sit as he heads down to the basement with Jim. I’m still flying pretty high and intensely study the artwork in Jim’s living room, a cheesy yet consistent collection of Southwestern scapes that I find oddly beautiful. I’m not so dim as to not realize what’s going on here, and it’s pretty ballsy: Walker Reade just led four cops to his drug dealer’s house.

CHAPTER 8

"Okay, it's two."

"So it is." Walker's sitting at his typewriter with a blank page inserted. I'm on the barstool next to him with his manuscript open in front of me. All fifty-nine pages of it. These I do have memorized. I have hours of downtime and I've looked at these pages from every angle. There are problems. Lots of little ones, and almost as many big ones—poorly conceived characters, lack of narrative direction, gaps of black-hole proportion, tepid humor, plot inconsistencies, and one big problem that has never before been an issue with Walker's work: it's kind of boring. I have pages of notes and ideas, but feel I have to measure them out—let them fall into place one at a time.

Unfortunately, Walker is in an entirely different head space. For about the tenth time, he peeks through the blinds, even though he lives in the middle of nowhere and everyone in this sleepy town is no doubt asleep on a Monday at two in the morning. But in the four days since our little trip up the mountain, Walker has been in full-blown paranoia mode, convinced that his untimely arrest is imminent. Every blind in the house is down, and we rarely venture out, even to eat. We are surviving on Marie Callender's frozen dinners and that Armageddon-ready supply of canned goods. To my great disappointment, Larry's visit was canceled. I feel like I'm missing something, as our interaction with the cops had all of the menace of a *Dukes of Hazzard* episode. The gun really *was* a screecher gun used to scare off birds; it doesn't even take ammo. No one got hurt, and no evidence was taken.

"So I have an idea about the story," I say.

"I don't want to hear it."

"Okay. Well, not an idea. It's a comment."

"*Sweetie!*" Walker is snapping at Devaney like she's a bellhop. She is sprawled on the circular couch in what appears to be a copper full slip and short shorts—her pajamas—watching *Pretty Woman* with the volume low. The irony, I assume, is lost on her.

"What?"

"Take a peek outside. Here . . ." He hands her a rifle from underneath the counter.

"Are you crazy, Walker? I'm not sure what you're lookin' for, but ain't nuthin' out there, babe."

"Alley?"

"How about I take a peek without the gun." I go into the breezeway, open the door, look through the screen at the half-moon, and smell the night air, hoping it will wake me up. No bogeyman under this bed.

"See anything?"

"Nope." I come back into the kitchen. "Not a thing. So, are you ready?"

"Ready for what?" He takes a long draw off his scotch and piles some cocaine onto the small tray next to him. Devaney's eyes light up. Walker does a line and passes the tray to me. I opt for the shortest line, my latest trick, and pass the tray to Devaney, who takes great pains to look exasperated at getting sloppy thirds.

"Writing," I say. "It's after two."

"You keep saying that. Who made this rule? Two."

"I don't know. Claudia said—"

"Claudia is a secretary."

"Okay."

"So why would I listen to a secretary about when to write my book?"

"Well, that's why I'm here, right?" I say matter-of-factly. "So I was thinking . . . It seems as if there's this disconnect between Luke and Polly . . . in chapter three . . . when they're—"

"That's life, sweetheart."

"I mean, there's just not much emotional resonance in the scene at the truck stop. But I was thinking—"

"Are you saying you don't care about the characters?"

"Well, no. I mean, not no. Not wholesale. I would care more in this section if—"

"Well, then why don't we just throw this sixty pages into the fire then."

"Oh, no. I wasn't suggesting—"

"That's exactly what you were suggesting. That they're crap."

"I don't think they're crap, but I thought you wanted me to be honest."

"I would prefer it if you were just not such an idiot."

"Okay." I have, by now, learned better than to chomp down on the "I'm an idiot" bait.

"You're wrong, missy. There's plenty of 'emotional resonance,' as you say. What orifice did you even pull that phrase from? We're not in Lit 201, sweetheart." Walker does another line and lights a cigarette before training his aviators on me, presumably waiting for an answer to that question.

I decide to not back down, like Claudia told me. "So if you

don't want me to have an opinion on this, what am I doing here?"

"Well, for starters, I need a refill on my drink. Scotch. Water. Now."

"Oh . . . okay."

"I have an idea," says Devaney. Throughout my first week here, Devaney has insisted on staying up with us. She mostly watches movies on TV, does a ton of coke, and elevates negligee wearing to a level of high art while alternately stewing in sexiness and insecurity. I can't imagine that she feels threatened by me, but she has the demeanor and impatience of a chaperone at a high school dance. I go to the bar and mix Walker's Chivas and water.

"Please, Devaney. Not now."

"So you want to hear her ideas but not mine?"

"My guess is that your idea is lamebrained. You grew up on a farm."

"So?"

"So your thoughts on animal husbandry, or whatever, are not going to help me."

"On what?"

"Okay, back to the movie, honey. And what are you wearing?" Walker is pointing at me and my black turtleneck sweater and blue jeans.

"I don't know . . ." I place his scotch down on the coaster next to the typewriter.

"I will never understand that kind of sweater. God gave you a neck, right? Didn't I just buy you some clothes? Devaney . . . get this girl something from the back." Devaney heads back to the bedroom, and I can hear her rummaging through drawers.

"I'm cold," I say. "Plus, can I respectfully add that this is supersexist?"

"Go ahead . . ." Devaney comes back with an orange,

off-the-shoulder jersey minidress. "Respectfully add that, then put this on."

"You want me to put this on?"

"You want pages? Trust me, it'll help. With, you know, *emotional resonance.*"

I head into the bathroom and start to change. As I rip off the turtleneck, I offer myself a pep talk of sorts. It's not like he's making me put on a bikini, and it might actually help with pages. Maybe if I start looking at this like it's part of the creative process, as opposed to an assault on my dignity, sense of self-worth, and feminism in general, we'll get something done. I look at myself in the mirror and smooth the front of the dress, which is sort of cute and fits me nicely.

"Well, well, Jennifer Beals," Devaney says when I come out. She is holding a rolled-up bill and takes another quick snort out of the tray. " 'What a feeling . . .' "

"Nice. Now, everybody shut up." Walker starts hunting-and-pecking at the typewriter. "While I'm doing this, I want you to work on the board." Walker has purchased a giant corkboard and wants me to cut out pictures from magazines that are pertinent to the story.

"Can I help?" Devaney asks.

"You can help light my cigarette." He takes another Dunhill from the pack. "There are also some glasses in the sink."

"Fuck you. I'm not the maid."

I start looking through magazines.

Walker literally types two letters—*Plink. Plunk.*—and looks outside again. "That bastard Ken is keeping me waiting."

"Who's Ken?" I ask.

"Town sheriff."

"Ken is your friend," Devaney says.

"He's the sheriff first. That bastard is coming after me."

"Well, he's not outside," Devaney says. "He's not hiding behind some tree."

"I'm looking for lights, you idiot."

I consider that perhaps some good old-fashioned reasoning might break Walker out of his funk. "It's pretty late. Why do you think you might be arrested again?"

"Golly, you're stupid."

"Just refresh me."

"I'm a big fish for this small pond, sweetheart. Catching me would be a real big deal for some people around here. Refreshed now?" Walker turns back to the typewriter. *Plink. Plunk.* He does another line of coke and hands the tray to me. "Here, you look tired."

I do another line because he's right—I'm exhausted—and I hand the tray to Devaney. The bump is less dramatic than it was when I first got here—still pulse-quickening but more predictable. Less David Lee Roth, more Sammy Hagar.

"And what are you drinking?"

"Wine. Red wine," I say.

"You're almost out." I get up and pour more wine into mine and Devaney's glasses and resume cutting out pictures that might have something to do with a truck stop, which is where Walker is in his story. The plinking turns into slightly faster key-striking, like a faucet with a washer that's slowly wearing away. Not exactly a newsroom hum, but I just need one page before bedtime. I've told myself that I'm not leaving without it. He's about a quarter of the way down the page—I'm so afraid of jinxing his progress I don't even look up—when he turns to me with "So, what do you think of the pages so far?"

A loud snort comes out of my mouth. I'm sure he's kidding.

"Something funny?"

"No."

Devaney starts to shift on the couch, her half-slip riding up. *Pretty Woman* is over, so we are all basically engaged in a slightly edgy, coked-up staredown as CNN rages quietly in the background.

"It's really good so far. I'm interested in what's coming next." I nod toward the page in the typewriter.

"You think I don't know what I'm doing?" He opens the cabinet next to him and pulls down two boxes. He doesn't say a word; he just takes out his Pulitzer Prize and his National Book Award and places them between us.

"Wow. It would be nice to win one of those someday."

"It would be *nice* if someone around here had a goddamn opinion and had the balls to say it. Now, you were saying?"

"Nothing. It's really good so far. What's coming next?" I am cringing internally, waiting for the other shoe to drop. Shockingly, it doesn't. Walker just types, working his cigarette filter between his teeth. Slowly the page starts to fill, each clunk of the return releasing something like relief in me. When he reaches the end of the sheet and puts in another piece of paper, it's like a little orgasm. He types two more lines and pulls the page out, handing them both to me.

"Happy now? Good-bye." He snaps his fingers at Devaney again, apparently her cue to head to bed. "Take this." He hands me the .22 from under the counter. "Get home safe."

"I'm walking across the driveway."

"Coyotes, sweetheart. Go on. I'll make sure you get over." I grab the rifle and the two pages. I'm barefoot in the orange dress, so I put on my clunky, black shoes and hightail it out of there. When I get to the door of the cabin, I flick the light on and off, and Walker's silhouette disappears.

Inside the cabin, I head back to my bedroom, where I have

the Mac set up on the card table. In these moments—as I wearily change out of whatever outfit, like an actress after the curtain—I usually assess my physical condition. Often a headache is building; sometimes I'm still wired from the coke. I'll brush my teeth, take some aspirin, use Visine.

I bring the pages into the kitchen. I might as well have them on their own gilded tray for how precious they are to me. I read them, reread them, then reread them again. Before I head back to the bedroom, I brew a pot of coffee because I know it's going to be a long one. It's almost as if the pages are in code. I seem to know what Walker is trying to say, but he's not actually saying any of it. These are different from the first pages I saw, which just needed minor tweaks. As I type the pages into the Mac, I take great pains to ensure continuity with the previous pages, and then, without even knowing that I'm doing it, I crack the code. I take these two measly, mediocre pages and start working them with a thrilling urgency, like I'm tearing the wrapping paper off a present, where I know what's inside is something invaluable. Something I've waited for. I'm rewriting whole sentences. Re-forming whole paragraphs. Suddenly—as the sky turns from dark to light gray—there *it* is, as if the dawn's glow is a stage light bringing Walker to the fore: old-school Walker. It's crisp. It's taut. The voice is there—the distinctive, adrenalized, paranoid, genius-on-speed voice, so often imitated the past few decades, so rarely duplicated. I print out what is now a page and a half, and I'm pretty goddamned pleased with myself as I watch the sun continue to rise out my window. I'm so pleased that I barely consider that I might be overstepping my bounds. I'm so pleased that I go back out to the living room and hit Lionel Gray's fax number without a second thought and turn in for the night.

CHAPTER 9

"Lionel is *happy*," Claudia intones, bursting into the kitchen, where Walker and I are both trying to get our heads on straight at three in the afternoon—him with a pipe full of hash, a couple of lines of coke, and a barely orange screwdriver; me with a giant glass of water, a cup of coffee, and a piece of dry toast. We're both reading the *Denver Post*; rather, Walker is studying the op-ed page; I am pretending to read the Lifestyles section but am just pleased to focus on something that won't talk to me. Claudia delivers this news from Lionel in a singsong voice I haven't heard in my almost month here. I can tell she's trying to perk up Walker, who remains mired in a paranoid funk even though it is, by now, a couple of weeks since our run-in with the local Keystone Kops. But the positive reports from New York can neither stir Walker from his grumpy haze nor me from a rabid headache that has taken up residence in my right eye. We drank entirely too many margaritas last night, and I'm paying for it today.

When I first arrived here, I harbored visions of days spent expanding our minds—a paisley album cover brought to life—and evenings spent turning those pearls of cosmic insight into genius. Walker would tap out the lines on the heels of my gentle prodding.

He would be the literary lion, me the lion whisperer. Instead, ever since Walker's brush with the law, what we're doing are piles of cocaine and drinking to ridiculous excess, but, to me, it's all become more grim than fun, more desperate than inspired. Instead of prodding a Thoroughbred, I'm dragging the horse one interminable furlong at a time, with a broken leg, on a muddy track.

When Walker's funk had first come on, I had set in place a protocol that has served me well. I resolved to let my natural stubbornness guide me each night and I'm now refusing to leave Walker's side unless I have at least one page in tow. Sometimes this means I leave at midnight, but more often than not it's closer to sunrise. Then I go back to the cabin, and the real work starts. I assume that I should have more mixed feelings about what I've been doing to Walker's pages—the editing, the rewriting, the channeling—but I don't. It has, in fact, been extremely rewarding to take the skeleton of his story and hang fresh meat on those bones. I'm even less conflicted to know that Lionel, with fifteen more pages in hand, is happy with them—until, on this day, the phone rings, and Walker puts the speakerphone on.

"Walker, ol' boy. How are things?" It's Lionel's unmistakable Plimpton-on-Percocet baritone.

"Lionel Gray . . ." Walker seems on the verge of ending this sentence with one of his usual bons mots—"you bastard," "you moron"—but even Walker knows who's writing the checks. "What's going on?"

"What are you doing over there?" Lionel asks a tad cryptically. But when he continues, his tone is one of pleasant surprise. "I like what's coming out of the fax. When can you talk edits?"

Staring at the speakerphone, neither Claudia nor Walker notices the blood draining from my face, or my jaw slowly hinging downward.

Walker looks to Claudia, who mouths, "Later today."

"How about six?"

"Works for me. I'll call you then."

After Lionel hangs up, Claudia goes over to Walker and starts kneading his shoulders. "This is great, Walker. He wants to talk edits."

"Who cares? My demise is coming. My arrest is imminent. And no one cares. You're drinking"—he waves his hand up and down at me—"*coffee*, for Christ's sake. And you"—he turns and waves his hand the same way at Claudia, but he has no words—"you'll see."

"Walker, no one is going to arrest you. It's been more than two weeks," says Claudia. "If they were going to arrest you, they would have done something by now."

"That bastard Ken is keeping me waiting."

"Ken would have told you if something was going to happen. Do you want me to call over there? Talk to Raine?" Raine is Ken's wife. She has the clipped good looks of a former model and now runs a farm on the other side of town.

"Call over there? Are you crazy? Where's my drink? *You*. I'm talking to you."

"Me?" I snap to attention and turn to Walker with an expression best described as Deer in the Headlights Realizing Too Late That It's Fucked. I have gone from reading the paper to sitting on the floor in front of the coffee table working a three-hole puncher through Walker's manuscript—the one without my changes—and putting it into a ringed binder. I know, by now, that when Walker starts to rage it's best to look busy. But I could spend the next three hours punching out holes with my teeth—nothing can change this one unassailable fact: Lionel wants to talk edits on a manuscript that for all intents and purposes Walker hasn't even seen.

"No, the other bartender. Get my fucking scotch."

I slowly get up and pour Walker a Chivas and water. The headache that has settled in is now compounded by blind panic.

"Look alive, sweetheart. What's wrong with you?"

"Just a little headache. So . . . like, do you want me here for that call?"

"What? Like . . . no."

"Why not?" My mind is furiously bailing water. Perhaps, I figure, if I'm here, I can try to smooth things over. Distract him. Pump him full of ether. Something.

"Because it's none of your business."

"Isn't the book technically my business? I am your assistant."

"Yes, and this is where your job ends. Now, shut up and give me that thing."

In my agitated state, I've put too many pages in the hole puncher, which is now stuck. Apparently I'm even capable of messing up pretend work. "In a minute," I say, hoping he'll forget about it.

"I'm calling Larry," says Claudia, gesturing to Walker. "You need a haircut, by the way."

"Larry? Call *Lesser.* All of this time, why haven't we talked to Lesser? What are we thinking? Do I have to think of everything? Claudia . . . *Claudia!* Get Lesser on the phone. For fuck's sake. Now!"

"Who's Lesser?" I ask, still trying to pry loose the manuscript.

"His lawyer," Claudia says, reaching into the kitchen drawer for a pair of scissors. "One of them."

From out of a drawer she grabs the small towel she uses to

catch hair clippings when she trims Walker's hair, wraps it around his shoulders, puts on her reading glasses, and stands behind him with a spray bottle of water. She lets one spritz go, and Walker turns like a ninja, grabs the bottle, and starts spraying her repeatedly in the face.

"Jesus, Walker. Fuck!" Claudia is trying to wrestle the spray bottle from him but is only getting more soaked.

"Are you the biggest moron to ever walk the face of the earth? I said to call Lesser."

Just then, Devaney walks in, in her pj's—a tank top and silky pj bottoms. She possesses a seemingly endless array of sleepwear, but evidently little sense of the effect this perpetual pajama party conveys. If she wants to be taken more seriously around here, an actual pair of pants might not hurt this late in the day.

"What the fuck do *you* want?" says Walker.

Devaney shoots him a withering stare, then goes to make a pot of coffee. She takes a mug from the cupboard and pours two fingers of Bushmills into it, then stands by the pot to wait, her hand resting on one hip, lips pursed. Meanwhile, Claudia is wiping her face.

"And what are *you* doing?" Walker says.

"Me?" I say.

"Stop saying that! Christ, who the hell else do you think I mean. You're here, right? You are *supposed to be helping me.* Why are there so many people here and *no one is helping me!?*" Walker takes a handful of cigarette filters and starts throwing them at me one by one. "You and your office equipment or whatever the hell useless thing you're doing over there."

"Walker, stop. Please," I say.

Claudia grabs his hand. "Walker, enough."

"*Everybody, out! And you* . . ." Walker points to the manuscript in my now-sweating hands. "Leave it."

I put the manuscript next to the typewriter—it sits there like a hand grenade with the pin pulled—and Claudia and I hightail it to the cabin while Devaney takes her Irish coffee, runs outside, and hops into her car—a crappy Toyota Corolla.

"Where's she going?" I ask.

"Who the hell knows," Claudia says. "Come on."

Once we're in the cabin, Claudia sets about fixing us a late lunch. She lights up two cigarettes and hands me one. Hers smolders away in an ashtray as she takes a loaf of rye bread, a spiral ham, a hunk of Brie, a bottle of grainy mustard, and two Heinekens out of the refrigerator. Claudia's commitment to smoking is impressive and unwavering. I half expect to find her eating a Dunhill for breakfast some morning.

"You look like shit," she says.

"Headache."

"Did you take anything for it?"

"No."

"Didn't you see, in your room . . ."

"What?"

"The giant plastic jar acting as a bookend."

"I thought that was decorative."

Claudia goes back to my room and returns with the oversize jar that has been holding all of the books up. It's labeled in her handwriting ASSISTANT ASPIRIN.

"That's pretty funny."

"It's from Mexico."

"Is it not the same as US aspirin?"

"Stronger. *Way* stronger."

"Is it safe?"

Claudia just smirks as if to say I picked the wrong time to care about that. "Two will do the trick. Here." She hands me both pills—in an alarming shade of red—and gets a glass of water. "But don't take more than two."

"Thank you. But how come Walker is never hungover? The man is twice my age."

"Basically, he just keeps drinking. It's not hair of the dog, exactly . . . it's, well, the whole dog. He's been doing this a long time. . . . The most functional . . ." Claudia stares off, her face a map of compassion, sympathy, anger, resignation, pity, sorrow, and fatigue. "Why don't you eat something, then go lie down."

As casually as possible, I ask, "So . . . like . . . what happens when Lionel calls to go over edits? Is it, like, you know, big-picture stuff or line edits . . . ?"

"You know, a bunch of bullshit. Lionel rewrites him a lot at this point, so he just covers his bases. Why?"

"No, no reason. Just, you know, curious, you know, about the process."

"It's not exactly a process. It just has to get done one way or another at this point. I already talked to him anyway."

"Who?"

"Lionel. Jeez, you are out of it."

"What'd he say?" I almost don't want to hear.

"He said what you sent him is not perfect but it's workable—they're workable pages. But look, Alley, I need to know what you're doing over there so I can support it. Keep it going."

"You know what we're doing over there. A whole bunch of nonsense until two a.m., then hands on the typewriter. I'm just not leaving until I have the one page."

"You're persistent. That's good. Whatever you're doing, just keep doing it." Claudia seems to be fishing. I'm just not sure if I'm supposed to take the bait. "We've got to get Larry out here. He always perks up Walker."

Claudia lights another cigarette off the one already in her mouth, and the act is already so familiar, so comforting, that it almost makes me want to cry. It's not like Claudia and I are mapping the human genome together. What we have amounts to little more than chain-smoking and meal preparation—or chain-smoking in lieu of meal preparation. But I'm attached to her in all of the ways I can't be with my own mother. I don't want to leave, but I fear within the next twenty-four hours that's exactly what's going to happen. For God's sake: I'm editing Walker Reade's book without his permission. How on earth did I think I was going to get away with that?

"What's going on, Claude? With Walker."

"It's just one of his moods. It'll pass."

"It looks like full-blown delusional paranoia."

"It'll pass." She waves her hand sharply, letting me know this part of the conversation is over. Claudia's job description would fill a phone book. In just the few weeks I've been out here, it has included cleaning the toilet, procuring fireworks, faxing pages, cooking, grocery shopping, scheduling media interviews, cutting Walker's hair, paying bills, going to the liquor store, general cleaning, polishing handguns, soaking cigarette filters, playing music, arranging personal visits, cleaning peacock cages, repotting flowers, organizing social gatherings, liaising with fans, mixing drinks, brewing coffee, holding off creditors, mollifying magazine staffs, publishers, editors, and assistants, handling PR requests, and laundry. Not to mention the constant ego stroking and reassurance that is her bread and butter.

"I do not envy your position," I say, as Claudia makes us

both ham-and-Brie sandwiches at the kitchen table. Her hair is still wet.

"Beats data entry."

"I don't know, data entry sounds relaxing and predictable."

"Exactly. C'mon. We're all adrenaline junkies out here. You, too."

"No, I'm not. I'm doing this as a means to an end." I take a church key from the drawer and open both of our beers. I ponder mine, hesitating at my lips. "This might be a bad idea."

"The hair. Just half. And you'll see . . ."

"See what?"

"That it's hard to stay here, but it's hard to leave, too. I have my house, but I can't be there more than a weekend without going nuts." Claudia owns a small ski shack in Crested Butte—a place she's only been to once the whole time I've been here. Her son, Cody, uses it as a massage studio.

"How long have you been out here exactly?"

"On and off twenty years. I've been fired eight times."

"Christ, you're a regular Billy Martin."

"Walker and I go way back." She takes a long draw off her cigarette but doesn't say anything else. We sit quietly, eating our sandwiches, drinking our beers, smoking.

"What are your thoughts on Devaney?"

"Minimal," Claudia says. She takes a long pull on her beer and then crushes the butt of her cigarette into the dolphin ashtray. She's barely touched her sandwich.

"She seems nice enough."

Claudia's either not biting or she didn't hear me. She stares out the kitchen window, distracted by a peacock that struts purposefully by. "I have to run a few errands," she says abruptly. "Why don't you rest up for later?"

"Okay." It seems appropriate to "rest up" for what will surely be my imminent evisceration.

I wash the dishes and tidy up the kitchen. Then I do what I always do when I'm feeling stressed-out. I grab my manuscript from the bedroom and lie on the couch next to the potbellied stove, throwing a quilt over my legs. The feel of the manuscript's heft always relaxes me—reminds me that I'm capable. That I did this without anyone else's help or guidance. The book is eighty-five thousand words and I'm on my third revision. When people ask me what it's about, I take great pains to tell them that it's not autobiographical, even though it's a fish-out-of-water story about a girl from a blue-collar family who navigates the gin-and-tonic lifestyle of the Ivy League. Even I have to admit it sounds autobiographical. Some things are undeniably real: the humiliation of doling out food to my dormmates my freshman year when I worked in the food hall and how learning to tend bar effectively turned the tables. There's the girl who finds her place at the writing center, the attentive professor who decides to mentor her, the failed romance with a rich boy. Like they say—write what you know. But I'm distracted, glancing repeatedly at the clock, which now reads five thirty. In a half hour the jig—and the gig—may be up.

I'm just taking my cap off the red pen when Devaney walks in with her coffee mug and a bag of doughnuts from the Aspen Bake Shop. She throws them on the couch—either a peace offering or a bribe. Her platinum bob is mussed just so. She looks like a rock star.

"Do you think I'm stupid?"

I can't tell if she's searching for an honest assessment or on the verge of making an accusation. "Um, no."

She opens the bag and shoves it toward my face, offering a napkin with her other hand.

I take out a cinnamon-sugar doughnut that smells like apple cider and take a bite. "God damn."

"Good, right?" She reaches in and takes a doughnut for herself. "Because Walker thinks I'm stupid."

"No, he doesn't."

"He says it all the time."

"He says it all the time to everyone. 'Moron . . . stupid . . . idiot . . . dumbhead . . .' It's like a verbal tic."

"I want to become more involved in the writing process," she says finally, as if she's at her annual review.

"You are, Devaney."

"No, I'm not. I just sit there and drink and do drugs."

"That's kind of the process. It's a shot in the dark. What am I doing that's any different?"

"Then why does he need both of us?"

I'm not sure I like where this conversation is heading. "Well, I do edit his pages, Devaney. I have some experience."

"You do?"

"A little." I leave out the part about how this might actually land me on the first plane home tomorrow.

"Show me how to do that."

I can't tell if Devaney is trying to make me dispensable or if she is looking to get on a career track that doesn't involve carrying menus and batting her eyes at tourists all night. "That's not my decision to make."

"But you get to spend nights with him."

"There's nothing to worry about, Devaney. I'm not interested." The moment these words pass my lips, I realize they might not be entirely true. "I may spend the nights with him, but you go to bed with him."

"Yeah, and that's a hoot and a holler."

"I don't really need to know—"

"How exciting do you think *that* is after all the booze and the drugs? I couldn't talk that thing up if I was in PR."

I pause and look at her for a minute. "*That's* funny. Really funny. Maybe you *should* be a writer."

"I'm telling you. I think I would be good at this."

"Wait here." I head to the back bedroom and grab one of my nice notebooks—an empty one with a leather cover. I give it to Devaney and grab one of my favorite Uni-ball pens from my purse. "The best thing I ever did was start keeping a journal. Otherwise you forget stuff."

She looks at the notebook and flips the pages. "Thank you. Here." She offers another doughnut, which I take, and she grabs the last one. I go into the kitchen and take two highball glasses down and fill them with ice. Claudia and I have a full bar in our pantry, and I pour Devaney and me two fingers of Irish whiskey each.

"Might as well not mix this early in the day," I say, handing her a glass. "Plus, this will be amazing with these doughnuts."

Devaney takes a slug of the whiskey, then grabs the pen and clips it over the front page of the notebook. I briefly consider that by tomorrow Devaney could be using that very pen, and the notebook in her hand, to do my job.

CHAPTER 10

"You wanted to see me?" I'm standing in the doorway between the kitchen and the breezeway, not wanting to come all the way in. Walker takes a sip of his scotch, sits back in his chair, and looks me up and down.

"Why, yes. I wanted your thoughts on the long-term impact of glasnost and perestroika on the Russian economy. While you're at it, I want you to write a report on the significance of the relationship between Gorbachev and Reagan vis-à-vis the end of the Cold War."

"Really?"

"No, you moron. I'm ready to write. Why else would I ask you over here?"

"No reason." It occurs to me that this call might not have happened after all. "You talk to Lionel?"

"Yes, the beast has been fed."

"What did he have to say?"

"What do you care?"

"I'm your assistant, right?"

As my question hangs in the air—half query and half plea—the CD player changes, a disc of sixties favorites. The opening notes of Buffalo Springfield's "For What It's Worth" start. Ping . . . ping . . .

"There's somethin' happenin' here / What it is ain't exactly clear . . ."

Walker is hunched over his typewriter, staring at a blank piece of paper like it owes him money—or drugs. As the opening lines to the song play around us, I'm struck by the notion that I don't actually know if Buffalo Springfield was a man (like Bruce Springsteen) or a band (like Steely Dan).

"You're too young to really understand this song," Walker says. "I remember exactly where I was the first time I heard it."

"Where?"

"Shhh . . . Just listen. *'There's a man with a gun over there . . .'*" Walker sings along softly, then lets out a barely audible sigh. "I feel sorry for your generation. You little fuckers don't know anything. You have no good music, no good wars. One way or another you're about to get an awful president."

"I'm sorry, what constitutes a good war?"

"One that doesn't need to sound or look like a video game for you to process it. 'Operation Desert Storm'? Please. The whole thing looked like a day at the arcade. And that's what you think war is. Targets and night vision and explosions."

Though I feel the need to defend my generation to Walker, I did, in fact, watch footage of targets in Baghdad being hit while nursing a pitcher of beer and a small pepperoni at the pizzeria across the street from my dormitory.

"You want a real war? Try anything with a *World War* before it. Or Korea. Or Vietnam. Those were wars. Long and tragic."

"Okay, what's wrong with the music?"

"Christ, I don't even know where to begin with that one. Listen to this . . . and then put in some MC Hammer or Madonna or whatever. Those people might as well be making music for dogs—that's how far off my aural spectrum they are. It's not even music. It's just sounds and mugging for the camera and stupid-looking pants. You listen to some Bob Dylan or Joni Mitchell, then throw in Manilla Ice, or whatever his name is, and tell me how good it sounds."

"Fair enough."

Walker closes his eyes, leans his head back, and lets the music work its spell. An hour later, we are drinking, laughing, and enjoying an intimate, drama-free evening. I am confused as all hell. If this is Walker's way of building up to the moment he confronts me for having defiled his pages, then he's an even bigger screw-job than I'd imagined. But as the minutes tick by, and the booze does what the booze does, I begin to exhale. What I feared might be my last night might, instead, just be another night. Or at least it is until Devaney comes storming in looking like she's either going to a slutty catering job or she's prepped for the first four minutes of a porn scene involving a "job interview." She's in a smart, black pencil skirt and a high-collared, white lace top with black vanity glasses and four-inch heels. Her lips are a blinding shade of crimson, and her hair is up in a tight bun. She perches herself between me and Walker with the notebook I gave her open on the counter. The pen she holds says Aspen Bank and Trust on it. She grabs herself an ashtray and pours herself a shot of straight tequila over ice with a wedge of lime.

"Devaney, what in the hell are you doing?"

"Whut?" Walker has the notebook of his pages in front of him, and when Devaney goes to grab it, he swats her hand away hard. "Ow!"

"Get out of my business, girl."

"That hurt."

"Well, what are you trying to do?"

"*She* thinks I'd be good at this."

"Dev, I think you misunderstood . . ."

"Misunderstood what?"

Both Walker and Devaney are looking my way for an explanation.

"Don't look at *me*."

"Yeah, don't *look* at her," Devaney says, hitting Walker on the shoulder.

"Christ, how did I get babysitting duty tonight? Please shut up. I want to hear this song. Here." Walker dumps out a bunch of coke and passes Devaney the tray, as if grudgingly relinquishing a dog treat.

For a split second Devaney reaches for the coke, then catches herself. "You can't just, you know, shovel me full of drugs to shut me up. I have a brain, too, you know."

"Turn around and let me see it."

In a cringe-inducing move, Devaney actually looks behind her at the seat of her skirt. Even though Walker and I can barely stifle a laugh, I can tell he immediately regrets saying this. Walker can get mean, but it's almost never in this way. Especially when the opponent is unworthy.

"Why are you laughing at me?"

"Jesus, girl. I just need to get some work done."

"I want to know exactly what my, you know, what my *role* is around here."

"You are here for the hang. It's that simple."

"The hang?"

I'm pretty sure Walker didn't mean to make Devaney sound as meaningful as a picture on the wall, but there it is. "Yes. You are supposed to sit on the couch and give me something halfway decent to look at while I try to pull this book out of my ass."

"That's it?"

"What do you mean, that's it? Plenty of women would love to be my muse."

"Your mule?" Devaney's ready to take those heels and shove them down Walker's throat. Her country is up.

"No. *Muse,*" I say softly, feeling sorry for her. She looks from me to Walker, wondering if that's a good or bad thing. "You inspire him, Devaney."

"Christ, can everyone please shut up. The board, Alley, the board."

Ah, yes . . . the board. I was trying to avoid the board tonight. It's not that I hate pretending to shuffle images and words around on a corkboard in a desperate attempt to look busy, but I am starting to feel like a third-grader in collage mode. I have paste, I have glue, I have tape and tons of pushpins. I have big scissors, little scissors, Magic Markers, even some string. I noodle around with the fax/copy machine to make certain words larger before putting them on the board. Walker wants me to represent this book in a visual way for "inspiration," so I spend lots of time clipping out photos and words from old *Vanity Fair*s and *New Yorker*s. Currently the board has the feel of an overwrought letter written by a serial killer.

"I can do it," Devaney says.

Walker holds up a hand to stop her. "Out."

"What? You're kicking me out?"

"I don't have time for nonsense, girl. This is serious business."

"Fine. I'll give you serious business." She takes the tray of coke and does two lines, then clip-clops in her heels outside, where we hear her car start.

"Well, that went well," I said.

"And what are you trying to do?"

"I'm sorry, I thought I was being encouraging."

"This isn't Miss Mabel's School for the Editorially Challenged and Infinitely Stupid, sweetheart. And you are not here to make friends. With anyone."

"She's *your* girlfriend. Am I not supposed to be friendly?"

"Friendly but not conspiratorial. You're here for me. Not her."

"So that's *my* role then?"

"Yes. You are the less pretty version of Devaney who happens to have a diploma."

"Um, thank you?"

"You're welcome. Where were we?"

"We were outside Oklahoma City." I gently take the binder from Walker, which contains the pages as he gave them to me—the pages that he ostensibly went over with Lionel and, in so doing, should have learned that they did not match. But he didn't? Or is he pretending he didn't? Or did he, and he's pretending that nothing's amiss? Or did he, and he's pretending that nothing's amiss so he can blast me into oblivion next time we're on the range? In lieu of an answer to these burning hypotheticals, denial appears to be my only recourse. And with twenty-plus years in an Italian Catholic family, that's one trick I've got down.

The new working title of the book is *Roadhouse*, which I suppose is better than the old title: *Truck Stop*. Regardless, it ain't exactly mining new territory—it's a road-trip story, plain and simple. Since the story lines of both versions of the book are basically the same, I've been able to nudge Walker in the same general direction. Two guys, Luke and Tomás, are on the run from the authorities for a crime they didn't commit. They are, of course, committing all sorts of crimes along the way, mostly involving illegal drugs and guns. There are political undertones, political overtones. There are plenty of women—some of whom will go along for part of the ride, one of whom will be their undoing. The main problems, as I see them now, are that the structure is too loose and the fun feels forced—two issues that I'm afraid are beginning to creep into our own daily reality.

To get Walker's juices flowing, I do what I've done most every night I've been here: I ask him questions about the characters. I remind him about certain plot points he's trying to develop. Even though the structure of this book is hanging by a thread, I tell myself it will all work if he just keeps going.

Walker shakes his empty glass while still staring at the typewriter. The clink of the ice cubes is my cue for a refill. I fix his drink, then go over to the board and start rearranging.

"This is a big romantic moment between Tomás and Cece, right?"

"Sort of. One of them," he says distractedly. "You know, I'm a little hungry."

I head over to the freezer and pull out a frozen sausage pizza. Walker nods his approval, then pulls out a pipe and puts a giant bud of pot inside. In the thousands of moments so far just like this one, I find myself amazed at how we are able to pass the time by doing almost nothing. Many nights after making dinner, mixing drinks, doing some drugs, messing around with the corkboard, throwing in a movie, going in the hot tub, and shooting some guns, I'll be shocked to look up at the clock and find it's 1:00 a.m. It's astonishing how much white space we can fill in between plunks of the typewriter. It *feels* like we're doing something when in fact we're just skirting the inevitable struggle that happens at two when I demand—or at least try to demand—that Walker's fingers go on the keyboard.

I would like to believe that our actions are in pursuit of the perfect cocktail of drugs, alcohol, and experiences to produce a halfway decent paragraph or two, but it's hard to deny the generations' worth of evidence that what we're engaging in does little more than impair a person's mental faculties. Even Walker Reade's. Back in the days of *Liar's Dice*, one could argue that the drugs enabled his genius. If they were not the whole point, they were a big part of it. But now they seem to produce what they would in most any fifty-two-year-old man: a desire to give up and call it a night.

Still, despite the tiff with Devaney, this is by far the mellowest evening I've spent here—so mellow that every once in a while Walker will turn from the blank page in the typewriter to me and seem almost surprised that I'm still here. The pot was a bad idea, taking an already unmotivated writer and rolling him into the pit of distraction. Walker puts in a new CD and starts changing the channels on the TV. I try to direct him to the board and start talking about the characters he's supposed to be writing about. I ask him questions about their motives. Other questions, too, hoping this will spur along, if not a wellspring, at least a trickle of creativity.

"I feel like shit about Devaney," Walker says finally.

"Where do you think she is?"

"I don't know. Probably the bar at her restaurant."

"Do you want to call over there? Do you want *me* to call over there?"

"Yeah, maybe. Yeah."

"What's it called?" I reach for the yellow pages.

"Cantina."

"Do you want me to talk to her?"

"You get her on the phone. Then I'll talk to her."

I call the restaurant and can barely hear the hostess with all of the noise in the background. Once Devaney is on the phone, I head to the back office, just past the hot tub and the gun room, to give Walker some privacy. No one here spends time in this room. On the wall is a picture of Walker receiving his Pulitzer. There are pictures of his children. Even his first wife. There are pictures of him with celebrities—rock stars, actors, presidential candidates. I'm amazed at how young Walker looks in these pictures, but it's more than that. He looks like he's having fun—a lightness in his eyes, a sparkle in his smirk. There's no thinly veiled rage, no look of disdain. Or maybe it's because he's keeping good company in these pictures. There are no Devaneys, Alleys, or Claudias for him to slum with. He looks like his true self. Or perhaps what I imagined that to be.

"Alley!"

"Coming."

When I walk into the kitchen, Walker looks visibly relieved. "She's on her way."

"Good. Let's maybe try to knock out a page before she comes. It'll be easier, right?" He nods, but then the phone rings. Walker puts the speakerphone on; it's Larry, who sounds like he's having a party of his own.

"*Hey, big guuuuuy.*" Larry sounds drunk—extremely drunk—and happy. My guess is the happiness is related to the half dozen supermodels that are likely responsible for the din of high-pitched giggling on the other end of the line.

"What craziness are you up to, you bastard?"

"I have a break in two weeks," Larry says. "Is there room at the inn?"

"For you? Always. Why don't you bring some of your friends?"

"Maybe I will. Alley still out there?"

"She's right here. You're on speaker."

"What's up, Larry?" My voice is straining under the weight of forced disinterest.

"Hey, girl. So I'll see you soon." There's a crash on the other end of the line, then a splash. Then a collective squeal, mostly female. Something fell. Someone's in the pool. Someone is yelling for Larry to come in. It sounds like fun. Sounds like Hollywood.

"Okay. So I'll see you, big guy."

"Later, you bastard." Walker stares at the phone after he hangs up, then jingles his glass again. I pour him another scotch, and he types a respectable page in ten minutes flat. We're both relieved: Our reinforcements are in various stages of being on the way. One for him, and one for me.

CHAPTER 11

"Alley alley oxen free, what's up?" Larry Lucas says while raising a hand for a high five, as if we've known each other for years. He's fresh off a private plane from LA, although in his khaki cargo pants and olive-green vest over a white T-shirt, he looks more like he's been airlifted from a humanitarian effort in Sudan.

"How's it going, Larry?" I just stare at his hand. I am giddy that Larry is here but sense it will be better to not act like it.

"You leavin' me hangin'?"

"A little bit."

"Enjoying the ride." Larry attempts to recover from the snub with an elaborate "cool guy" move—stretching his arms above his head, converting the hanging high five into a full-on raising-the-roof stretch-flex. It's self-consciously dorky, awkward, adorable—and undeniably hot. The man's arms are ripped.

I learned during my first night at Walker's that Larry is strict—and vocal—about "eating clean." He drinks green tea at every turn. He works out with a trainer six days a week. He employs a "life guru." And he shoves his face in a tray of blow whenever he can. "I like the getup," he says, referring to the "cowgirl meets high-priced escort" look I'm currently sporting:

cowboy boots, a too-tight ruffle top, and a beige pencil skirt. My recent diet of cocaine and cigarettes has done wonders for my body; I'm actually starting to look good in these ridiculous clothes.

"From the Walker collection," I say, flipping through an old *New Yorker*, acting uninterested. Even though Larry makes $10 million per picture, I never lose sight of the fact that I just gave up an unpaid internship and a bartending job to make zero dollars. So I'm not about to blow this gig for this guy, even if I can bounce a quarter off his fine-looking ass. Little do I realize that by "acting uninterested" toward Larry Lucas—a man who routinely receives marriage proposals and women's panties in the mail—I am acquiring a certain mystery I neither intend nor possess. And it's apparently turning him on.

"Hey, big guy," Larry says, laying a man-hug on Walker. "What're we doing? Let's get this party started."

"People are coming over tonight. We got some more pyramids," Walker says.

"Meantime . . . ," Larry says.

"Meantime, we have work to do," I say. Our little team has had a decent two months, but only because of my unwavering commitment to a page a day, no excuses.

"No pages tonight, sweetheart. We have company," Walker says.

"I thought we didn't keep bankers' hours around here."

"Nice try, but not tonight." Walker turns to Larry. "I thought we could go fuck with Johnson."

"*All right!* Let's do it. . . . Alley, you coming?"

I look to Walker for guidance.

"Go pick out a gun for later, sweetheart, and meet us by the car. Larry and I have to get some supplies from the garage. Grab a bottle of something while you're at it and maybe a little snack for the ride." Translation: *We are about to load the car up with something illegal and would like to get drunk while we're driving. I'm also a little hungry.*

While Larry and Walker head for the garage, I procure a picnic basket from behind the bar and open the fridge. I toss in a whole key lime pie, a chocolate torte, a hunk of Brie, two Bosc pears, a few clusters of grapes, a bottle of chilled muscat, and a bottle of champagne. Then I grab a sleeve of crackers from the pantry. I throw in paper plates, napkins, knives, forks, and plastic cups from behind the bar along with bottles of Tanqueray and tonic water, and a Ziploc filled with ice cubes and limes, just in case. I go to the gun room and pick out my .22 rifle and head out to the Caprice—gun in one hand, picnic basket in other, resplendent in my ridiculous "Annie Oakley working the pole at Scores" outfit. Larry and Walker are laughing conspiratorially and loading up the backseat with enough fireworks and Roman candles to invade Grenada. Walker has also packed up the bullhorn/cassette machine from our excursion to Henley's. They look up at me as I approach. It's late in the afternoon, and Larry is backlit by the setting sun—as if he needs the help.

"I'm Italian. I know what those are," I say, pointing toward the fireworks. "My uncle Nunzio can actually get those for you cheap."

"Hop in, sweetheart." I slide in between them in the front seat. Walker takes a joint out of his shirt pocket and lights it up, pulling a long toke and passing it to Larry. "Pour us a little something before we get out of here."

I take the bottle of champagne out of the picnic basket and pop the cork. Larry hands me the joint and grabs the champagne bottle, taking a long swig off it.

"I have glasses . . ."

Larry already has a slightly crazed look in his eye, and he's only had one toke of pot and a taste of champagne. "Glasses? Let's go."

I take a hit off the joint, and Larry hands me the champagne. After a swig, I hand both to Walker. It never occurs to me to *not* hand the person driving this car alcohol and drugs, but only because it's Walker who's driving. Indeed, the window on Walker's sobriety is so tiny on any given day, we wouldn't do anything at all if I started discriminating on the basis of this criterion. The more alarming part—only because I might be in complete denial—is that he seems to function perfectly well when under the influence—any influence. It's remarkable. And seemingly physiologically impossible. But there it is. For whatever reason, I feel perfectly safe.

We head down the mountain in the Caprice, me wedged between the two men—Walker with his hand on my knee, as usual, and Larry with his hand under my ass. It's unclear how intentional Larry's move is, and if so, what the intent is. His hand is turned up, so I suppose there's little room for debate that he *is* trying to grab my ass.

"To Johnson's," I muse. "Hmm . . . let me see . . . Lyndon B.? No, he's dead. Arte? Is he dead, too? Johnson, Johnson . . ."

Larry laughs. "Should we keep her guessing, Walker?"

"Yes. Who's got the joint?" Larry passes the pot to Walker, who takes a long hit and passes it to me.

"Magic?"

"*Don*," Larry blurts finally, triumphantly, unable to contain his enthusiasm for this fact. "We should give that ass-clown a clean, close shave, Walker. That would kill him. Take away his Miami Device. Pin that fucker down with a Gillette straight razor. Now that's cold."

"Really? We're going to Don Johnson's house? How do we get into Don Johnson's house?" In my mind I'm envisioning massive gates, security, Tubbs, something.

"Well, we're not going to head in for a cup of tea, sweetheart. Stay loose." Walker guns the Caprice, a terrifying act on this mountain back road.

Larry lets out a manly battle cry, and I wonder if movie stars always feel like they have to act like they're in a movie.

When we reach Don Johnson's sprawling ranch, Larry and Walker get down to business.

"Is he home?" Larry asks Walker.

"Of course he's home. Where would that has-been have to be?"

Larry and Walker set about arranging the Roman candles along the perimeter of the property. Walker takes about a dozen coffee cans out of the trunk.

"What are those for?"

"Shut up and mix us a drink."

"It's the middle of the afternoon. What on earth is he going to see of these fireworks?"

"It's not about the seeing," Larry says in his best "spiritual guru" voice. "It's the *hearing*."

"You are a terrible actor," I say, ribbing him.

"Um, fuck you." Larry laughs. "I'm in AA, baby."

"What does that mean?"

"Academy Award. Choke on *that*."

"You're such a geek." We're all high.

"Make us up a picnic, sweetheart. Over there somewhere." Walker points down a hill at the edge of the property. "Go on."

I grab the ever-present blanket out of the backseat, along with the picnic basket, and head down the hill while Walker and Larry start laying out a cache of firecrackers. From a distance, I watch Walker remount the bullhorn/tape player onto the back of the car and pop a cassette into it. At the bottom of the hill I spread out the blanket and pour three glasses of champagne and three glasses of muscat. No reason not to double-fist with this crowd. I start taking out the contents of the picnic basket and notice Larry and Walker doubled over with laughter. Really high.

Finally, with great theatrical flourish, Walker presses play on the recorder. Jan Hammer's "*Miami Vice* Theme" begins blaring. Walker and Larry work quickly, like a team of highly trained yet harmless terrorists, lighting all the Roman candles and then all the firecrackers. They place the coffee cans over the firecrackers so that when each round goes off, it sounds like a series of jet planes exploding. Walker and Larry run down the hill, laughing like six-year-olds, to where I'm sitting, and we wait, double-toasting with our glasses as the entire arsenal goes off. Then, just as Henley appeared out of the shadows, there is Johnson, in a red velour bathrobe—Crockett on his day off.

"Reade! Walker?" he yells. "Where the fuck are you, you crazy bastard?"

Walker relights the joint and passes it around as we pick at the food. He and Larry giggle as Don Johnson makes his way down toward the fence.

"Big fun, right?" Larry says to me, winking.

"Right," I say, smirking.

"*Walker, what the hell are you doing?*" Don Johnson is not happy but still looks good in that robe and brown suede slippers. His face, as advertised, is covered by his signature five-o'clock shadow. He might, in fact, still use the Miami Device. As with most of the celebrities I'll meet, he appears shorter and older in person. Walker heads up to the side of the fence to talk to him.

Suddenly Larry and I are alone, and Larry apparently sees it as an opportunity to "reveal" himself to me. He talks about his Midwestern upbringing as if he grew up on a farm and rose at the crack of dawn to milk cows. Like he chewed on straw while staring at sunsets, contemplating the simpler things in life. I know from my gossip magazines that he is, in fact, from a suburb of Detroit, which, I suppose, is technically the Midwest but not exactly, say, a clapboard farmhouse in Kansas. I tell him that I come from a family of Italian plumbers, which he loves, as if there were some everyman nobility in my being kin to people who snake drains for a living. I know he just signed on for some $10 million role, so I don't know why he's wasting his time trying to convince me he's normal. He's just not. He's astoundingly rich, just like most of the people who come out here. I don't know why he thinks I mind that.

"So, Devaney still out here?" Larry asks.

"Yeah, she's out with some girlfriends right now. Why do you ask?"

"I don't know, I don't want to step on anyone's toes. I didn't know if you and Walker . . ."

"There is no 'me and Walker.' Step away." This invitation might be ill-advised given Walker's and Claudia's admonishments, or maybe it's just uncharacteristically forward on my part. But the pot is making me not care. Now that Larry Lucas is real, in the flesh, talking about sunsets, kind of pursuing me, it seems silly to not at least nudge back a little. What I've said is the truth: Walker has a girlfriend—and it's not me.

"Do you mean that like 'Go away'? Or 'Go ahead, step on the toes'? Or 'There are no toes to step on'?"

"Christ, you're high. Don't overthink it. There are no toes to step on."

"So you're telling me to go for it?"

"Do we have to discuss it so much? And I'm not exactly sure I like the use of the phrase 'go for it' in reference to me."

"Right, let it happen. Let it come to you, right?"

"Oh my God. Just shut up."

It occurs to me that while Larry can score any piece of tail he wants in Hollywood, he might still have the soul of the awkward theater geek he undoubtedly was in high school. He can get any piece of tail—he just might not know exactly how to get it. This will become a familiar pattern out here at Walker's: Celebrity arrives. Celebrity does too many drugs. Celebrity's outsize ego crumbles to reveal a vestigial social awkwardness and deep-seated neuroses.

"How did you and Walker meet, by the way?" I ask.

"I optioned the film rights to *Liar's Dice* a couple of years ago. It's stuck in development hell, but I hope to make it soon. I called to ask him some questions and he invited me out. When Walker Reade calls, you don't say no."

"Tell me about it."

Walker and Don Johnson are sharing a joke, then Walker turns and yells down the hill, "Christ, Alley, get the man a drink."

I bring up two glasses—one muscat, one champagne—and hand them to Don Johnson.

"Thank you," he says, making eye contact, scoring huge points. Most everyone I've met out here so far has seen me as little more than Walker's appendage du jour. They neither know, nor do they care, that I scored 1480 on my SATs. They grant me all of the personal regard one might afford an armchair. I'm loving Crockett right now.

"You're welcome."

I make my way back to the blanket where Larry sits. "You look nice. Coming down that hill, the light behind you . . ."

"Yeah, like a tampon commercial for the American West."

"You're not one for 'moments,' are you?"

"I am if you need someone to kill them."

Larry takes a grape and puts it in my mouth. His finger lingers on my chin. "You're going to do something amazing. I know it."

"I wish I was as certain. What are you working on now?"

"I get to be a superhero." He lowers his voice and cocks his head to the side, one eyebrow raised, and intones in a mock stage whisper, as if he's already spent hours practicing it in front of a mirror, "I'm Captain Avenger!"

"Oh, God."

"Well, in all seriousness, I'm trying to make it . . . *dimensional*, you know? It's easy to just get lost in the suit."

"Are there nipples?"

"What do you mean?"

"On the suit—are there nipples?"

"No . . . But there definitely . . . *should* be." His face contorts in wonder, as if he were a caveman discovering fire. "Of *course*. He's a man after all."

"It's just a joke, Larry."

"It's an *excellent* point."

Walker is making his way down the hill now as Don Johnson heads inside.

"Hey," Larry says to me, "let's have fun tonight."

I'm not sure exactly what that sentence means. It could mean "let's play a board game" or "let's have sex" or "let's do a ton of drugs and shoot guns." Right now I don't much care. Larry Lucas is kinda into me. Whatever it means, I'm there.

"Don't worry about that," I say. "We don't have much choice."

When we return to the house, Devaney is there, having spent the afternoon eating brunch with her girlfriends from the restaurant.

"Walker, baby, I'm pooped. Let's go have a nap or something before tonight." She's rubbing up against him and smells like a mimosa.

"That's not a half-bad idea," Larry says. "Recharge the ol' battery. Who else is coming over?"

"Lesser, Arlo, and Paul." Lesser, as I now know, is one of Walker's many lawyers. Arlo is a local Bahamian graffiti artist/heroin addict. And Paul is a young, gay film director.

"Awesome," says Larry. "Let's regroup here around eight, have a little bite, do the pyramids. Sounds like a plan."

Devaney is practically dragging Walker back to the bedroom. Apparently, when Larry stays out here, he gets the assistant's bedroom at the cabin if no one else is there. If there is an assistant, he takes the couch at the cabin.

As we walk over, Larry takes my hand. "Whaddya say? A spoon?"

"Let's just get this all out in the open. I'm not sleeping with you. The spoon is fine."

"You're such a badass."

"That's generous."

Claudia is out. Larry and I, both tired from the midafternoon pot and alcohol, crash in my bed. Larry scoots behind me and nuzzles my neck. The unexpected third dimension of Larry is the way he smells. He smells exactly how he does in my fantasy—like lemon Pledge and the Pacific Ocean. Like he just came out of a dryer full of Bounce. It feels good to have his arms around me, his chest against my back. For perhaps the first time since I've been here, I feel like I can relax for a minute. Or maybe it's more like deflating—I can almost feel myself getting smaller under his touch. When I turn toward Larry, he's already breathing steadily, the noise as comforting as a pendulum swing. Anything predictable out here is welcome, and that's what Larry's sleeping face pulls from me right now: relief. It only takes me a few seconds to join him in a deep, dreamless slumber.

CHAPTER 12

The circular couch in Walker's living room often resembles some kind of freaky game show or a weird, mashed-up dream involving random celebrities. Who will be in Seat #1 tonight? One of the best criminal-defense attorneys in the country or Sean Penn? Ed Bradley or the waitress from the local tavern? A former leader of the yippie movement? The national news anchor with relatability issues? A governor who once dared the national media to uncover his adultery? A musician famous for once setting the entire floor of a Detroit hotel ablaze with a can of Sterno and a Bic lighter?

Tonight's crew encircling the round table includes Lesser, a stereotype of a Jewish lawyer—if all Jewish lawyers billed $10 million a year and did fistfuls of drugs; Arlo the artist, decked out in head-to-toe hemp, including some twenty woven bracelets he's clearly using to cover up his track marks; Paul, who directed Larry in his first nonteen film and resembles a young Robert Redford, if Robert Redford liked to bottom; Devaney, clad in a bikini top and jean shorts, looking as if she's come directly from the Central Casting White Trash Convention; Larry, trying too hard in Mardi Gras beads but still looking fine; and me. Walker is in his normal spot at the counter behind us. We've dropped the pyramids and are enjoying the limbo between the taking of the acid and the kicking in—all sitting there, watching *American Gigolo* on the TV, waiting for something to happen to us. We just don't know exactly what that's going to be.

"No matter what Richard Gere does," says Paul, "he will just forever be known as the guy who maybe did or maybe did not have a gerbil stuck up his ass. It's sad."

Arlo looks at me and simply says, "This is deep, right?"

"Right."

"I mean, no matter if he wins an Oscar," continues Paul, "or donates everything he owns to Tibet, or Christ, he could levitate, fly, cure Crohn's disease. He's still going to be known as the guy—maybe—with the gerbil."

"Truly deep," Arlo says, not kidding at all.

"Larry, you are going to do the thing that's never been done," Paul says.

"What's that? Fuck himself so he can see what it's like to fuck himself?" says Lesser. It's kind of awesome that everyone here gives Larry endless shit about his insufferable Method acting.

"Make an indie superhero movie."

"The budget is almost seventy-five million dollars," says Lesser.

"How do you know that?" Paul asks.

"I'm a defense lawyer. I care about money."

"I know that more than anyone," Walker says, lighting a cigarette. "Alley, some drinks."

"Dirty martini, honey," Lesser says.

"Gin and tonic," says Paul.

"Two," says Larry, getting up. "Let me help."

"I got it," I say, shimmying awkwardly over the back of this ridiculous fucking couch—a move that I have yet to execute while retaining even a modicum of dignity.

"Arlo?"

"Okay," he says, fixing his eyes on me intently, punctuating each word with overly dramatic hand gestures. "A *Red Stripe* . . . on *ice* . . . with *lemon* . . . and a *straw*."

"Uh, we have Coors."

"I know. *Why must I be the only black man in Aspen?!*"

"Dev?"

"Red wine." I don't love taking drink orders from Devaney, but she is Walker's girl, and this is the type of situation where that means something to her. When other people are here, Walker is typically on his best behavior. She can, for a few hours, relax.

I'm mixing and opening and pouring when I'm suddenly awash in a profoundly comforting, all-consuming warmth, like I'm sitting on Aretha Franklin's lap while swaddled in a plush, rabbit-fur duvet. Then, one by one, I can tell the others are feeling it, too—or some version of it. Even though it's the same type of acid Walker and I took on the day of the tennis dress and the potted fern, different things are happening to me today. Visual things. I hand out the drinks as quickly as I can, flop-fall back over the couch, and sit next to Larry, taking a deep breath. The warmth begins to give way to hallucinations, and I'm trying to roll with them. Nothing too scary, but Arlo is right: this *is* deep. Suddenly, yet not entirely unexpectedly, a giant spinner appears in the middle of the circular coffee table. In my mind I ask a question and spin the spinner. I can't tell if the spinner is real, but it seems to be working, so I don't question it too much. When the real-but-not-real spinner stops spinning—sometimes it takes a *really long time*—the person it lands on has to answer the question. This goes down three or four times with each question landing randomly on different people, whom I then pepper with spine-chillingly important queries: What's really inside your eyeball? Do you like chunk-light or white tuna salad? If you had the opportunity to kiss a bird on the mouth, would you? Then I ask, "What in the hell am I doing here?" and spin the black needle. Round it goes, past Devaney, past Lesser, past Arlo, past Paul, before settling grandiosely, with one final, thunderous tick, on Larry, who's sitting directly to my right, and whose pupils are huge and black. He looks like a deer but still smells fantastic. Almost *like* Fantastik.

"Larry," I say, moving closer, "what in the hell am I doing here?"

Larry just starts laughing. We are all tripping hard. Arlo is humming Marley from the other side of the couch, his eyes closed. Paul and Lesser are laughing so hard they aren't making any noise. Every once in a while one of them will erupt in a snort and wipe tears away.

"Like, how do you mean, Alley? Do you know how many different ways you can take a question like that?" Larry asks. "Like I'm thinking there are more ways to take that question than to *not* take that question."

"What? Just answer the question."

"Maybe the answer is right in front of you."

"Christ. Talk about there being a kabillion ways to take something. Fuck."

"Kiss me, Alley."

"No way. You kiss me."

"Um, kiss me."

"You kiss me."

"Is our first kiss turning into a fight? This is interesting, man."

"I know. Why don't we kiss each other?"

"Someone is still going to be kissing someone else. It always happens that way. One person is always way more into it, you know."

"Maybe we shouldn't kiss then. All of the inequality, the injustice, in kissing. This could be horrible."

"I know. . . . Let's just close our eyes and fall headfirst into each other."

"You mean, like, accidentally kiss."

"Right . . . no, you know, driver to this car. Just two lips that happen to touch."

"You mean four lips."

"Well, two sets of lips."

"I don't want to hurt my head."

"We won't. We could put a pillow or a napkin or something on our foreheads, then just fall."

"If we have a pillow, then we won't be able to reach each other. A napkin won't provide enough protection."

"How about a shirt? A T-shirt?"

"A thin T-shirt. Maybe. Do you have a thin T-shirt?"

"No. Walker, do you have a thin T-shirt?"

Walker is putting lipstick on Devaney—and not only on her lips. "What? What the fuck. Check the bedroom."

Larry practically rolls over the back of the couch and zigzags across the floor toward the hallway. He disappears, presumably going into the bedroom, and comes out—he could have been gone a minute or an hour, I can't tell—with a white T-shirt. All I know is the T-shirt looks really, really white. He jumps back over the couch like it's a hurdle and lands just short of the coffee table. Disaster narrowly averted. He throws the shirt in my direction.

"Holy shit, Larry. Blind me much with that shirt?"

"This is gonna work. Come here."

"How much fucking bleach was used on this shirt?"

"Don't worry about it."

I sit close to Larry and he rolls up the T-shirt, placing it on his forehead with one hand and positioning my head with the other.

"Okay. Ready? Close your eyes."

I close them.

"Now, just trust me. Fall forward."

I hit the T-shirt, and Larry's and my lips lock. The kiss has no discernible beginning, middle, or end. It seems to go on forever in some moist kissing vortex. There is a lot of saliva and a lot of tongue, and even some teeth, and from the sounds around us, my guess is that it doesn't look particularly sexy. It sounds like it looks pretty gross, actually.

When I pull away from Larry, I realize everyone is staring at us, but not in the same way as if you were, say, in a restaurant. Each individual trip is playing out, so I'm not exactly sure what Arlo, who is now alert with a bemused look on his face, is seeing, or Lesser, who is no longer laughing and appears concerned. Then I see Walker's face, which, tripping or not, cannot hide what he's feeling. Even with all that is happening around him—Devaney licking his ear, Arlo yammering on about Basquiat, Paul fingering one of the African masks suggestively—there is that true part of Walker that is not at all tripping. And that part looks utterly betrayed. I wipe my mouth, crawl over the back of the couch, and head to the bar to mix more drinks. I put Walker's fresh Chivas and water in front of him. He makes eye contact with me as I do this and simply yells, "To the range!"

Larry lets out a hoot like he's at a pep rally, and the group clambers over the back of the couch, following Walker into the gun room. Devaney and Arlo express a preference for the hot tub when they see it, so it's just the five of us carelessly handling a bunch of firearms as we jostle and jockey in the small room to choose our pieces. As we make our way outside, Walker flips a switch, illuminating the range with klieg lights.

"Has it ever occurred to you," I say to Walker, "that this is a terrible combination?"

"What?"

"I don't know, guns and drugs . . ."

"Of course it has, you idiot." Walker sets up five exploding targets at the far edge of the range, and the five of us line up. Larry and Paul have both chosen Glocks; Walker has a .38 Special; Lesser is handling a hunting rifle; I have my .22. We are all wearing headsets for protection—something I should clearly have done the last time we were out here.

"Ready . . . aim . . . *fire!*" Walker shouts. We all shoot, and three of the five targets explode. Lesser, who is apparently far more competent in the confines of his corner office, clearly hasn't spent much time hunting, and Paul is holding the gun pretty much the wrong way—it didn't even go off. But the three that do explode look amazing on acid—a slow-motion, Technicolor burst of cartoon flames.

"Nice shot, Al," Larry says to me.

"You, too," I say.

As Walker tries to teach Lesser and Paul how to shoot, I hear Devaney calling for him from the hot tub. But she doesn't sound like her normal self—like Blanche DuBois after a couple of bourbons. Instead her voice is tight with panic. We all leave our guns on the ground and hightail it to the hot-tub room, where we find Arlo facedown in the Jacuzzi. All five feet two, 105 pounds of Devaney is trying to wrestle him out of the tub, but because Arlo is still wearing all of his clothes—what amounts to a giant, wet hemp sack—he probably weighs almost 250 pounds. Forget that we're tripping—this is definitely as bad as it looks. The guys all pull together and get Arlo faceup at the edge of the hot tub.

"Shouldn't we do something like pump his stomach? No, chest," Paul stammers.

"No, CPR," Larry says. This, I consider in a moment of lucidity, is what happens when you confront an actual emergency in the presence of actors and directors. "Wait, is he breathing?"

Lesser leans down close to Arlo's face. "I can't tell. Something is breathing." We are all, of course, still massively tripping.

"Nine one one," I say.

"No!" everyone hollers together.

The collective scream succeeds in yanking Arlo's eyelids open. He doesn't spit out water or suddenly inhale, like you see in the movies. He simply says, "I saw something."

Devaney excuses herself and scurries out the sliding glass door to puke. When she comes back, her nose is bleeding.

"Jesus," Paul says.

"You're a mess, girl," Walker says. "Come on. Party's over for us."

"That just freaked me out," she says.

"Arlo, are you good, old boy?"

"More than good, old boy. I'm going home to paint." Arlo gets up and wanders out the sliding glass door as if nothing whatsoever has happened.

"Make yourselves at home," Walker says, leading Devaney back to the bedroom. I'm almost touched that he would give up this party to tend to Devaney, who is visibly shaking, looks an unnatural shade of green, and is on the verge of tears. Walker puts a towel on her as she chatters away in her American-flag bikini.

Lesser, Paul, Larry, and I head back into the kitchen.

"Okay. That was bad," I say.

"Everyone is fine." Paul says this, at first, like he's a guy who's seen some shit and this is nothing—but he then repeats this every five seconds or so like it's some kind of Tourette's mantra.

As I sit on my normal perch near the end of the counter, listening to Paul make like LSD Rain Man, I'm struck by the notion that I've never felt fully relaxed in this room. I can't tell if I'm still tripping, and this epiphany is therefore meaningless, or if I am, instead, experiencing some kind of posttrip clarity. Paul, rather suddenly, snaps out of his fugue—like someone has yanked the needle off his record—then grabs *The Seventh Seal* and tosses it in the VCR, before he and Lesser flop on the couch.

"Christ," Lesser says. "Can't we watch something funny?"

"You'll see," Paul says. "It'll be good."

For a second I consider that the two men might hook up, even though Lesser is married with three kids.

"You want to head home?" Larry asks, tilting his head toward the door. When Larry rubs my leg and looks up at me, I can tell he is having his moment of clarity, too. His hand traces down my cheek and comes to rest on my chest. I place my hand over his, and although I might be accused of buying into all of the cheesy clichés that characterize Larry Lucas's early movies, he can, no doubt, in this moment, feel the beating of my heart. I am holding his hand there so he can. We are sitting at the counter, so Lesser and Paul can't see us, which makes it all the more sweet.

"Yeah," I say.

"Good night, boys," Larry says. "We're out." After handshakes and bro-hugs all around, once we're outside, out of sight, Larry puts his arm around me. "Want to give it another try?"

"What?"

"The kiss."

"Yeah, of course I do. Let's go."

"No. Right now. Under all of these stars. Kiss me, Alley," he teases. This time I don't argue with him. I don't even want to. I lean in and kiss him—there's no question it's from me to him. No question. Until he returns it.

"Wanna spoon?"

I shake my head no and take his hand. "No more silverware. Walk me home. There are animals out here, you know."

As we make our way back to the cabin, Larry puts his hand in the back pocket of my jeans.

"That's very high school of you. Is my black Goody comb back there?"

"Something's back there."

"You know, I first fell in love with you in high school. Those movies . . . How does it feel to know an entire generation started masturbating to pictures of you?"

"Pretty excellent, actually."

When we enter the cabin, I notice that Claudia has made up the couch for Larry. There is something pointed in the amount of bedding she has laid out, as if to telegraph in no uncertain terms that this is where he should end up. There might as well be a mint on the pillow. We head back to my room. All is still behind Claudia's closed door; I can hear her snoring lightly.

I close my door behind me. "Do you want a drink?"

"I think I'm good. You've done enough bartending tonight." It's endearing how nervous Larry seems as he looks around my room. "That your family?" He points to the photos on the bookshelf.

"Yeah. Three older brothers. In an Italian family, it's like having a pack of bouncers at your disposal."

Larry points to the manuscript on my desk. "That Walker's book?"

"No, that's *my* book." I take the three-ring binder with about a quarter as many pages as mine and hold it aloft. "*This* . . . is Walker's book."

"How are you *doing* out here?" He says the word *doing* the same way one might to an inmate during visiting hours.

"Jesus, Larry, talk about a kabillion ways you can take something. . . ." He laughs, but I don't have the wherewithal to get into the depths of my loneliness out here, the anxiety each day brings, my fear of failing. "I'm fine."

"What's your book about?"

"Oh, you know, it's like *War and Peace* meets *Less Than Zero*."

"Really?"

"No. I'm not telling."

"Why?"

"Oh, I don't know. What do you want me to say? That it deals with the very familiar themes of alienation and loneliness? That the main character, who is definitely not me, has yet to feel she fits in anywhere? That sometimes it seems as if writing this book is the only thing I have to look forward to?"

"So . . ." Larry puts an index finger up to his lips and raises an eyebrow. "I didn't peg you for being an opportunist. But maybe you are," he says in a mock-mysterious way that's supposed to be funny.

But it irks me. "How, exactly, am I an opportunist?"

"You want your own book published, right? That's why you're here."

"Well, not the *only* reason. And even if it is, that's how these things work. You have to know people. Network. Connections. And this is currently the only one I have."

"Calm down, calm down. In case you haven't heard, I am a very important major-motion-picture star. You think I've never milked a relationship? I get it. You're out here alone. This book's, like, all you've got. It's like"—here Larry pauses for dramatic effect and sets his eyes in a sexy look of deep understanding, a move I've seen him pull a hundred times on-screen. And I realize, with no small amount of pride, that Larry Lucas is working me—"it's like . . . your friend."

"Well, if you want to sound supergay about it. Yeah, I suppose."

"I'm not trying to sound supergay about anything. I'm trying to sound very heterosexual. Because I'm feeling very heterosexual about you."

It's the best-worst pickup line in history, and I no longer care. Larry sits cross-legged on the bed, facing me, and takes my hand. The moment is an almost-perfect re-creation of the famous kiss in his classic teen romance *Sweet Seventeen.* And I am totally fine with that.

He brings his face close to mine, searching, until he finally just says, "I like you, Alessandra."

"I like you, too, Larry."

He leans in to kiss me, removing my shirt and bra. I take off his T-shirt, and when our skin touches, it feels as if we are too close—a combination, I think, of coming down off the acid and keeping him at a distance for so long. I feel the same way when he finally enters me until, with one honest and tender look from him, I relax. Every moment with Larry has felt like we're in a movie, except, oddly, for this one. This one feels entirely real.

CHAPTER 13

Claudia smothers her emotions so much that it's hard to tell when she's unhappy. The emotion manifests, instead, in subtle ways, like a crinkle between her eyebrows or a distracted look on her face. Sometimes her tell comes through the smallest verbal tic—her voice rising slightly at the end of a sentence. So when Larry and I present ourselves the next afternoon at 3:00 p.m., both nursing an acid hangover, she simply says, "Good morning, you *twooo* . . ." And I immediately feel like an ass.

One of the primary reasons Claudia is well suited to working for Walker is her ability to suspend all judgment. She witnesses more debauchery than Caligula at Mardi Gras. When in Rome? Hell, she lives in Rome. When people are here, they can do as they please, unless things are catching on fire—and even that's not always a deal-breaker. So the fact that Claudia is bothered by Larry and me is no small thing, indeed.

Before she heads over to Walker's, she says in an overly saccharine way, "You, my friend, are going to get a call soon. So be ready." She says this to me a lot—"Be ready"—like going over to Walker's entails some specific preparation, like stretching or putting on sunscreen. Instead I light a cigarette, pour coffee for

Larry and myself, and take some Mexican aspirin—which are probably the best preparations I can make.

"Alley alley oxen free," Larry says softly, taking my hand across the kitchen table.

"What in the hell does that even mean?"

"You know, kids say it when they're playing games."

"I'm aware of that. But what does it mean?"

"I don't know. I think it's a German derivative. I looked it up one time for a role."

"Jesus. Really?"

"Yes, really. I'm all about the Method, you know. You have to immerse. Know all you can know. Then you can set it free."

"Oh my God. I'm entirely too hungover to keep a straight face."

"Such the cynic! Maybe you think I'm full of shit, but I'd bet it's the same way you write. Anyway, you should come out to LA and visit sometime."

"Full of cynics!"

"You'll fit right in."

"I'd love to. I've never been." I don't tell Larry that the trip out here was only my third time ever on a plane.

"Last night . . . was really, really nice."

"I know." I'm afraid to say much more than that. Afraid of seeming too eager.

"I'm starting production soon, but I'd like to stay in touch. Get you out to La-La land. I mean it."

"I feel like I'm already in la-la land."

"You seem to be holding your own."

"Does this look like keeping up to you?" I'm huddled over my coffee, waiting for the aspirin to kick in. "I try, but I can't."

"You should do like Bill Clinton."

"How's that?"

"You know, that whole 'I didn't inhale' thing. Smoking pot at Oxford. Said he didn't like it and he didn't inhale."

"Yeah, Dan Rather, I heard about it. But . . . well . . . actually, that's not a bad idea."

The phone rings and I pick it up. It's Claudia. Apparently the party has already started at the house. Walker wants us both over.

"We're on," I say.

"Who's there?" Larry asks after I hang up.

"I guess Paul is back. Devaney. Rene Wang."

"Rene? I *love* that guy. Let's go."

"There are three Asian haircuts and two Asian pairs of glasses. For, like, way more than a billion people. Think about that," says Rene Wang, who is about three inches from my face and unbelievably high. His black-rimmed glasses look enormous. He holds a huge joint like a cigarette and tips it my way. I'm starting to realize Walker often smokes pot first thing in the morning for a reason—it helps with hangovers. I know that's a bad sign, thinking that my excessive illegal-drug use might be cured by another illegal drug. But for better or worse—okay, maybe just for worse—that is where I am. I take a drag off the joint and pass it to Larry.

Rene, Paul, me, Larry, and Devaney are all arrayed on the circular couch. It appears that Devaney is over last night's trauma—either that or she's drowning it in the red-wine glass she now holds. Walker, as usual, is on his barstool behind us. Claudia is puttering about the kitchen, tidying and making coffee.

"What are the three haircuts?" Larry asks.

"Asian number one: bowl haircut. Asian number two: crew cut. Asian number three: slightly longer, spiked crew cut. Glasses number one: mine. Glasses number two: Yo-Yo Ma. I have Asian number two hair and Asian number one glasses. It's like Garanimals. You just mix and match." Everyone is getting really high now, and Rene is dancing at the far end of his personality spectrum, basically running the show. "Alley, what's your plushie fuck fantasy?"

"What?"

"Sorry. Change of subject. Your plushie fuck fantasy?"

"I can't even figure out what you're saying. What do all of those words together even mean?" I'm fairly high as well. Apparently, Paul crashed in town last night and has come over today to continue the party. Thanks to either gay priorities or good genes—or both—he appears perfectly coiffed and psychically fresh. Rene, who spends the summers in Aspen producing art installations and performance art for festivals, was invited over this afternoon as well. He is, as noted, often called an "enfant terrible," which I'm pretty sure just means that he can be a tremendous asshole when you least expect it.

"I'll repeat the question in the most direct manner possible: If you could have sex with a life-size stuffed animal, what would the animal be?" Larry says.

"Jesus."

"Just answer the question," Rene says, inching closer toward me. "Don't think about it too much."

"Or maybe think about it a lot. It's important," Paul says, as if it's a matter of national security. We are all really, really high.

"I don't know. What's yours?"

"Easy," Rene says. "Cat."

"Cat? Too easy. A cat is almost like a girl," Larry says.

"That's my nickname back home."

"Girl?" says Larry.

"No, Cat. Like, Alley Cat."

"Oh, right," says Larry.

"So what's your plushie, Cat?" Rene asks again.

"I don't know. Maybe a penguin?"

"Whoa."

"That says something about you, you know, so you better mean it," Paul says. "Your plushie fantasy is very revealing."

"She's frigid," Walker says. He's reading the op-ed page of the *New York Times* while drinking a cup of coffee. "It's official."

I hear Devaney snicker behind her red-wine glass. Everyone is in some version of pajamas except for Paul—even Rene, who didn't even sleep here last night.

"Girl penguin or boy penguin?" Larry asks.

"Boy penguin, of course," I say.

"What if the plushie was a girl? What would you want it to be?"

"I've never had sex with a girl." All of the guys' eyes roll at once. "But if I had to pick. Um . . . Frog?"

"Christ, you're twisted," Rene says.

"What does *that* say about her?" asks Paul.

"I don't know," says Larry, winking at me.

"She's jumpy," Walker says.

"Most girls pick a lion or tiger or something dominant," Paul says. "For a guy, that is. For the girl it's usually something cute and soft—like a rabbit."

"I don't know. A frog seems vaguely nonthreatening. Why am I the only one here who has to answer this stupid question? What's yours, Larry?"

"Lamb."

"Isn't it slightly twisted that it's a *baby* sheep—like a barely legal plushie?" Rene says.

"What about a guy?" I ask.

"Still lamb. And I'm not apologizing for it. Paul?"

"I'm not fucking a girl plushie. My boy plushie would be a dog."

"Typical" is all Rene says.

"Dev, you want to weigh in?" In situations like this one, it's my job to bring Devaney into the fray—to make her feel like she belongs.

"No, thank you," she says, sounding a little like Dolly Parton. "I don't like stuffed animals."

"Well, presumably none of us *like* them," I say. "We're just high. How did we get on this again?"

"I was talking about the fuck-you pajamas," Rene says. He has just regaled us with a story about his girlfriend, Elise. When she's mad at him, she puts on gray, amorphous long johns to go to sleep but doesn't say anything else.

"Then how do you know she's mad at you?" I ask.

"You haven't seen these pj's. They say it all. They're, like, made out of hemp or bamboo or something. Trust me, it's just aggressive. Nothing passive about it."

"And this has to do with stuffed animals because . . . ?"

"Because sometimes if I pretend Elise is a plushie, it doesn't seem so bad. That's how thick and impenetrable these pj's are."

"Dude, that's messed up," says Larry.

"But they're gray, so she's like, I don't know, a rhino plushie. A hot rhino."

"There's no such thing as a hot rhino," Paul says.

"Don't talk about my girlfriend like that. You don't even like girls."

"I like girls. I just don't like to sleep with girls."

"You might if they looked like a hot plushie rhino."

"What does *vaguely nonthreatening* mean?" Larry asks me. "Is that your criteria for sleeping with someone?"

"What? Did I say that?"

"Yeah, like, two conversational threads ago," says Paul.

"Don't get your panties in a knot," I say. "It's my criteria for sleeping with a hypothetical stuffed-animal woman for the first time. Is this conversation even real?"

"We need drinks, sweetheart," Walker says.

I point at all the guys.

"I guess a beer," says Paul.

"Vodka soda," says Rene.

"Vodka, ice," says Larry.

"My scotch, honey," Walker says.

Devaney is still nursing her red wine.

I head over to the bar and start mixing.

"What're we doing today?" Larry asks Walker. "Maybe we should blow something up."

"Not today, I don't think."

Everyone looks at Walker, but it's Claudia—poker-faced Claudia—who can't hide her surprise the most. Blowin' shit up is Walker's stock-in-trade.

"We have the fixin's in the garage, Walker," she says. "Could be fun."

"Nah." Walker isn't visibly distraught, but this simple refusal to create a bomb from scratch—something he is famous for—has everyone slightly confused. "Gotta get some work done. Let's have a round, then we've got to get at it, Alley. Throw the game on for now."

This is the most enthusiasm, if you can call it that, that I have ever sensed from Walker about working. He excuses himself and heads for the bathroom. We are all quiet after he leaves, so much so that you can hear the clinking of the ice in the glasses.

"Twist or lime, guys?"

"Lime," says Rene.

"Nothing," says Larry.

"Okay," says Paul. "Who is the most powerful man in Hollywood right now?"

"Costner. No contest," Larry says. "*JFK*, *Robin Hood*, *Bodyguard* in the fall."

"I don't know," Paul says. "What about Gibson, De Niro, Eddie Murphy?"

"Eddie Murphy?" says Larry.

"Yes, Eddie Murphy. Do you know how much his films gross? People just keep seeing Eddie Murphy movies, and I don't know why."

"He's genius," says Rene, taking another toke. "What are you talking about?"

"I mean, you could have a two-hour film of Eddie Murphy rolling around in his own fecal matter and it would do eighty million dollars," says Paul.

"Well, that might actually be funny," Rene says. "Think about it." Rene, Larry, and Paul pause for a beat, then all start laughing at the same time. Then they start laughing really hard—then they can't stop. Devaney is looking on, unamused, while Claudia smiles ever so slightly.

"It's only funny because we're high," Paul says, wiping tears from his eyes.

"Yeah, well, so are all the people who go see Eddie Murphy movies," says Rene.

In Walker's absence, Claudia takes the opportunity to talk to me privately, pulling me aside. "Look, Walker seems to want to write, so in about a half hour I'm not-so-delicately getting everyone the Christ out of here. Devaney and me, too. Be ready."

"Got it," I say.

Walker emerges from the bathroom visibly energized. You can almost feel the heat emanating from his skin as he passes by.

"What are you idiots talking about now? Can't you see there is important shit going on? Jesus." CNN is on with the volume off, and Walker resumes reading the *Times*.

Images of Bill Clinton, George Bush, and Ross Perot appear, and Larry takes his cue to stop acting like a moron and engage. "You think he's going to beat Bush and Perot?"

From what we've seen so far, Clinton seems to be the alpha dog. Throughout the primary season, dozens of journalists have called Walker for quotes, and this has been his assessment, hands down.

"Of course he's going to win," says Walker. "It's like putting Elvis up against a weasel and a chicken. It's done. If women didn't have the vote, maybe those other two would have a chance."

"Excuse me," I say. "Are you saying that women are this shallow? That they're just voting for this guy for his sex appeal?"

"Yes."

"That's insulting."

"That's politics," Walker says. "The tipping points are never on merit. We always vote for the one we want to see naked. Think about it."

"Okay," Larry says. "Bush versus Dukakis."

"Works there," I say, warming to the theory. "Dukakis . . . just so . . . hairy."

"Reagan and Mondale."

"Yup. For sure. Even Mondale didn't want to see himself naked."

"Reagan, Carter."

"Much as I hate to say it, yeah."

"Carter versus Ford."

"Yeah, okay."

"Nixon and McGovern?"

"Not sure about that one," I say. "I mean, I'm not sure Nixon ever got naked. I kinda picture him showering in a suit."

"Look, it mostly works. And trust me, it will work here. Now, you all are going to have to excuse me," Walker says dismissively, waving away his couch-dwellers. Then he points to me. "You stay."

If I've gleaned one thing in my few months at the compound, it's that Walker reserves his venom for the women in his life. Claudia, Devaney, and I are the buffers for his rage. I avoid trying to pop-psych it. It might not even have to do with our being female as much as that we're not famous and are responsible for the minutiae of his life—the care and feeding of the modern American icon. Familiarity out here breeds utter contempt. It's odd then for Walker to call out his guests, whose company he sees as a sign of his continued relevance. It's so unusual that Larry, Paul, and Rene exchange looks and then immediately start to gather their things to leave.

"All right, big guy," says Larry. "Can't wait to read the rest of that book."

"Thanks, Walker. We'll see you," says Paul.

Rene shakes Walker's hand and gives him a gentle pat on the back.

"Take care, fellas," Walker says. "Let's do it again soon."

"Okay, everyone. It was great having you," says Claudia.

"I'll be right back," I say.

"Where in the hell are *you* going?" Walker asks.

"I left something in the cabin. I'll be back in two minutes."

"Hurry up—and check the pig while you're at it."

I'm sure it's fairly obvious to everyone present that I want to say good-bye to Larry, but it's equally obvious that it had better be as quick and as chaste a good-bye as possible. The second Larry and I enter the doorway of the cabin, he pulls me into a dramatic dip and kisses me.

"Don't be a stranger," he says.

"*You* don't be a stranger. I'm in prison till this sucker is done." I curl my head into Larry's neck and drink in the smell of him. "How do you smell so good? Even after drinks and pot and a weird night's sleep you smell like you just came out of the dryer."

Larry just runs a finger down my cheek and lifts my chin to meet his gaze. "Stay sweet, Cat. I'll call you next week."

I watch him the entire walk to his rental, staring at his ass, his back, the way his pants drape on his legs. I'm swimming blind out here, and I figure if I'm going to grab on to something passing by, I can think of worse things than Larry Lucas.

CHAPTER 14

Much to my distraction, Walker has put *Deliverance* in the VCR—a movie I've heard about but have never seen. Since four, when Walker chased away the riffraff, he and I have shot guns, hung out in the hot tub, ordered take-out Chinese food, tried on a variety of women's wigs, and consumed a mountain of fresh cherries that I flambéed with brandy and served over vanilla ice cream. I've mixed several scotch-and-waters, and Walker has done numerous lines of coke. I have taken Larry's advice and snorted my way around a few lines, moving them into the main pile completely undetected. I've pulled a Clinton on a few hits of pot, and my drink tonight, a "vodka on ice," is mostly water.

When the gang dispersed, it was ostensibly because Walker was itching to work. But now at 2:00 a.m., a blank piece of paper sits in the typewriter. Devaney has long been in bed, and both Walker and I are still wearing wigs: I have on a red Mamie Eisenhower bob, Walker a long platinum number. We're chitchatting about the book, smoking cigarettes, actually having something like fun—Walker appears relaxed, not at all like he was this afternoon. Then Ned Beatty gets guy-raped.

"I'm going to put this near the top of my list of bad date

movies," I say. "Along with *The Accused*, *The Sound of Music*—unless you're gay—*Carrie*, and, let's see, *Cape Fear*."

"You're starting to talk like them."

"Who?"

"The dick-erati. Larry, Paul, Rene."

"You're the one who hangs out with them. What am I supposed to do?"

"Not be such a fucking sponge. Have a mind of your own."

"I have a mind of my own."

"Only when it's inconvenient."

"What is that supposed to mean?"

"You question me too much. I'm in charge here, and I don't want you to forget it. I don't want any distractions either," he says pointedly.

I'm presuming he's referring to Larry, but he won't come right out and say it. I've been here long enough to know that an argument is as much a diversionary tactic as shooting a gun or setting last year's Christmas tree on fire. It's just one more way to get out of writing. But I'm not biting tonight. We need to get stuff done.

I set about tidying up and grab some magazines to cut out pictures for the storyboard. Walker's still staring at the piece of paper in the typewriter. Unless we start playing board games, we have officially run out of things to do.

"We need something else to drink," he says. I'm not sure if it's possible to become inured to one particular type of liquor, but the scotch in front of Walker might as well be Hi-C for all the effect it's having. "How about something sweet. Something with tequila."

"You want to go old-school? How about a good old-fashioned tequila sunrise?"

"Sounds good."

"Then can we put something, you know, Latin in the VCR? This movie is depressing me."

"How about *Tequila Sunrise*?"

"Love it." This is right up Walker's alley—drinking tequila sunrises and watching *Tequila Sunrise.* The man loves nothing more than a good theme night padded with narcotics.

"After you mix the drinks, I need you to work more on that board. Nothing is really coming." I have arranged and rearranged the storyboard several times tonight to make it appear as if I'm actually doing something during all of the downtime. The storyboard is divided into four quarters: One quadrant deals with the comings and goings at the truck stop—it's kind of a character dump but a locale in which Walker can write set pieces. One quadrant deals with what happens on the road trip (a linear device, but not one unfamiliar to the Reade oeuvre). One quadrant is just generally about the main characters—Luke and Tomás—how they came to be running from the law, and their backstories. The last quadrant involves all of the substories, the girls, the political radicals seeking to align themselves with the men, the merry band of minor characters. The board has taken on a life of its own; Rene has actually asked to show it in a local gallery.

I put the movie in the VCR, then go over to the bar, where I grab a bottle of Cuervo, a bottle of grenadine, and an unopened jar of maraschino cherries. I pull orange juice from the fridge and fill two highball glasses with ice.

"Wow, it's getting late," I say as offhandedly as possible—it's almost 3:00 a.m.—but as soon as it comes out of my mouth, I know an explosion is coming.

To my surprise, Walker chuckles and says, "It usually comes like bankruptcy."

"What does?"

"The writing."

"How's that?"

"Gradually, and then suddenly."

"What's that from?"

"Come on. Hemingway? *The Sun Also Rises*? Christ, didn't they teach you anything at that school?"

"I'm sorry that I don't memorize everything, Walker."

"He also said, 'There is nothing to writing. All you do is sit down at a typewriter and bleed.'"

"That's a little melodramatic, don't you think?"

"You obviously haven't written anything of any worth then."

"I won the *Playboy* contest."

"I repeat . . ."

"And I've written a novel of my own."

"Didn't we cover this? I don't care."

"Not even a little?"

"Not even a little. So please don't tell me the only reason you're here is to get whatever infantile, self-important nonsense you've cooked up published. I'm not going to help you."

"Of course not," I lie. "I already told you at the tavern . . . I'm not even working on it anymore," I lie again.

"Good. Now get me a beer."

"I will. If you start bleeding."

"I already have, sweetheart." His fingers slowly inch their way to the typewriter. I busy myself with cutting out more pictures. I get his beer. I go to the bathroom. I do whatever dishes are in the sink, then go back to moving things around on the storyboard. I don't want Walker to feel like I'm looking over his shoulder, and I am amazed at how little time it takes for him to finish a page, which he removes from the typewriter with a great flourish.

"Read it."

I start reading the page, but it doesn't fit in anywhere with what he's writing. Four sentences in, I realize that it's the first page of *The Great Gatsby*.

"Is this *Gatsby*?"

"Ah, so they did teach you something at that school."

"Do you have this, like, memorized?"

"Like, *yeah*," Walker says, mocking me. "It's the greatest masterpiece of this century. It gets my juices flowing—makes me remember how to write one."

"Great." I don't know what else to say but hand Walker another piece of paper from the area that I've turned into a makeshift office-supplies stash. The typewriter starts plucking to life, but slower this time, like raindrops on the roof at the onset of a gentle shower. I start to mix two more tequila sunrises. Walker types for a full ten minutes straight, his fingers quickening now, pummeling the keys, then he pulls out the paper and puts in another piece and keeps going. His platinum wig is so long he has to keep flipping it out of his face, first one side, then the other, like Cher used to do on the *Sonny & Cher* show. He's typing and drinking and flipping and chomping on a filtered cigarette. He's swaying slightly—it's a thing of beauty. It's what I imagined when I first got out here but have so rarely seen. This, I think, is what it must have been like when he was in his prime, a writer in full.

When he's through with the second page, he whips it out of the typewriter and hands me both pages. "To Lionel!"

"You got it. Great."

"I need to get some shut-eye, sweetheart. Thanks. Here." He hands me the .22 and goes to wait by the window until he sees the front light of the cabin flick on and off.

Then I get down to business. Just as I've done every time I've received pages from Walker, I fix myself a pot of coffee, light a cigarette, and sit at the kitchen table instead of the couch, so I don't fall asleep. I get the lay of the land, reading through it slowly, then match whatever is there to the previous pages. Not that all of Walker's pages are created equal. Those written at the tail end of an acid trip have a certain rhythm, with another for those written completely sober (which is almost never). If Walker is coked up, everything moves quicker, but the pages are not necessarily good. The best pages come when he's only been drinking; Walker Reade puts the "fun" in functional alcoholic. I usually take a half hour to smooth things over, then type my changes into the Mac Classic, print them out, and fax them to Lionel from the mini-fax on Claudia's desk. Then I try to go to sleep.

But tonight, as I look over these two pages, I begin to sweat. It's like that moment in a movie where the doctor says, "It's airborne," or the scientist says, "They're here," or the cop says, "The call is coming from within the house." It's that moment of blind panic when your worst fears have come true. The pages aren't exactly "all work and no play makes Jack a dull boy," but they're not far off. They're a mashup of the two different story lines—it almost reads as if Walker were half-asleep, as if he were having a dream about his unwritten book. I can make out some of the Walker Reade DNA, though, so I get to work, connecting the dots until a picture appears, fairly proud of what I've turned it into. I type the whole thing into the Mac from my paper edits, print it out, give it one more read, and fax it to Lionel as the sun starts to come up. I try to convince myself that these pages were just an anomaly, an off day. If not, I'm officially scared.

I lie down on my bed and realize, as always, that I'm completely exhausted but that sleep is far off. I've ingested too many substances, drunk too much coffee. It's hardly a surprise. After several months on the vampire shift, I'm finding it so hard to come down that I've devised a three-step sleep plan: (1) masturbate, (2) read, and (3) make notes about Walker's book. Sometimes I'm asleep after step one. If after step three I'm still wide-awake, I'll take out my own book. Tonight, though, my thoughts turn to Larry—his hands, his smell, his hair—and I decide that it can't hurt to repeat step one. This time when I'm through, I barely exhale before I'm out cold.

CHAPTER 15

"There were no nipples," Larry says.

"What?" My voice is giddy with relief. This is the first time I've heard Larry's voice in almost a month.

"On the suit. You were right." Larry is calling me from the set where he's filming.

I'm at the cabin, and Claudia is puttering about the kitchen as I sit at the desk in the living room. It's a small cabin so it's almost impossible for her not to eavesdrop. Still, I try to contain myself. "No way."

"Way. No nipples on the suit. Like I'm some kind of eunuch or something. So I had my agent call the director, who sent it up the chain, and I had to threaten to walk."

"Why?"

"Well, it was a six-hundred-thousand-dollar fix. They totally had to scrap the five suits they'd made and design new prototypes for the action figures. The producer tried to call my bluff. Said they'd get Nic Cage to replace me. But I'm a bastard in a fuck-you staredown. They caved. Now those nipples are so big I could fucking lactate in that suit."

"So it's going well?"

"I feel . . . transformed. Superhuman."

"Well, that's kind of the point, yes?" I can tell Larry has already immersed himself fully in this role. He sounds different. More steely. More crime-fightery. More actorly.

"Listen, we're going at it hot and heavy the next couple of weeks, so I might not be in touch."

I decide not to dwell on his not having been in touch in almost a month. "No problem."

"But we'll have one break. So I'll probably head out there."

"Great. I can't wait."

"Gotta run, Al."

"Bye."

When I hang up, Claudia steps into the room, a cigarette dangling casually from her hand. "You all set there? I have some work to do."

"Sure, Claude." The phone rings, and I hear Walker barking into the receiver at Claudia.

"Her mother" is all I can hear Claudia say, and I know she's covering for me. "She'll be right over, Walker." She nods at me. "You're on."

"All righty."

"Alley . . ."

"Yes?"

Claudia looks at my beaming face and the ridiculous outfit I've put on in anticipation of Walker's call—a red cha-cha number with black patent-leather pumps and an updo—and smiles. "Never mind."

* * *

"What the fuck are you smiling at?"

"Well, hey, *hello*. . . . You don't like it much when I'm happy, do you?"

"I like when you appear desperate. It makes me feel less so. Who the fuck were you talking to all this time? I've been trying to reach you for a half hour."

"My mother. I have a mother, you know."

"Yes, well, I need you right now."

"You are only about twenty yards from the cabin. If it was that urgent, you could have just come over."

"Just stay off the phone, okay?"

Devaney makes her entrance in a blue polka-dot bikini. She's apparently heading to the hot tub. She's wearing bright-red lipstick and raccoon makeup on her eyes. Her body is ridiculous.

"Devaney, get this girl some of your makeup." Devaney looks me up and down, seemingly unsure that it will do any good. "Now!"

Devaney heads to the back bedroom.

"I thought I was sufficiently dolled up for you, Walker."

"You look sweet, but you need something on your face. Something . . ."

Devaney comes out with four different lipsticks, a tube of mascara, an eyeliner pencil, and a compact full of ten different colors of eye shadow.

"Do, like, the girl thing," he says to Devaney.

Devaney sidles up close to my face; her breath smells like lime, like she's had a few margaritas. Her hand is steady, though, as she lines my eyes in black, then paints on gray shadow.

As she fluffs on the mascara, she smiles. "This is actually helping." I squint, ever so slightly, at the buried insult. "Wait till you see this." The red lipstick she's painting on matches my dress.

I can see Walker peeking over her shoulder. "Let's see. I knew it. See?"

I head into the bathroom and check myself out in the mirror. It's not that I've never worn makeup before—just not this much and never with this lack of subtlety. I look like I'm selling it on Cinco de Mayo. But I have to admit, whatever I'm selling, the price probably just went up.

"Now, some drinks," Walker bellows as I emerge from the bathroom.

"What does everybody want?" I ask.

It's one of those nights when we're not really doing anything, but everything we're doing is ostensibly leading to writing. More important, everyone is in a good mood.

"Do y'all know how to make frozen margaritas?" Devaney asks me. The editor in me cringes—as it does every time—when she refers to me, a single human being, as y'all.

"Yes, I'll get the blender." I get to work, mixing ice, tequila, triple sec, and lime juice.

"Come here, Chiquita," Walker says, removing a red rose from a vase Claudia has put in the living room. As I'm blending, he cuts the rose and tucks it behind my ear, fastening it with a bobby pin from my updo. I salt three large margarita glasses and pour in the mixture, handing one to Walker and one to Devaney. "To the hot tub!" Walker says.

Devaney hops in, and Walker takes off his shirt, settling in with his shorts on. In moments like this, I'm struck by the notion that for a man who's ritualistically abused his body for decades, he looks remarkably good, with a natural athletic build. I lounge on my side on the edge of the hot tub in my outfit, cradling my head, watching Walker and Devaney splash about. For perhaps the first time, I can see how they might actually be in love instead of just mutually using each other—how Walker might see in Devaney a nice down-home girl from the South, like the ones he probably spent the fifties necking with in the back of his Ford Fairlane in Kentucky. He clearly likes that she can hold her own out here, and I'm endeared when he moves in and gives her a peck on the cheek. For Devaney? The attraction is clearly more complex—if not an actual complex. Father? Mentor? Protector? God only knows.

"Alley, we need a movie and some food and a little bit of the drug. Do you mind?"

"No, not at all." Translation: *We're going to write at some point tonight but I'd like to cop a feel with my girlfriend in private right now.*

I head to the kitchen and peruse the movies. In light of the margaritas and my cha-cha dress, I'm thinking *Scarface.* I go into the pantry and grab a can of black beans. In the fridge I find tomatoes, a red onion, a jalapeño pepper, some cilantro, and more limes and set about making a black-bean salsa. After that's done I take some nacho chips from the pantry and spread them on a cookie sheet, sprinkle some shredded jack cheese on top, and broil those until the cheese is melted, then spoon the salsa all over it. Since Walker has a chronic sweet tooth, I grab a six-pack of red-velvet cupcakes that Claudia brought back yesterday from the Aspen Bake Shop. As I'm hauling everything into the hot-tub room, I can see that Devaney has her bikini top off, and the two of them are canoodling in the corner. Devaney's back is to me, and Walker catches my eye when I freeze, waiting for direction. He motions for me to come in. Devaney, I notice, is lolling about in the water. She suddenly seems extremely smashed.

"You might want to get out, honey," he says to Devaney. "Let's get you out of here. Maybe get you some food."

I hand Walker a cupcake, and he feeds a piece to Devaney. He wraps a blue, oversize, plush towel around her, and she leans against the wall.

"More please," she slurs. "That cupcake is dang good. Gimme some . . ."

I put in *Scarface* and start nibbling on the nachos. I kick off my shoes and put my feet in the hot tub, pressing them against a jet.

"You're positively glowin' tonight," Devaney says. "Doesn't she look good, Walker?"

Walker looks me up and down. "*Very* nice."

"She got *laaaaid*," Devaney says. "Wasn't that, like, a ton of weeks ago? It must have been gooood."

"Can I just eat my nachos, please?"

"That sounds *sexual*." Devaney laughs. "Eat my nachos. *Ha*."

"You coming in?" Walker asks me.

"I don't have a suit."

"You don't need one," he says.

"I am not getting buck naked. Sorry," I say, considering for a moment that I actually might.

"Come in with the dress on."

"I'm not ruining this dress."

"Where is the drug, by the way?"

"Oh, sorry." I head back into the kitchen and take the yellow envelope from beside Walker's typewriter and grab a tray from the dishwasher. I can hear Devaney starting to drunkenly berate Walker, and I can tell by the cadence of the conversation that things are heading rapidly downhill.

"You *laaaaaaak* her," she drawls, imbuing the word *like* with about fourteen syllables.

"Put a shirt on, Devaney."

"*Fuck* you. I don't *waaaaant* to."

"Cover up, sweetie. You're getting sloppy."

"You think she's smarter than me, don't you."

"Devaney, the nacho chip on this tray is smarter than you right now." I know the comment will hit Devaney in a way Walker doesn't understand. It's every boyfriend, probably her dad, too, telling her she's an idiot.

"She does stuff to yer book, you know. After you go to sleep. *Rewraaaaatten* and stuff."

I step into the room with the tray and they both go quiet. I decide it's best to let her comment hang in the air, as if I didn't hear it, where it will hopefully die a fast death.

"Who do I have to fuck around here to get some drugs!" Walker barks.

I put the tray down on the side of the hot tub.

"I guess her," Devaney says. She gets up and stumbles into the wall.

"Dev—"

"Y'all shut up. I'm *faaaaane*."

After Devaney leaves, Walker sighs, stares at the bubbles, then does two lines of the coke and hands the tray to me. In a desperate attempt to fill the vacuum left in Devaney's wake, I do a fake line, then put my pumps back on and step down into the hot tub until the water is at my waist. The dress billows up around my hips.

"Forget about that craziness. She was doing tequila shots before you came over," he says. "What are you doing?"

"I don't know. I think I like your idea about coming in with the dress on." Walker smiles, and I ease my way into the water until I'm up to my neck. I'm glad Devaney is gone. I don't care what she had to drink—she tried to sell me out. Plus, I need pages, and there's no easier way to get them than by being a good sport.

"Now float," Walker says pointedly—a man with a plan. He reaches out of the hot tub and grabs a Polaroid camera from underneath the TV. I lie on my back, and my updo immediately undoes. The rose falls out, too, but Walker places it delicately on my chest as my long, black hair spreads out behind me. Walker gets out of the hot tub so he has an aerial view with the camera. "Close your eyes," he says, then clicks the Polaroid. When the camera spits the picture out, he waves it in the air as he sits on the side of the tub.

"How about this one?" I put the rose in my teeth, and Walker laughs, sipping on his margarita. I glance sideways, flirting as he snaps the photo. He lays them out side by side, waiting for both to develop. When the first one appears, it is beautiful and unsettling.

"Eeeew. I look dead."

"You look beautiful."

"Not mutually exclusive."

As the second image develops, Walker and I stare at it. I'm thinking, with this thick makeup, my wild hair, the crazy dress, that sly look, that I resemble nothing of the person who first arrived here in her Amish funeral-director clothing and sensible urban shoes. I kind of look like a babe. I can tell Walker is thinking the exact same thing.

"What do you say? Want to work a little?"

"Yeah . . . ," Walker says quietly. "I guess."

I get out of the tub and wrap a towel around my soaking dress. "I need to get some dry clothes from the cabin."

"Don't go back over there. Borrow some of Devaney's. I'm sure she's passed out in the bedroom."

"You sure?"

"Yes. Go." Walker does another line of coke and wraps a towel around himself, settling in at the typewriter.

Even though I've been out here about three months, it dawns on me that I've never been in Walker's bedroom before, and it's markedly different from what I expect. I'd pictured low futons and lava lamps—beads, tapestries. But Devaney is fully ensconced on a sensible mattress with tasteful bedding. Paintings from local artists are on the walls, and the whole room is minimal and tidy, save for an enormous deer's head that's hanging on the right wall as I walk in. I start going through the dresser and quickly discern that Devaney owns the top two drawers, which are filled with colorful off-the-shoulder shirts, short skirts, and entirely too much jersey material. The drawers smell like her.

Devaney reels up suddenly like a corpse come to life. "Just *whaaaaaat* do you think yer *doooooooin'*?"

"Can I borrow some clothes, please? I'm all wet."

"Fuck you and shut up." Devaney passes out again. I take an orange, off-the-shoulder shirt and a gray jersey skirt and hang up my wet dress in the small master bath on the far side of the room.

When I come out, Walker is sitting at the typewriter doing another line, and a cigarette is burning in the ashtray. "My drink, sweetheart. A beer, too."

I walk behind the bar and pause to consider the specific nature of my enablement of Walker's phenomenal alcohol and drug use. If I were to attempt to peel back the layers of it all, it would probably go something like this: Psychedelics on the outside—the ostensibly quirky substances that afford him his sixties cred. Then the other drugs—prescription, pot, etc.—the soothers, like having a social drink would be for normal people.

Walker, for all of his massive intake, would never do heroin or crack—those, as he says, are for crazy people and crackheads. A fine distinction, to be sure. Close to the center would be the alcohol—a physical necessity, plain and simple. And at the pulsing core of this volcano would be the coke. Call it what you want—an addiction, an obsession—there is no satisfying his need for it. It's the one thing, up close, that makes me feel for Walker. The one thing that puts the lie to the cartoonish antihero role he's created for himself and his lifestyle. The one that reduces him to a mere addict.

I mix him a Chivas and water and get a Heineken out of the fridge. A blank piece of paper rests in the typewriter, and Walker keeps rubbing the top of his head—I'm unsure if the coke is making him jittery or if he's simply trying to think of the next word to write.

"Christ. Where were we?"

"Sacramento. Remember?" The road-trip structure of Walker's book is the perfect vehicle for someone with perennial writer's block—a linear structure where crazy things can happen at each stop. There are arcs and threads. Anarchic moments. Drug-fueled mayhem. Sociological insights. Paranoid rants. He's clearly writing by muscle memory though. I mean, it's not exactly Proust.

Walker takes a sip off his scotch and turns the TV to CNN with the volume off. He leans to his right and puts in a Creedence Clearwater Revival CD. Everything tonight has been like most other nights—shenanigans, drinks, drugs, music, CNN, one meltdown/fight—yet tonight, for me, it's all beginning to feel a bit tired. If debauchery can turn monotonous, I sense we're almost there. It's hard to believe that I've only been doing this for a few months; Walker's been at it for thirty years and is, astoundingly, still up for it.

He does another line and turns toward me. His cheeks are pulsing red. "What in the hell are you looking at?"

I exhale none too subtly, bracing myself. Some version of this happens almost every night about four lines in with little to no warning.

"Why are you breathing like that? *Huh?*" He barks this last word so loudly it's begging for an answer.

"What do you need, Walker?"

"I need to know why you're breathing like that."

"Really?"

"I'm sorry, am I not speaking loud enough? Huh? Idiot? *Speak!*"

"I'm breathing like that because I know exactly what's going to happen here." No matter how many tirades come my way, they still send my body into autonomic mode, except I don't know the right answer: fight or flee? It's usually the first, halfheartedly, then the second, inevitably.

"You and your stupid little *Flashdance* shirt. You're no Devaney, honey."

"I don't want to be Devaney."

"Trust me, you could learn a lot from a girl like that."

"So, we're not writing tonight? If you don't want to write, maybe you can just say so and then we can all go to bed."

Walker turns to me, breathing heavily—so hard that I study the tray to see how much coke he's had. A lot. But what is about to happen is born less out of any physical distress and more engineered by pure rage. Walker takes a plate from the cabinet next to him and without even so much as a pause hurls it, Frisbee style, just past my ear and into the opposite wall. It hits with a dramatic crash that makes us both jump. I'm frozen in my seat, stunned.

"I did *not* just try to hurt you, so don't go telling the papers, you . . . you . . . *moron.*" Through everything over these past few months, I have seen Walker as little more than at turns a merry prankster and an obstinate child. Despite the substances and the guns, I've never felt unsafe. Until this moment. Leaving seems impossible. Staying seems worse. I make eye contact, hoping to soften whatever part of him is still sane, and wait.

"To the range!"

"I don't know, Walker. Is this a good idea?" I am positive this is the worst idea in the world, but I feel like I'm walking on a minefield in stilts. I'm suddenly unsure about every move.

"Probably not. Here." He hands me the dwindling tray of coke. I look at it as would someone at the all-you-can-eat buffet who has stuffed herself beyond reason. I almost can't even face what's in front of me, especially with Walker watching intently as I do one line, then another. There's no fake-snorting these babies, and the kick is immediate and bracing. He puts his glass of scotch in front of me, and I mimic an affectation of his: dipping two fingers into it and snorting them as well.

"Let's go."

While the idea of Walker's handling a gun right now is terrifying, leaving him alone seems worse. We head to the gun room and he chooses a Glock for himself, then hands me my .22. Out on the range he sets up a paper outline of a man like I've seen on television—the kind cops use for target practice—then stumbles back to where I'm standing at the perimeter of the range. Without a word, he draws his gun and lets fly fifteen, maybe twenty, shots. *Boom . . . boom . . . boom . . .* Paper Man is demolished. I sit down on the bench. Even though the klieg lights are on, Walker is in the shadows at the edge of the range. The next thing he does is executed so fluidly, so offhandedly, that at first I think it is Walker's own hand held up to his right temple—that he might be scratching his head or thinking about something.

Then I realize it is not his hand at all.

The shape of the gun fully registers at the same time I hear the horrible click of nothing. There is not even time for me to overreact. It all happens so fast, I'm trying to figure out how to react at all. I stare mutely for five seconds.

"Jesus, Walker. What the fuck did you just do?"

"Just playing around, sweetheart." The gun is now by his side, but suddenly nothing here feels normal, safe, or finished. Walker is almost limp, like a man in shock. Reflexively, I find myself trying to move us back into the house. I need to channel the other Walker—the one without an ungodly amount of cocaine in him. The one who might think that what just happened was crazy, too.

"Let's go inside. Let me mix up some drinks. We'll get a movie in."

"What did you think I was trying to do?" he asks slowly, cautiously, seemingly curious to hear the answer himself.

"I don't know. You might be trying to scare me? For some reason . . ." I am lost out here. I know nothing about guns, so I approach the one in his hand as if it's still full of bullets—even if it's just one. For the first time ever, I consider the notion that this gun could be turned on me.

"I'm trying to see how much you can handle, little girl. Things are about to get hairy out here. Are you going to leave?"

"No, Walker. I don't want to leave."

"Really? You want to stay out here with a coked-up, crazy son of a bitch with a gun? You're even more stupid than I thought. Are you that desperate for relevance?"

Absolutely, I think to myself. "Maybe."

"Do you think I don't know how many bullets are in that gun?"

"No, I think you do. But what if you were wrong? What if you miscounted?"

"Then I'd be up shit creek." He slumps down on the bench like a parachute falling to the ground. I never knew someone so coked up could look so exhausted. In a seeming non sequitur, he says, "Let me tell you something about Larry."

"What?"

"Working for someone famous and fucking someone famous does not make you famous."

"What does it make me?"

"A fortunate groupie. Ask Devaney."

"Devaney never appears to feel that fortunate," I counter, trying to start a conversation.

"Do you think she'd rather be making Goldie Hawn's brunch reservation?"

"Probably not."

"And would you rather be slinging drinks to the bridge-and-tunnel crowd?"

"Definitely not."

"Do you think you're the first one of my assistants Larry has fucked?"

"Not anymore."

"Fucking my assistant is like climbing Mount Everest for Larry. You know . . . because it's there."

"Great," I say.

"I just want you to remember that you're not going to get very far without me."

"I wasn't planning on leaving, Walker."

"I've heard that one before."

"I'd rather be slinging drinks to you, actually," I say, trying to regain some sense of control, trying to find some firm ground underfoot. "Let's go in. I'll make manhattans. We can watch *Manhattan*. Fuck the book tonight. We need a break."

"That's not a bad idea, sweetheart. Manhattans and *Manhattan*. I like it." As we make our way back into the house, I'm trying to appear like I'm not rushing.

"I'll put the guns back if you want," I say evenly.

"Sure. Sure . . ." Walker hands me the Glock. I carry it and my .22 back to the gun room. My hands are shaking as I put them away. I take a minute to gather myself. I want to do something like they would on a detective show—unload the clip or put the safety on—but I might as well be handling an H-bomb. I don't know how to do any of these things, so I just put the gun on the shelf and poke it back with my finger, as if I'm checking to make sure it's dead.

"Alley!"

I head back out to the kitchen. Walker is seated on the circular couch, looking like a guest in his own home. *Manhattan* is just starting, and Walker does another two lines of coke. He hands me the tray, which is now almost empty, and I do one real line and one fake line. I've gotten good at that by now.

"The drinks . . ."

"Coming right up." I head to the bar and throw a shot of Canadian Club down first, just to settle my nerves. I like using Canadian Club for my manhattans, and I'm glad to see an almost-full bottle. I pull out sweet vermouth and a jar of maraschino cherries from under the bar and start mixing.

I sit next to Walker and we sip our manhattans. He puts a pillow on my lap and lays his head down. I put my arm around his chest; he holds my hand. I'm relieved that we're inside, safely ensconced on the couch. More important, he seems like some version of himself that I recognize. Still, as Woody Allen's mythical version of Manhattan appears before me, my thoughts turn to Larry. On the downside, it took him a month to call me.

On the upside, he did call, and he's coming out at some point. I chalk his curious silence up to his preparation for his role, then I dissect every part of our brief conversation.

He was nice enough, I suppose, and I think that maybe this is what happens when you're involved with someone famous. They're beholden to projects and distance. Priorities are different. Perhaps this is just what grown-ups do. About a half hour into the movie, our drinks finished, I look down to find that Walker is sound asleep, and all I can think is *How?* How on earth, with that much cocaine in his system, is he snoring like an apneic old man? I, for one, am suddenly wide-awake.

CHAPTER 16

I wake to the sound of a gun going off. I've heard these noises other afternoons and easily slept through them. But not now. I throw my sweatpants on and stagger out to the front patio of the cabin, where I'm relieved to see Walker and Arlo in deep discussion at the edge of the range. Claudia is sitting at her desk on the phone, possibly on hold—she gives me a short nod—and much to my relief, she doesn't seem the least bit alarmed.

Walker and Arlo have an array of firearms on the ground and two guns at the ready. Arlo is definitely one of the many types that come in and out of here, including (1) film stars and directors, (2) waitresses and bartenders, (3) lawyers, (4) Aspen socialites, (5) local artists. Arlo is in the latter category, and is also, not to put too fine a point on it, insane. He's a graffiti artist, and I've been to his studio once with Walker. The place had so little ventilation that I left light-headed from the paint fumes after just ten minutes. This might be why Arlo is insane. It might also be the drugs. He shoots an astonishing amount of heroin—a drug I've never seen Walker touch—along with your more standard psychedelics, and basically spray-paints the shit out of anything placed in front of him. A few of Walker's friends would, like Walker, surely perish without the help of a devoted female. Arlo's wife, Gabriella, appears determined, against all odds, to ensure that he occasionally consumes food and does not pass out or vomit or OD or die anywhere compromising. When Arlo catches my eye, he waves me over. I look to Walker first for approval. He nods.

"Arlo, what's up?"

"Check it out." Arlo's eyes are pure black. The pupil, the iris, everything.

"What's this?"

"My new enterprise," Walker says.

I look out onto the range and see four enormous pictures—Ronald Reagan, Marilyn Monroe, Jimi Hendrix, and John Lennon. The life-size photos are all mounted on separate pieces of plywood and all have gunshots through them. Four others just like them are on the outskirts of the range. Those have the gunshots, plus red-paint splatters that look like blood, and Walker's signature scrawled at the bottom.

"What are they for?"

"Collectors," Arlo says. "I have some collectors interested."

"In what?"

"My artwork," Walker says, as if he's been an artist his whole life. "Why the hell I didn't think of this sooner, I don't know. You artist bastards work an hour and you're rich. What in the hell have I been doing?"

"I don't know. Enriching the culture? Answering your true calling? Winning Pulitzer Prizes? Making real art?"

"Spare me the American Lit lecture, sweetheart. We have bills to pay. Here's how it's going to happen."

"Who are these collectors?"

"An oilman from Texas wants these four. A Hollywood producer wants the other four. You believe that?"

"Not really." It appears that something like five minutes of effort have been put into said artwork. Walker might as well be signing baseballs.

"Ten grand apiece."

"Wow."

"He has the gift," says Arlo, who is clearly high on some substance I couldn't even begin to imagine. I have this idea that Arlo shoots and snorts things he finds lying around his studio, just to see what will happen. Walker, however, seems stone-cold sober.

"The gift . . . ?"

"Have you ever listened to the radio in the car and you've never heard of the song that's on, but you think it's got a great beat? You're enjoying it. Then you realize you turned on the Christian rock station?" This is Arlo's bailiwick: acting all crazy but being sort of right.

"Sure."

"You know how there's 'pretty' and then there's 'porn-star pretty'? Something is slightly off—like she's pretty, but one eye crosses or her nose has a bump on it?"

"Got it," I say.

"This"—Arlo points to the paintings—"is porn-star pretty."

"Arlo, stop talking like a crazy Rastafarian. You get one bong hit in these Jamaicans, they lose their fucking minds."

"I'm Bahamian, man."

Claudia pokes her head out of the cabin and yells over to Walker, "Don't forget, Hans is coming over!"

"When?"

"Five. Then Lionel wants to talk edits."

"Fuck. Come on, Arlo. We've got to finish."

"Hans Bauer?" I ask.

"No. Hans Christian Andersen. Of course, Bauer. How many Hanses do you know?"

"And Lionel is calling again?"

"What are you, my traveling secretary? He is a book editor. Every once in a while he wants to talk about my book. Is this a problem?"

"Of course not." *Uh, definitely*, I think. When Lionel had first called weeks ago, only a handful of pages were new—I figured, at the time, that I got away with it because I wasn't doing that much to them. But the past two dozen–plus pages I've sent to Lionel are significantly rewritten. It's not that I didn't think Lionel would ever want to talk edits again. Every single thing I've done out here has just been reactive. But now I need to think. "I'm going back to the cabin. Nice seeing you, Arlo."

"No way," Walker says. "You need to help. And stop giving me that look."

"What look?"

"That hurt sad-bunny look. Like I'm some sort of sellout. Do you have any bills to pay?"

"No."

"Well, I do. Now shut up and help me."

"What do you want me to do?"

"Go get those out on the range."

"No way am I going out to the range while you two have firearms in your hands."

"For God's sake, girl. This ain't my first rodeo. Get out there and do what I tell you. I'm not going to shoot you, okay?"

"It's not you I'm worried about." Arlo is sitting on the bench with a gun in his hand and his eyes closed. He's rocking back and forth and laughing quietly.

"Duly noted," says Walker. "I've got it covered."

"Would it help my case if I were to say something like 'This isn't my job'?"

"No. Your job is to do what I tell you, so don't start with that."

"I'm not going anywhere until Arlo is divested of anything that discharges a bullet."

"I said I've got it covered. Now go."

"I'm waiting."

"Christ. Arlo . . ." Arlo looks up. "Give me the gun, old boy. We're wrapping up."

Arlo hands him the gun and lies down on the bench.

"A real menace," Walker whispers to me. "He can't even tie his own shoe right now."

We both head out to the range and start pulling the plywood pictures off their stands. I have John and Ronnie. Walker has Marilyn and Jimi.

"This is a slippery slope, Walker. What's next? Your own cologne? A signature cigarette holder?" We both pause for a moment, realizing that last idea might not be so bad.

"Hell, Jerry Garcia is silk-screening fucking ties," Walker says finally. "Unless you want to be on the next plane out of here, I'd shut up. You would like to eat, correct?"

"Why is Hans coming here?"

"He's in town for some music thing. We have to talk some other business, too."

"About what?"

"Other business that is none of your business. Now, what do you think?"

We have all four of the new "canvases" on the ground now. Walker gets the red paint and starts to splatter these, then signs the bottom with a silver marker.

"Maybe a little more red on this one," I say, pointing to Hendrix. Walker takes the brush from the red-paint can. As he hunches over the images, I take in the curve of his back and the soft hairs on the back of his neck. I'm struck by a wave of tenderness that's close to pity.

Then he says exactly what I'm thinking: "So, it's come to this." He stands up and we walk around the pieces, now dripping red and drying in the sun.

"Not bad." I take his hand and squeeze it. "They're kind of cool."

"Is that bastard asleep?" Arlo is curled up on the bench and snoring away. "Claudia!" Walker yells. He squeezes back briefly, then drops my hand. "Come on. Let's go get cleaned up."

CHAPTER 17

Hans Bauer has the sheen of success. I find that with most of the rich people I meet out here—the actors, the politicians, the artists. They all glow in a certain way, and not from some inner confidence. It's a literal glow—be it from the superior food they're eating, the weekly massages, the premium skin and hair products. It's like how a horse's coat becomes shinier with a special diet. Indeed, it looks as if there's a halo around Hans's long, gray ponytail as he comes inside with his wife, Carol, and plants himself on the circular couch like he's a roommate come back from vacation.

Up until the time I came to Walker's, I worked at Hans's magazine, *Beat*, as an intern. I worked ten to six, five days a week, for free, for almost a year—hence the bartending job—and I have never spoken to Hans directly. He and Carol are staying at their ski cabin, in town for a jazz festival.

Hans offhandedly orders a vodka on ice from me, like I'm still working for him anonymously out here. Carol asks for a glass of wine. They sit, stiff as mannequins on the circular couch, drinks perched on their laps, with all of the jocularity of patients awaiting biopsy results. My mind is elsewhere as I'm trying to devise a plan for the ensuing call with Lionel.

Claudia, however, is working overtime. "So, Hans, the excerpt is good, yes?"

"Sure."

"It'll be out when?"

"September."

"Good, good. The cover, right? You'll have to let us know how the issue does."

Carol seems truly absorbed in the soundless CNN ticker at the bottom of the television. Claudia lights a cigarette, and Walker takes a long draw off his scotch and water.

While I know that Hans and Walker's relationship is complicated, it feels unbearably so in this moment. The two of them go back twenty-five years, to the genesis of *Beat*, when they ran it out of Hans's apartment in Berkeley. Walker was the countercultural id of the magazine—Hans its musical superego. Over the years their relationship has become one of symbiotic dysfunction. Walker famously napalms deadlines and undermines budgets. Hans obsesses over the bottom line of what has become a small publishing empire. Each feels like the other owes him his career, and both quietly seethe that the other guy doesn't get it.

As we sit here, making minor conversation, there is this feeling that things could go in any direction—they could just as easily hug each other as end up in a brawl. What I hadn't expected was for the conversation to be largely directed by Claudia, or for it to be less a conversation than a plea.

"We were thinking, Hans," Claudia says casually, "about excerpting the whole thing. Like a serial."

Hans's face goes blank. "Could be good."

"Really?" Claudia fills up Carol's wineglass and asks Hans if he'd like another Stoli.

"No thanks."

"Well, we should talk terms—"

"Well, *we* probably wouldn't do it," Hans interrupts.

"Oh."

"Let me think about it. I'll put some feelers out." Hans puts his vodka glass on the circular table with a finality that says they'll be on their way. "All right, guy." Hans and Walker shake hands and give the half hug. Carol and Claudia air-kiss. "We've got to get going. Good seeing you, as always."

Hans removes his glasses and puts on a pair of sunglasses. Together the two pieces of eyewear probably cost twice my monthly New York rent. The whole time Hans and Carol have been here—let's call it a half hour—I've been perched on a barstool at my usual spot at the end of the long counter, trying to stave off my anxiety over the coming call with Lionel. I've been getting drinks and lighting cigarettes and doing a significant amount of nodding. Carol took a brief shine to me out of politeness—we discussed wine for about five minutes after she learned I was a bartender. But the whole time we have been with the Bauers, something has seemed off that I can't quite put my finger on. Devaney is not here, so the dynamic is strange. But that's not it. Then I realize, when Walker takes a long drag off his Dunhill and looks quietly down at his typewriter—a private moment—that he has barely said a word.

Aside from the initial pleasantries, Claudia and Hans have done most of the talking. Once the Bauers leave, a hush comes over the room. It's the kind of hush I recognize as the prelude to a bad explosion.

"Jesus Christ, Claudia, I have an idea," says Walker. "Why don't we just prostrate ourselves at Hans's feet and lick his shoelaces. That would be way less humiliating."

"He didn't say a definitive no."

"What about that wasn't definitive? He was being polite."

"I thought we had agreed this was a good idea, Walker."

"Yes, you moron. To me and you this is a good idea." He motions toward me.

"What?"

"Not in front of the children, Claude."

"She's been here over three months, Walker. Do you think she doesn't understand what's going on?"

"Understand what?" I say.

"That we're broke, you idiot."

"Define broke." Personally, I'm used to living on $1,000 a month—Walker's weekly coke habit.

"What's to define? We have no income until this book is finished," Walker says.

"What are your other revenue streams?" I ask.

"Let's see, there's the mail-order maple-syrup business . . . the tie-dyed T-shirt business . . . our roadside tomato stand . . ." Walker punctuates each item of this list by pelting me with cigarette filters.

"Ow. I'm just asking. What about speaking engagements?"

Claudia looks over at Walker.

"I told you, no more," he says.

"It's a lot of money, Walker. It's easy money."

"I'm not getting on an airplane. So what does that leave me? The Aspen Rotary Club?"

"I find it hard to believe you're afraid of flying," I say.

"I'm not afraid of flying, you halfwit. We just had the ATF out here for tea. What do you think is the first thing that happens when Walker Reade walks into an airport?"

"Oh . . . We could drive," I say.

"Okay, that leaves us the Grand Junction Rotary Club and the Denver Rotary Club. Now what?"

"Walker, there are a million universities within driving distance," Claudia says. Indeed, the college crowd has always been Walker's most reliable market. College campuses are like little factories producing generation after generation of Walker Reade disciples. "There's Vegas."

Walker squints, staring at something out the window. "Look, I just fucking hate the things. Makes me feel like an animal in the zoo, for Christ's sake. All that 'step and fetch it' business."

"What about these paintings you've been doing?" Claudia asks.

"It's something. It'll be our bridge. But it's not going to last."

"We'll just finish the book," I say.

"*We'll* just *finish* the *book*," Walker says. "Then we'll cure malaria . . . ! Then we'll part the Red Sea . . . ! Then we'll try to find your brain! Why are you so stupid?" Three more filters.

"Stop pelting me with those things."

"How many pages do we have?" Claudia asks.

"One hundred forty-three," I say.

"That's not bad," Claudia says.

"That's just entering the woods, you fool."

"It's better than nothing," Claudia says.

Better than nothing—but, at the risk of heresy, I can't help but think it's not nearly as much as it could be. It is fascinating to me how Walker writes. It's older than old school—like how Dostoyevsky or Dickens did it, page to page, editing afterward on paper. Storyboards and typewriters. Although, to his credit, he does seem to have at least some sense of where everything is going.

"Alley, go check the pig," Walker says.

"Nothing is going to magically appear in that pig until you settle up," Claudia says.

"The back."

Claudia heads back to Walker's bedroom and emerges five minutes later with a large yellow envelope, which she places next to his typewriter.

"Finish the book," she says, putting on her sunglasses. "What else can you do? Lionel's calling in a half hour. Figure it out. I have to run a few errands."

Claudia looks down on the table at a pile of magazines that Carol has forgotten. I can see something register on her face, but I presume it has to do with something ridiculous on the cover, like stars who look like their pets or The Sexiest Men of 1992.

"How about I pick up some Mexican for tonight?" Claudia says. "It's cheap."

Walker and I both nod, and she heads out.

When Claudia leaves the room, as I have come to learn, it's like a mother leaving her children in a room full of knives. When she's gone, trouble often follows. What happened last night feels like a secret we have to keep from her—we both know this without talking about it. After Walker fell asleep, I tucked him in on the couch and went back to the cabin, where I spent a restless evening replaying the range scene in my mind, over and over, from every angle, like the Zapruder film. For the first time, I feel in over my head, but Walker's words linger. Desperate for relevance? Well, yes. Why else am I here? I've yet to be paid a dime in compensation, and I'm on a ship that's not just taking water—the hull is blown wide and there isn't a bucket in sight.

"Sweetheart." Walker motions for me to sit closer. He lights two cigarettes and hands me one. We both inhale deeply. "About last night. I'm just a little stressed-out. You know, lots of mouths to feed. So, I don't want you to worry. Just . . . Claudia will worry. Just, let's keep this one between you and me."

"I totally understand. We'll get through it. I'm here to help you get through it."

"Can you mix me a drink before the call, sweetie?"

"Absolutely. What do you want?"

"I don't know. How about a martini. Make it dirty. And go get the manuscript for me, okay?"

"You got it. You want me here for the call?" If I'm going down, I want it to happen in front of me.

"Nah. Take the night off. Just . . . We need a break." He hands me the envelope, bloated with cash. "And deposit this in the sow on your way back home."

"Okay."

As I make my way over to the bar, I catch a glimpse of the cover of the magazine that Carol had left—one of my favorite trashy tabloids—and finally see what Claudia was staring at. I wouldn't normally so much as glance right now. When Walker wants his drink, I know better than to stall with a gossip rag. But the cover subject is compelling. The photo is slightly grainy, but the posture—the false humility you can read in the shoulders—is unmistakably Larry. "Secrets from the Set!" screams the cover line for an article about all of the goings-on during the filming of *Captain Avenger.* Under those words, Larry is embracing his costar: September McAvoy.

I start to mix the dirty martini, stirring slowly so as not to bruise the liquor. I've put ice water in the glass to chill it. I am mixing this drink as methodically as I can to give myself a second to think. I can figure out a lot of things: Why Larry would prefer the company of a Hollywood It Girl to me. Why Walker played

Russian roulette last night. Why I'm surely heading home after Lionel's call. But what I can't figure out is why Claudia didn't throw these magazines in the trash. Why she didn't just let me have this small, bright thing to anchor myself. Why she didn't just spare me.

CHAPTER 18

Most mornings, when I wake up at the cabin, I have a few hours to myself. I smoke. I read. I work on my book. I drink what amounts to a midsize bucket of Maxwell House. I almost always down two of the Mexican aspirin—and resist, with great difficulty, the desire to take more. If Claudia isn't over at Walker's, I chat with her. Occasionally I'll talk to my mother—enduring a one-sided grilling about when, exactly, I'm heading home—take a shower, lay out all of my crazy clothes and, these days, my makeup. These hours are filled with a certain dread. Being at Walker's is fun of a sort, but even the fun is stressful. It can easily be a disaster, rife with broken glasses, lamps, or dishes, verbal abuse at high volumes, and no recourse in sight. Those nights—most nights—I just take it until I get kicked out, which can take hours. Inevitably, around two in the afternoon, I develop a fairly acute somatized stomachache in anticipation of The Call, and once the phone rings and Claudia gives a firm nod my way, I dress with all the enthusiasm of a Salem witch heading to the gallows. But this afternoon that feeling is magnified tenfold. Unless Lionel and Walker talked last night about nothing more than Jordan vs. Drexler, there's no way I wasn't found out.

To make matters worse, by 5:00 today, I notice that my 3:00 call hasn't yet come. By 6:00 I'm officially worried. Through it all, I'm attempting to distract myself the Italian way, making an all-day sauce. Claudia is, as usual, poring over a checkbook at the kitchen table while I brown sausages. I don't know if she's perennially balancing it or, like a midnight snacker who checks the fridge repeatedly, she's hoping the contents might change. I pour her a cup of coffee, and she turns to me with an expression I sense is a product of recent events. On her desk is a photo taken earlier this year of Walker with her—with no deep creases around her eyes, no look of perpetual concern.

"Can I ask how bad it is, Claude?" I start cracking eggs into a bowl of ground beef to make meatballs.

"It's bad. We took a second mortgage on the property, but I'm starting to think it wasn't a good idea. Walker needs to be told no, not given more debt to play with. I'm just not very good at saying no to him. But, you know, we're finally there. It has to be done."

She taps the tip of her pen on the table and takes out a Dunhill blue, offering me one. I decline. I'm about to get up to my wrists in meatball mix. But I get an ashtray from the sink for her.

"I have a crazy question."

"What?"

"Would he ever give up the drugs, the drinking? You know, clean up?"

"Alley, he's fifty-two years old. This has always been his life—it's who he is. To cut him off from that would be like caging a cheetah in a zoo."

Claudia clearly thinks sobriety would kill Walker. My guess: Walker thinks it would render him moot. Actors and musicians, they clean up, the world applauds. But nobody would applaud if

Walker Reade cleaned up. His work, his persona, everything he represents, is inextricably tied to his substance abuse—his "fuck you" to the system. But if this kind of defiance was romantic twenty-five years ago, it sure as hell ain't romantic now. It's nothing more than expensive. And it's tamped down whatever genius was there. The irony is that Walker is convinced he can't function without the drugs. And he doesn't think the world would give a damn about him if he tried.

I try to imagine Walker cleaned up, and although I've only been out here a short time, I can't conjure what that would look like. Even when he first wakes up and is ostensibly a clean slate, the need is palpable, pulsing—some explosion, good or bad, is always close to the surface, unless mitigated by various substances. The scotch is mixed before the coffeemaker's last gasp. The coke is rationed out like medicine.

"Do me a favor, Alley." Claudia is considering how to phrase what she's about to say. She takes a long drag off her cigarette and blows the smoke out her nose. "Just keep an eye on him. . . . Just let me know if anything weird . . . well, weirder . . . happens."

"You got it, Claude." I sense that Claudia is in deeper here than she could ever be in any marriage. Her life effectively depends on Walker, and I know that she, like me, is not collecting a paycheck. The seesaw out here doesn't budge unless they're both on it—something they both seem to know without saying it.

I've also learned, by now, a few things of my own about codependency. I have become accustomed, when called over sometime in the late afternoon, to assessing Walker's mood—sour, happy, mad, manic, depressed—and summarily flipping mental switches to accommodate. How will I talk to him? What will I put in the CD player? If he's happy, he'll want to go shoot guns. If he's depressed, he'll like a movie and a sleazy outfit. When he's manic, I've learned to get him in the hot tub with dessert and booze and some Lyle Lovett.

Then I have to surmise, depending on the glasses in the sink, the detritus in the ashtrays, and what's happening on the coke tray, what else I might be dealing with. The hallucinogenics make him happy. The coke makes him mean. The pot makes him relaxed. The booze evens him out. If something has happened with Claudia or Devaney—a fight about money, a tiff about sex—everything can change on a dime. Then there's the book.

We now have almost 150 pages, but the quality of the work is clearly getting worse by the day. Ever since Walker's first call with Lionel, my Spidey sense has been on high alert. I've parsed every loaded look and cryptic phrase for meaning, to the point of driving myself half-mad, but I still don't know if Walker is aware of the extent to which I'm rewriting his pages. It almost feels like he's testing me, handing me progressively weaker work to see what Lionel says about it. Not only that, but I've constructed my own house of cards with this book. For months now, I've been keeping the two manuscripts—one with what Walker has actually written, which he works from the following night, and one with what I've sent to Lionel, which are the pages with my rewrites. And the strain of keeping both narratives at the ready, in my mind, is wearing me down.

For the sake of the historical record: I'm not writing Walker's book for him. I've retained the basic arc that Walker is going for—the shape of the story, the way his personal rage is building the characters, the conflicts, the sex, the politics. But his details, his dialogue, what he's conjuring, aren't sharp enough. I simply can't let them be. I've tried to convince myself—usually as I'm lying on the floor of my bedroom finishing up a pot of coffee—that I'm just the messenger here. No matter what I do to these pages, they are Walker's. But in my bones I know I've gotten in too deep. And if I'm just the messenger, my main concern right now is not getting shot for it.

I put the meat into the pot of sauce I've made and finally, at 7:15, the phone rings. Claudia nods my way. A wave of relief washes over me, followed by a wave of dread.

"Leave this simmering for three hours and make sure it doesn't stick. Put it in the fridge after that. This'll be amazing tomorrow."

"Will do. Good luck."

When I get to Walker's, it's as if all the energy has been sucked right out of the room. I take my usual place at the end of the counter and light a cigarette. I am expecting the rage switch to turn on at any moment. Something—or someone—is going to fly across the room. The manuscript that I gave him yesterday is sitting on the counter next to the typewriter, and he hands it to me without looking my way. I'm not sure what I expected to come out of his mouth, but it's not this:

"Will you look at this?" When the TV is on, tuned to CNN with the sound off, as it is almost all the time, Walker will busy himself with running political commentary. He narrates the events himself. Caspar Weinberger's face comes on, along with an inset of Oliver North. This can only mean one thing: the "Iran-Contra" diatribe.

"Oh, my God, will this shitball of deception never stop gathering moss?"

"It's been a lot of years," I say.

"And for what? All of this money and time that's only going to lead to one thing."

"And what's that?"

"A pardon party. It's a disgrace. The only person I feel sorry for in this whole mess is the girl. She's going to get chewed up and spit out."

"Fawn Hall?"

"Yes, that one."

"Chewed up, spit out, or shredded," I say.

"That's pretty funny."

"Why do you feel sorry for her? She was an accessory to a crime."

"Because she's only guilty of being loyal. It's extremely dangerous to be a good girl for a bad man. You'll find that out soon enough."

I laugh. "I don't know. It might work out for her. Everyone knows who she is."

"Trust me. He's going to end up a senator and she's going to end up in rehab. You'll see. Do you even know what this whole thing is about?"

"Of course I do." I'm not going to lie: I'm intimidated as hell talking to Walker about this stuff. I sound amateurish, like I'm reciting from an infographic in *USA Today*. I'm the first to admit that when it comes to politics, I'm guilty of listening to everything I'm told and believing it. Walker's political incisiveness, on the other hand, is like a stain that won't come off—it colors everything, including his writing, and it's not going away anytime soon.

"Proceed," he says.

"You know . . . selling arms to Iran . . . money to the Contras. Blah blah. The Sandinistas . . . bad. Et cetera."

"Yeah, I figured."

"I'm sorry. I have a hard time getting into this stuff."

"That's what they're all counting on. That you simply won't

care enough to be outraged. You want to know what this is really about?"

"Sure."

"It's about seeing how much they can get away with not telling you. This is just a test. Thieves start out by taking candy bars, just to see if they can. Then, when they realize how easy it is, they move to cars and jewels and banks. This is a mere trifle compared with what's coming your way. And the bitch of it is, your generation won't ever see it coming. You'll just sit there with your video games and your Mac Classics or whatever while the bastards rob the store blind. And you don't even know you own the damn store. It's pitiful. Fucking pathetic. The beginning of the end of a goddamn failed empire."

"Okay." I finger the manuscript, and all at once I'm reminded of what should be happening right now. I should be getting fired. But I'm not being fired. Or at least this is one hell of a tangential way of going about it. Perhaps his "edits with Lionel" are simply pep talks? Regardless, the pause in Walker's rant is the opening I need to resume the job of pretending that everything is normal. Which I do. By nagging. "Are we going to work tonight or are you just going to tell me how pitiful I am?"

"I'm not sure yet."

"C'mon, Walker."

"You got someplace to be?"

"No. But what are you waiting for?"

As if to annoy me on purpose, he taps one letter at a time, slowly, with both index fingers.

"Have you seriously been a writer for thirty years and you still hunt-and-peck?"

"Shut up."

"I can teach you how to type. Things would go faster."

"I repeat, do you have someplace to be?"

"No, I'm just tired."

He hands me the tray of coke. "Here. Wake up."

I look down at the tray with pure ambivalence. I do one real line that barely registers and then fake-snort the other one, moving it around on the tray, and hand the tray back to him.

"Did you just pretend to snort a line of coke?"

"No," I say reflexively, slightly panicked. I'm surprised by how straightforward his question is, and I'm pretty sure he's surprised by the straightforwardness of my lie. We stare at each other for a beat, then two, then he does two more lines and the scotch snort.

"Now, where were we?" he asks.

"Well, um . . . This is the scene we talked about at the tavern last night. Christ, it's so straightforward. Just start it. One or two lousy pages. I could write this in fifteen minutes."

"You're starting to annoy me. Would you rather be ordering up Hans Bauer's pool boy?"

"Sorry, Walker. No."

"Do something, damnit."

I get up and shuffle over to the library of films and choose *Mamma Roma*, starring Anna Magnani. "Italy's national treasure?"

"Sure. Here." He hands me the tray again and trains his aviators on me as I do both lines for real.

"Italian movie. We need grappa."

"Yeah, I need a drink."

As I head to the bar, I finally begin to feel the coke a little bit.

"Where's Devaney?" I ask, suddenly realizing I haven't seen her in a few days.

"Her mother"—*peck, peck*—"took ill." *Peck, peck.* He's typing intently, but one letter at a time. "She's back in, I don't know, Iowa or wherever she's from, for a few days." *Peck, peck.*

"Isn't she from Tennessee?"

"I don't know."

I go to the fridge and take out four lemons and a tray of ice. "You don't know where your girlfriend is from?"

Walker lets out a big sigh. "I'm her meal ticket, sweetheart, not the IRS."

"She's from Tennessee. Come on, Walker, she's always *fixin'* to go to the bathroom and stuff. Where did you get Iowa?"

"When did you get to be so annoying?"

"She didn't tell me she was leaving. That's all."

"Well, she's not buried under the porch, if that's what you're getting at." *Peck, peck.* "She left this morning. You were sleeping. Please just mix my drink and shut up. I'm working."

I juice all of the lemons into a bowl, then fill a cocktail shaker with ice. I mix in four shots of grappa, two shots of lemon juice, and some simple syrup, then throw the top on and shake. I fill two highballs with more ice and strain the cocktail into the glasses. I take a paring knife and make two long twists with the lemon peel for garnish. I press play on the VCR and put Walker's drink down next to him, rubbing his back a little as he types.

"Thank you, sweetheart." Walker does another line and hands me the tray; I do another line as well. He takes a sip of the drink and says nothing but starts drumming on the kitchen counter. Then the drip of the typewriter keys turns into a steady rain . . . then a downpour. My freshman year of college was the last time I used a typewriter, the saving grace of which was an autocorrect tape that would fix typos with the press of a key. By the next year I was all about the computer lab and floppy disks. But Walker, when he's on, makes me long for the satisfying thwack of typewriter keys, telegraphing progress.

"Oh, God. Is that her?" Anna Magnani has made her first

appearance on-screen, and I'm slightly offended that Walker thinks I resemble this earthy, somewhat ugly *paesana*.

"That's her."

"She's ugly." It's just true.

"'A woman who cannot be ugly is not beautiful.'"

"Where the hell did you get that one?"

"Karl Kraus . . . Or was it Picasso?"

"Yes, well, sometimes ugly is just ugly."

I watch the film a bit more and begin to see what Walker's getting at. Certain Italian women are all angles—I'm one of them. It's mostly a matter of catching the nose just right, the jawline. The lighting has to be good, and certain makeup doesn't hurt. Wearing black seems to help—the less going on the better.

"Plus she's a hooker," I say. "Is this really your impression of me?"

Walker chortles, a bit too strongly. "Not that part."

"And what is that supposed to mean?"

"Honey, you're more frigid than an ice-cream cone in the Yukon. Is this really a big secret?"

"I beg your pardon?"

"Can you just stop acting like you're offended at everything? You're wound a little tight, sweetie. Do I have to call the Channel Seven news team?"

"I'm just trying to be professional," I say, though the second it comes out of my mouth it's laughable. I'm sitting at Walker's kitchen counter wearing a low-cut, purple jersey minidress and heels with a grappa cocktail and a tray of coke. It's not exactly the steno pool.

"Yeah, right. Okay, how do Italians make love?"

"Weird question. While rolling around in sauce? While losing a war? I don't know."

"Come here."

I'm at the opposite end of the counter from Walker and don't budge.

"For Chrissake. I'm not going to do anything you don't want me to do." The last part of this sentence makes my neck hairs stand on end, and I'm realizing that grappa and coke is not the best combination if I'm trying to maintain a professional distance from Walker. Not only that, I am noticing things about Walker that I hadn't before. I'm taking note of his forearms, his hands. Or, again, maybe it's just the grappa. The liquor is pulling me down and the coke is pushing me through the roof—the combination yielding a wide-eyed clarity and the desire to do something crazy. What is about to happen seems inevitable.

With my pulse doing a cha-cha, my conscience doing backflips, I slowly walk over to where Walker sits on his stool, pretending to look over his shoulder at the half-typed page that sits in the Selectric while a cigarette burns in an ashtray next to the typewriter. I am trying to merely take stock of this situation rather than be in it—it's just easier for me to do it this way. On the counter behind him is a fruit bowl that also holds a bulb of garlic, which he places in front of me.

"I'm not eating that."

"That's right," he says. "You're not."

He removes a clove and peels it. Taking the knife I used for our lemon garnish, he cuts the clove in half. And that's when I remember our conversation from the tavern when I first arrived. I haven't cut my hair since I've been out here, so my dark curls fall over my chest. Walker brushes my hair away from both sides of my dress, and he traces lightly with his fingertip over my neckline. His touch releases something in me, something I have been careful to keep locked up here. I'm focused, curious about what's going to happen next. Walker pulls the fabric of my dress aside to expose my right breast. I breathe heavier now as he rubs half of the garlic clove on my nipple, then encloses his mouth around it, his tongue licking softly. I pull him close; I want him to stay there.

There is always the unexpected with men the moment you become physical—their skin feels softer, they smell better than you think they will, their touch is gentler. Walker's right: I am wound tight from a lifetime of watchfulness and ambition. I think way too much. But I'm also capable of being in a moment, and right now I'm in this one. Walker's lips on my breast send my mind blank, and for a minute I just let it be what it is. All thoughts of Devaney, Larry, my book, my career ambitions, what's appropriate, what's not—they're effectively barricaded. I can almost see them screaming from behind a fence: *Don't you dare do it! Here are the reasons why!* Then Walker becomes more persistent—so persistent that the unexpected, the seemingly impossible, happens. From nothing more than Walker's mouth on my breast, I come. There is no maybe about it. I am in the throes of an all-out leg-buckling, wave-riding orgasm with no end in sight—clutching at Walker to keep from collapsing—when there is a knock at my mental door. And all at once, the barricade comes crashing down. My head, which had slumped forward on Walker's shoulder, pops up.

"I've gotta go," I say abruptly, barely spitting the words out before I'm running back to the cabin in the middle of the night. Normally Walker makes me take the .22 and watches as I head across, mostly, I think, for dramatic effect. I have yet to see a coyote hunkered by the door, desperate for a bite of free-range editorial assistant. But this time, if there were, it would be moot—I'd outrun it. I bash through the door of the cabin, and Claudia, who had been snoozing on the couch, sits bolt upright. We both scream, and I quickly smooth the front of my dress.

"Alley?"

"Claudia. I'm sorry. I didn't think you'd be up . . . or out here . . . or . . ."

Claudia tilts her head to one side, now fully awake. Her look suggests that this is not the first time she's been woken in the middle of the night by a crazed assistant. "Calm down. Sit."

I'm breathing heavily as I take a seat at the desk. "I'm okay."

"Did he hit on you?"

"Yes. Kind of. Yes. I guess. Yes."

"Calm down." I'm on the verge of mania as Claudia lights two cigarettes and hands me one. "Did you want him to be hitting on you?"

I'm surprised that Claudia doesn't know the answer to this question, but no doubt she's seen this before: the formerly ambivalent woman suddenly succumbing to Walker's charms. I lie, "No. I don't think so. No."

"You're sure."

I lie again, "Sure."

"It's funny. Everybody at some point, at some time, falls in love with Walker." She says this more to herself than to me. "So just tell him to cut it out. He'll listen. Trust me. After the sexual-harassment suit, he's not going to touch you unless you want him to. He's many things, but he's not like that. Any pages?"

I am amazed that Claudia cares about pages at a time like this. "Half of one. We were just starting. I mixed a grappa cocktail. It was a bad idea."

"Calm down, Alley. Seriously, he'll forget about it tomorrow. Get some sleep." She gets up to go to bed herself.

"Okay . . . Claudia . . ."

"Yes?" She takes a long, slow draw on her cigarette.

"I just don't want to be that girl, you know? I want it clear to everyone that I'm not just going to be passed around out here."

"Trust me, you're not cut out to be that girl. Get some rest."

Claudia heads back to her bedroom and I sit on the couch to finish my cigarette. I would like to get some rest but know that with all of the coke in me, sleep is not an option. As I fidget on the couch, my hand goes to my chest. I'm still damp between my legs. If I close my eyes, I can still feel Walker's lips. Claudia says I'm not that girl, but I'm starting to become afraid of the one I really am. The one who's bumping into all the boundaries just to see what's there. The one who is ignoring the small chips in her dignity, morals, and otherwise good sense.

With sleep out of the question, I go back into my bedroom to work on my manuscript, which has remained an anchor of sorts the whole time I've been out here. No matter what has happened, it's what I've found solace in, something so unmistakably tied to all of my hopes for the future. The physical reminder of why I'm here—why I refuse to go home despite an environment that has turned increasingly insane. I had left it, as I always do, on my makeshift desk next to the Mac Classic. But after staring blankly at the spot for several seconds, it dawns on me: it isn't there. I rifle around my desk briefly—there are the two Walker manuscripts, exactly where I left them, plus a few other notebooks strewn about. Everything else looks untouched. I go out to the living room thinking that I might have left it out there or in the kitchen, but there's nothing. Just the hum of the refrigerator, the glow of the potbellied stove. I don't want to consider the unthinkable, but suddenly it becomes clear where it is—not exactly *where* it is, but what has happened to it. I don't wake Claudia. I don't want to face the truth. I just want to go to bed.

I sink onto the mattress and curl up like a possum. Now I'm tired—dead tired. What happened tonight was perhaps the one thing that would have pointed me home—awakened me to the fact that it's time to get out of here. Since I fled to the cabin, that thought has spread like a virus, become obvious even: *It's time to go*. But suddenly, like a sentencing, it dawns on me: now I can't.

CHAPTER 19

"Mom?"

"Alessandra?"

"Hi."

"Hi."

I'm sitting alone at Claudia's desk; she's over at Walker's getting his day started. It's midafternoon, and I'm fresh out of the shower. We have no hair dryer, so my thick, black mane is still tied up in a towel, and I'm in a plush, white terry-cloth robe from the Four Seasons Chicago. I stole it from Walker's one night after a foray into the hot tub—it was hanging on a hook along with plush robes from several other four-star establishments, an amenity he routinely steals, or at least used to steal when he was still traveling. I smooth my hand over the empty desk calendar and wait for my mother's usual script to kick in.

The few times I've spoken with her since I've been out here, she has been aggressively concerned, peppering me with questions about sleeping arrangements and the exact origin of my meals, which I'm forced to lie about. If my mother knew I was eating frozen Marie Callender's lasagna out of a microwave twice a week, she would be on the first plane out here with a

Tupperware full of braciole. But she sounds relaxed today—slower, less desperate—like she's eating something. From the sound of her aggressive masticating, perhaps a handful of peanuts. I'm waiting for the histrionics, the *Why haven't you called?* and the *I'm worried sick over here.* But instead she swallows hard, waiting for me to talk.

"I just wanted to hear your voice. How are things?"

"Good, good."

"You eating?"

"A little snack. Yeah. Everything okay?" This is as close as she comes to her usual overconcern, but her tone is light—positive, even. Her voice is a singsong. It's deeply off-putting.

"What are you drinking?"

"Ginger ale."

"How are Dad and the guys?"

"Great. They got a big contract. Your father is happy about it."

"What are you up to, Ma?"

She lets out a soft snort as if to ask, *What do you think I'm up to? Deconstructing* Guernica*?* I know the answer: She's cooking for a bunch of men who don't appreciate her. She's washing endless loads of laundry. She's cleaning the bathroom—again. Going to church and bingo. Aunt Sal and the girls are coming over to play cards on Wednesday. "You sound different."

"Different? I got a little job. Two days a week at the church office." Two days out of the house. It's not different she sounds. It's happy. "I'm good. Okay . . ." And just like that, for the first time ever, she's ending the conversation. We say our *I love yous* and she practically hangs up on me.

I head into the bathroom and put on eyeliner and red lipstick. I find a casual little black dress from a recent boutique trip with Walker, and the bright red pumps he bought me my first week here. Even though it's two in the afternoon I look like I'm going to a cocktail party. I don't quite know what to make of the conversation with my mother. Maybe J.D. got to her and she realizes what a great opportunity this might be for me. Maybe getting a job herself—her first one out of the house, ever—is helping her understand my desire for a career. Or, who knows, she just might be finding the freedom that comes with letting go—despite the unlikelihood that this life skill would suddenly manifest in her early fifties. Whatever's going on, I called her because I was looking for some strength, some inspiration, for what I have to do right now. I smooth my dress and wipe a small lipstick smudge from the corner of my mouth and replay the call in my head—something's still bothering me. I'm big enough to realize, finally, that maybe I was looking for someone to just be worried about me, and I don't think it's too crazy that I thought she was a lock.

When I enter the house, Claudia is scrambling a peacock egg for Walker, who is sipping a large screwdriver as he reads the paper. A George Strait CD is playing.

"Hey . . ."

"I didn't call you over here, did I?"

Even Claudia looks shocked to see me as she furrows her brow over the frying pan. "Let me just finish this egg, Alley, then I can help you out."

"Has anyone seen my manuscript?" I ask casually.

Walker continues to read the paper as if I'm not here. Claudia is concentrating hard on that egg, like she's working a nuclear-fusion experiment. She throws two pieces of wheat bread down in the toaster and grabs a plate. No one says a word. I take a highball from the kitchen cabinet and fill it with ice. I pour two fingers of Chivas and sit at the end of the counter where I light a cigarette. I'm watching Claudia and Walker almost as if I were watching a play—the one where the divorced couple reconciles but you know from the way she fixes breakfast, the way he reads the paper, that it won't last. Walker lights up a cigarette and turns on CNN. After Claudia places his breakfast in front of him, she turns to me and mouths, *Let's go*.

"Go where?" I say out loud. "Where the fuck is my manuscript?"

"You are slightly out of line, miss," Walker starts.

"I'm out of line? Last I knew I didn't steal anything from you. Why would you take it?"

"You are supposed to be working for me out here. Not on your own business."

"I *am* working out here for you, Walker. What exactly am I *not* doing for you?" I say this last sentence as pointedly as I can.

"I need you to focus."

"I am focusing. We're getting pages done, right? Lionel's happy, right?"

"Very," he says, a little pointedly himself.

Claudia doesn't leave but shuffles about the kitchen making herself busy, washing dishes, tidying up, cleaning cigarette filters—a uniquely gross process that involves soaking the lot of them in a bowl of detergent. I can tell she's debating whether she should step in.

"Just until you leave," she says.

"Shut up, Claudia," Walker says.

"I won't work on it, I promise. I just want to have it in my possession. It's mine." Something like desperation is in my voice;

the fact that something has been stolen from me seems very basic. In New York I had a copy on my Mac Classic, which was stolen, and I never put the file on a disk. It's the only copy I've got.

"We really need you to focus," Claudia says, winking at me.

"Didn't I just say to shut up? Go away."

"Come on, Alley." Claudia takes me by the hand.

"She stays."

Claudia hesitates, but I drop her hand and sit back down where my scotch is. Claudia looks at us both. To her right, the rock. To her left, the hard place.

"It's okay," Walker and I say to her in unison.

After Claudia leaves, Walker starts in on his breakfast.

"What is going on, Walker?"

"I just need to know I have your undivided attention, sweetheart."

"Walker, I already feel like I'm in a gulag out here. I don't do anything but wait for your call. I have no friends. I barely talk to my family."

"You made friends with Larry."

"I think we all know how that turned out."

"He's coming out here next week, you know."

"He is?" I try to say this as impassively as possible.

"So are you going to jump all over him?"

"No. Is that what you want? For me to say I won't jump all over Larry?"

"Yes."

"Fine. But I'm not going to jump all over you either."

"Fine."

I don't even know if it's worth bringing up Devaney. I don't sense that Walker's undying fidelity is something either of them is wagering on. “I’m here to learn from you, Walker. I’m fully committed.”

“Yeah, what do you think you can learn from me?”

“What it takes to be great.”

“And what makes you think I’m so great?”

“The National Book Award, the Pulitzer. The seven books.”

“Ancient history. Like me, sweetheart.” He seems to be on the verge of saying something but appears to not feel enough conviction to say it. “Anyway, what do you want from me? You’re here to help me. I’m not here to help you. Didn’t they teach you to write at that fancy-pants Ivy League school you went to?”

“Excuse me?” I’ve let these comments slide a few times since I’ve been here, but not today, not now.

“Bunch of spoiled brats. Didn’t they teach you rich kids anything?”

“You know what, Walker? Big fucking deal. I went to an Ivy League school. You don’t know anything else about me. And I’m sure you think that because I went to an Ivy League school that my dad is some sort of CEO or oil mogul or some ex-parliamentarian from Rome or something. But guess what: He’s a plumber. A snake-your-crapper plumber. And Larry knows that, because he asked. And my mom cooks all day long in a housecoat with a tissue up her sleeve to wipe the sweat from frying meatballs and squash flowers. They’re off the fucking boat, Walker. They don’t even know who you are. My grandfather was a brick*maker* in Italy. Not a bricklayer, but the guy who *made* the fucking bricks. I’m trying to think of something more mind-numbing than creating a brick from scratch, and I can’t. Maybe being out here snorting drugs and fucking around all day. You know why all of the drinks I mix for you taste so good? Because I’ve been slinging them on the side since I was old enough to mix one to pay for that fancy-pants Ivy League school, which I'll be paying off for ten more years unless you write this book. So . . . so *fuck you.*"

Walker chuckles and smiles a bit to himself. "So fuck me," he says, his smirk slowly giving way to a full grin. He takes a quick snort of coke and offers me the plate. I do one, too—it's a glancing blow.

"Trust me, I'm desperate enough without you stealing shit from me. I'm not going anywhere."

"You'll get it back when we finish."

"Is that supposed to motivate you or me?"

"Both of us. Go back to the cabin. I'll call you later."

CHAPTER 20

When I walk into the cabin, Claudia is dusting. I have never before seen the woman dust. I've seen her do other menial jobs under the guise of thoroughness. But I'm beginning to realize that Claudia focuses on mundane tasks—cleaning the fridge, balancing the checkbook—when she gets stressed, an all-too-common occurrence these days. Indeed, the more dysfunctional this place gets, the better it looks. I figure I'll really worry when she starts bathing the peacocks.

I know Claudia likes me; at this point I'd even say we're friends. But her loyalty to Walker is so complete that I think even she is confused by the depths of it. I can tell she feels bad by the aggressive manner in which she's polishing the hell out of her desk with an old, torn T-shirt. I feel sorry for Claudia most of the time—I don't know enough about her or Walker to draw a blueprint of the house of cards they've built together—but I have no interest in making her feel worse. She can barely look me in the eye.

"What's going on, Claude?"

"Filthy desk. How did this get so dusty?" She sits in the chair and puts her head in her hands.

I light up two cigarettes and hand her one. "I don't know. Is it maybe the fourteen packs of cigarettes we smoke every day? It's not dust. It's ashes."

Claudia lets out a long sigh. The now-charcoal-gray T-shirt is draped over her lap. "I'm sorry, Alley."

"Why? Did you give him my manuscript?"

She doesn't answer, only fingers a wood knot on the dark brown desk.

"Do you know where it is?"

"Yes, of course I do."

"Where is it then?"

"It's safe. I promise."

"Can't you just tell me?"

"If I tell you, you can't go take it back. Then it'd be hell to pay for both of us."

"Fine."

"It's in his bedroom. There's a safe in the closet. I'm not telling you the combination. But that's where it is. Trust me, it's safe. It's fireproof."

"It's not fire I'm worried about, Claude."

"He's nervous about this book. If he feels taking your manuscript will help, then that's what we have to do." She says this so offhandedly, I'm not sure if she knows she's said it out loud. She shakes her head and stands up. "I need some help."

At first I think she means this in some macroexistential way. But when I follow her outside, she merely waves to flats upon flats of flowers in front of the cabin from yet another trip to Von Gundy's—one Walker took with Devaney last week. A peacock strolls by with purpose, as if on his way to a pressing engagement.

"Why don't you get changed?"

"I'm good. I don't care if this gets dirty."

"It's pretty sunny, though. You want to be covered up. Your shoulders . . ."

"I'm good."

"We have pots over there." She points to a storage area behind the peacock coop. "Come on."

We lug over eight pots and six bags of potting soil. Claudia takes some pieces of broken pot and places them loosely over the drainage hole in the bottom of the pots. She fills them about three-quarters of the way with soil, and then we start with the impatiens. Outside, the sun feels good and the air clean, and I realize that I haven't had a lick of exercise since I've moved out here. I haven't hiked or biked or gone for a run. I've gone from smoking half a pack a day to two packs at least—and I am ingesting drugs so casually now that it's hard to tell if I have a problem; it just seems like a condition of employment. The drinking is what it is—constant, the mixing relentless. I would say the alcohol is like oxygen out here, but even that is more scarce at this altitude.

"Do you want gloves?" Claudia asks.

"Nah. It's kind of nice to feel my hands in the dirt."

"You seem to know what you're doing."

"My mother has a killer garden. Mostly vegetables—tomatoes, eggplant, zucchini—but I help her when I'm around."

"You should cover up. You're getting red."

"I'm fine. I feel like a vampire most of the time now. I think I could use the rays. Vitamin D. Something . . ."

"Don't forget, we're closer to the sun."

"I know." What I want to say is I feel this every day now—that I'm already too close to something hot and bright and capable of burning me at will. We continue to pot the flowers without speaking, Claudia's spade clicking against the ceramic. "When's Devaney coming back?"

Claudia eyes me. "What do you mean?"

"Nothing," I say, confused. "I mean, she's at her mom's, right?"

"Who told you that?"

"Walker."

"Hmmm." Claudia heads inside without a word. When she comes out, she has two Heinekens, a pack of Dunhill blues, a lighter, and an ashtray. She hands me a beer and a smoke; our hands are still covered in soil. I can tell Claudia is deciding—as she must do with everyone, I guess—what purpose Walker's behavior serves and whether it's okay for her to override his intentions.

"I don't think she is," she says vaguely.

"Is what?"

"Coming back."

"Really? Is her mother that sick?"

Claudia looks at me as if I'm an idiot. "I doubt anyone is sick."

"Oh. He didn't tell me. What happened?"

"What always happens. Walker picks people half his age because he thinks they're somehow going to be easier to handle or influence or that they're sexier or something. Then he hates them for being so dumb and inexperienced. Then he hates himself for uprooting their lives, so in order to not feel guilty, he treats them like shit until they run away. This goes for girlfriends and assistants, by the way. I give her credit, though."

"For what?"

"I honestly thought she would last longer. But the shorter they stay, the more I respect them."

"Yeah, but what does that make you?" I take a draw off the beer. "You've been here forever."

"Me? I'm an idiot."

"And what does that make me?"

"Jury's out."

I'm not sure what to make of this news. Like her or not, Devaney has been my buffer thus far with Walker. She's saved me from a whole host of duties that might start entering my job description in her absence. I wouldn't necessarily call her a friend, but we had the forced bond of prisonmates, and it wasn't entirely uncomforting.

"There's something I need to tell you," Claudia says.

"What?"

"I have to go see my son. He's up at the house, and from what I understand, he's pretty sick—mono or pneumonia. He's resting up there and I have to coordinate his care a bit. But I want you to keep an eye on Walker. I have to tell him later, when we're both there. I really want to leave tonight. He doesn't do well when I leave."

"Well, he said Larry's coming to town." While I feel bad for Claudia's son, the idea of being alone in the cabin with Larry gives way to multiple fantasies involving coffee and robes, long, hot baths, curling up by the stove while my feet get rubbed by a movie star, games of "hide the Oscar" in the bedroom. For the first time since I've been here, I feel the freedom of a teenager whose parents are about to go out of town for the weekend.

"No, he's not," Claudia snaps.

"Yes, he is. Walker told me last night."

"Well, he didn't tell me." This tone is uncharacteristic from Claudia. I'm trying to figure whom, exactly, she's mad at.

"I'm just the messenger, Claude," I say, holding up my hands.

She takes a long drag off her cigarette, blowing the smoke

out of her nose. "Yeah, well, I guess I'm used to being the messenger for everybody else around here." Then this: "I'm not sure about Larry sometimes."

"What do you mean?" I suppose she could mean he's a bad influence on Walker or perhaps just not good for me. But there's something else.

"You going to be okay here?"

"I can handle myself."

Claudia nods. I'm not new anymore; she believes me when I say this. "You better cover up, Alley. I can see it. You're burning up."

CHAPTER 21

When Claudia and I head over to the house around suppertime, Walker is watching a baseball game. A joint is smoldering away in the ashtray, and he's nursing a bottle of Heineken and, of course, a glass of scotch and water.

"Frick and Fuck," he says when we come in. "What now?"

I've never seen Claudia so nervous around Walker. "Cody's really sick," Claudia says matter-of-factly. "I have to head up to Crested Butte."

"When?"

"Tonight, Walker."

"Turn around," Walker says to me.

"Excuse me? No. Why?"

"Relax. I'm not about to goose you, sweetheart. You're all red." Claudia was right. My shoulders are cherry-colored from wearing that skimpy cocktail dress in the afternoon sun.

"I told her to cover up," Claudia says, trying to sound lighthearted.

"Why didn't you cover up?" asks Walker.

"I don't know. We're only a mile and a half above sea level, not six inches from the sun."

"I have to leave to go see Cody," says Claudia, staying on message. No doubt she's seen this before—the evasive recast of the situation.

"At least head down to the pig before you go." Most people would ask about Claudia's son, but Walker is staying on message, too.

"There's a problem with the pig."

"Christ, Claudia. I just need you to take care of it. Did it ever occur to you that I might be having company this weekend?"

"Actually, no. Because you didn't tell me."

"Come here," he says to me.

"Why?"

"Fuck. Why is everyone always questioning me? I am not paying either of you to ask questions. *I am paying for help!*"

"You are not paying either of us, period," Claudia says quietly.

I am expecting an eruption of volcanic proportions from Walker, but he simply stares Claudia down. And it occurs to me for the first time how much Walker needs her. She obviously doesn't want to piss him off, but I see that he doesn't want to upset her either, and I briefly wonder how long it's been since Claudia has cashed a paycheck.

"Just leave, Claudia. Everybody leaves. Are you next?" He looks right at me, motioning me to come closer.

I blanch. "No." I stay right where I am.

"Just get over here. I'm trying to help." He reaches up in the cabinet to his right—the one that houses CDs, pills, and a few awards, and pulls out a bottle of pure aloe. I'm always caught off guard by the mundane moment at Walker's. Just when I think it's all adrenal glands, ATF raids, lysergic acid, and speedballs, he'll pull out a simple bottle of aspirin, and the effect is always unintentionally hilarious. "Turn around."

"Was that a Grammy in there?"

"Yes."

"For what?"

"My banjo playing."

"Really?"

"No, not really. It's for spoken word, you fool. You should know this."

I turn my back to Walker and he starts rubbing the aloe over my shoulders. His hands are warm and soft on my neck. The aloe, bracing. If I knew Walker only by his touch, his smell, his lips, I would imagine him to be a much nicer person. One could say that Walker *is* a nice person—a nice person with a rage disorder, a coke addiction, an alcohol problem, abandonment issues, and clinical insecurities. It's almost too much to tease out. All I know is that the hairs on my neck are standing on end, and it's not because of the aloe. Perhaps Walker senses the effect he's having on me again, but I'm fully aware of Claudia's presence.

"I told you," says Claudia. "There's a problem. Jimmy's caught your paranoia. He's not coming to the pig. He says you have to do it old-school."

"Old-school? I'm not heading over there," Walker says, as something like actual panic crosses his face. Walker's hands stop kneading my neck, and the aloe suddenly feels sticky and cold on my skin. I'm not sure I like where this is headed.

"Shall I send one of the peacocks?" scoffs Claudia.

"Maybe we can send Alley," Walker says finally.

"I don't know," Claudia says.

While I appreciate that Walker wants to indoctrinate me, to show me that I belong here, drug runs are illegal. People get killed during drug runs, like, all the time. I'm not entirely sure this is the kind of street cred I'm looking for.

"Hello? I'm here. Don't I get some say in this?"

They both ignore me.

"Goddamnit, you can't just *go*, Claudia." Walker slams his fist on the table.

Claudia rolls her eyes. "You'll survive a few days, Walker. I'll be back on Sunday. Alley can do it. It's just one envelope."

"It's two, actually." Claudia's eyebrows go up. "I just said, Larry's coming into town."

"And how are we paying Jim? Gift certificate? Peacock eggs?"

"The back."

I briefly imagine my manuscript floating in a sea of hundred-dollar bills in Walker's safe. Claudia goes to the back bedroom and returns a few minutes later with an envelope.

"Here." She gives it to me, then Walker grabs my face in both hands and turns me toward him.

"Listen . . . very . . . closely," Walker says, looking at me as if we're speaking two different languages.

I am being told to do this, not asked. "Okay. What?"

"I'm going to give you directions to a mailbox. Put this in it. There should be two envelopes in the box. Take them out. Put them in the glove compartment and come directly back here unless you feel like you're being followed. Don't speed, don't drive ridiculously slow, and obey all traffic laws. If you're stopped by the police, act like an idiot."

"What if I feel like I'm being followed?"

"You won't be," Walker says.

"Then go to the tavern," Claudia says. "And call here."

"And then what, you moron?" Walker says. "You're not going to be followed."

"So I'm doing this?"

He scribbles directions on the back of a cardboard coaster, apparently seeing this question as rhetorical.

"See you all on Sunday," Claudia says, and hightails it out of there.

Walker simply hands me the keys to the car. He can't even look at me. I get into the Caprice and pull the seat forward as far as it can go. I briefly wonder if a joke is being played on me. I mean, if you're trying to look unassuming, this is hands down not the vehicle to be driving. Plus, everyone in a ten-mile radius knows it's Walker's car. I might get pulled over simply for being in this thing, much less having an ounce in the glove box. I turn the key and the engine thrums to life. It occurs to me that it's been years since I've even driven a car. I went right from a city college—where I didn't have a car anyway—to living in New York City. I put the Caprice in reverse and slowly back down the driveway. I stop at the bottom and unlock the gate. I can see now that the blinds are pulled down in the kitchen, and I think I see them flutter slightly. I back out of the gate, stop the car, then lock the gate again.

Even though Walker gave me a coaster with an address, I don't need it. I remember Jim's from when I first got here and we were stopped by the cops, even though it seems years ago. I drive about a mile up the mountain and simply can't help myself. I pull over at a scenic marker, open the envelope, and count $1,000 in cash. Ten hundred-dollar bills.

"Fuck," I say. It dawns on me, suddenly and not so subtly, that *I am doing a drug run.* I repeat it to myself a few times, but quietly—as if a DEA agent might be under the passenger seat next to the minibar Walker has fashioned there. I try to convince myself that this is just part of my job description and somehow divorced from the fact that *I'm actually doing a drug run*, but that doesn't stick. I could have said no. I could have drawn the line. I still could, though I have no idea what holy hell that would reap. But this has the feeling of decision time, and I check myself in the rearview. I look at myself for a while, like they do in the movies. I process the dark circles under my eyes, like a badge of honor, my red lipstick bleeding off my upper lip, where a few drops of sweat have formed. Then I do what that movie character would probably do: I look at the back of the coaster, just to double-check I know where I'm going, take a deep breath, and slowly, but not too slowly, step on the gas.

CHAPTER 22

When Walker calls the next afternoon to tell me Larry is here and to come over, I'm already showered and dressed. I had heard his car come up the drive but didn't want to seem too eager. With the many balancing acts I've had to perform here—with Walker, Claudia, Larry, Devaney, whoever else shows up—my strategy has been to let everything come to me. To sit back, be patient, and watch it all play out. But nothing I do is not thought through. I decide on a black jersey wrap-top, jeans, and boots so I can purposely appear as if I haven't tried too hard. I deliberately wait fifteen minutes before making my way across the driveway. But when I'm just a few feet from Walker's door, I hear something I hadn't anticipated: a woman's voice. I try to place it, finally settling on a horror movie I'd seen in college—*She's Not Sleeping*—in which the murderer commits her foul acts, unbeknownst to her, in a twilight sleep. The star of that movie: September McAvoy.

I take a deep breath as I enter the breezeway, not sure what's coming my way. When I turn into the kitchen, all eyes are on me—Larry's eyes apologetic, Walker's eyes steeled, September's eyes cheerfully screaming, *Let's be best buddies!*

But it's just so easy to hate September McAvoy. First of all, she's named after a month—but not April or May, or even June, which I could probably stomach. My guess is her real name is something plain, like Karen or Lisa. Or maybe it really is September, the product of some sort of unbearable hippie union. Maybe she was born in September. It doesn't matter. She's impossibly skinny and her teeth are impossibly white, and her long, blond hair glows like a Thoroughbred's mane, and she's super-duper fucking nice.

Then there are all the things about September McAvoy that I learn to loathe within the first hour of meeting her.

One, the second you walk into Walker's kitchen, she touches your arm as she greets you, so you feel slightly chummy. But you'd also like to hit her hard in the face. So there's that.

Two, she swears a lot for no good reason in an apparent attempt to make you think she's somehow street, even though her DNA has been more carefully cultivated than that of most Kentucky Derby racehorses. She's the offspring of a famous-actress mother and an equally famous-director father and is wearing boots that cost as much as your tax return. She fancies herself a "broad," saying things like "That fucking fella was, like, so fucking unbelievably crazy," while punctuating the air with her cigarette, even though she's in her early twenties.

Three, she has an affinity for highbrow/lowbrow drinks like Dubonnet on ice and Pabst Blue Ribbon. She asks me for both of these at the same time.

Four, she crinkles her nose a lot as some sort of signifier that she "understands," and when she smiles, she often puts her tongue between her teeth. She frequently performs these two actions in tandem—the nose-crinkle/tongue-teeth thing, an idiosyncrasy she carries to the big screen, is the primary reason why she's often referred to as America's Sweetheart.

Five, she smiles when she talks about everything, so she looks like some kind of hot ventriloquist, even when she's downloading with Walker and Larry about the cyclone in Bangladesh.

Six, she shines like a fucking birthday candle.

And seven, while I notice pretty much every move September McAvoy makes, the worst one is the simple placement of her hand on Larry's leg.

I'm willing to admit that I'm not objective when it comes to September McAvoy. Walker and Larry, for their parts, are sitting there acting as if everything were completely normal, so I figure the "mature" thing to do is to pretend as if everything were completely normal as well—and to drink entirely too much straight tequila.

"So, Walker," September coos. "I hear you have some guns." She might actually just be a dipshit.

"You know how to shoot, honey?"

"Just movies, baby. Just movies." Nose crinkle. Drink of PBR.

Larry is looking around the room as if he were in the principal's office. I am perched, perhaps like the principal, at the end of the counter, smoking as passive-aggressively as I can. I down another shot of straight Cuervo, completely forgoing the limes and salt.

"You got any weed, Walker?" Larry asks.

Walker rummages around in a drawer and produces an almost-empty baggie with nothing but shake. He hands Larry the bag and a pipe, then takes out one of the envelopes I successfully retrieved from Jim's last night. He cuts a few lines, does two of them, and passes the tray to September. After September does a line, she says, "So, Alessandra. You're helping Walker write his book?"

"Something like that."

Walker shoots me a look that conveys something along the lines of *Make some compelling chitchat*, and he does another line, then passes me the tray.

"How's the movie coming?" I ask her, snorting up two lines—*real* snorts, because clearly I'm not already enough on edge.

"*Film*," she says.

"I'm sorry, what did I say?" I pour another shot of tequila and start cutting limes from the fruit bowl.

"*Movie*. You called it a *movie*."

"Sorry, the dif?"

"Seriousness," she says.

"And what are you in the film? A cat?"

"Yes. Well, like Catwoman."

"Sounds serious. What does one do to prepare for a role as a cat?"

"Stop eating." She laughs. "Wardrobe really makes you stop eating!"

"I believe you." I overlaugh back. She looks about ninety-five pounds soaking wet, and I can tell by the way she does the line of coke that this has been her breakfast, lunch, and dinner for the past month.

"What the fuck are you doing in the film, Larry?"

"Uh, well, you know. I . . . the last time I was here . . . I told you . . ."

"You told me a lot of things the last time you were here, so forgive me for not knowing which stuff is true and which stuff is bullshit."

"Oh, jeez," Walker says.

"I think I'd like to see some of those guns," September says.

"To the range!" Walker bellows, though when he says it this

time, it's as if he were saying it in a vacuum. This foursome is feeling tired already, fueled by my rage, Larry's fear, September's stupidity, and Walker's jealousy. Plus, I've managed, in a short time, to become seriously drunk. Still, we all dutifully follow Walker back to the gun room like schoolchildren forced into some lame field trip. Walker retrieves a bunch of guns and hands each of us one. As September and Larry make their way out to the range, I fix Walker with a death stare.

"You probably don't want a firearm in my hands right now," I say.

He wipes a drop of tequila from my chest. "What's that?"

"Fuck off." I swat his hand away.

When we get to the range, September continues to act like an idiot. She has that easy, breezy way some girls have of being stupid to make men feel close to her. I'm disappointed to see that it's working on Walker, with her various incarnations of "How do you hold this crazy thing?" I decide to sit on the bench far away from them before someone ends up with ammo in his or her head. My mother always said that Italians can't drink tequila or gin, and I realize now that she's right. I feel like I could crush some living thing with my bare hands. I'm Mussolini in '42.

Larry makes his way over to where I am, even though every syllable of my body language is screaming at him to not come a step closer.

He holds up his hands. "Truce?"

"Not a chance."

"Can I at least sit?"

"At your peril." We watch Walker and September go through their own dance. All sorts of lines are being blurred—no doubt

September is trying to impress Larry, and Walker is trying to impress me. "What is she, your month of the month?"

Larry chuckles. "That's pretty good."

"Can you tell me why on earth you would bring her out here? Don't you have anything at all to say?"

"Don't look at me. Walker insisted. He got her on the phone himself."

"I mean, don't you have anything to say to me?"

"Alley, come on. Now you're showing your age. This is Rome out here. When in Rome, you know . . . Nothing out here is meant to last."

"Why do people keep saying this? Half my family is from Rome. And no one I know treats people this way."

"Why do you think I come out here?"

"I don't know. Free drugs. Idiot pranks. Sex with jailbait."

"It's all fantasy out here. There's no work or competition or worries. We just let it all hang out."

"Like I said, free drugs, idiot pranks, and sex with jailbait."

"Maybe you're right. But don't be mad at me. It's not like I made promises I couldn't keep."

Maybe Larry's right that I'm showing my age—that only twenty-two-year-olds see sex with someone as a promise. "I'm not sure who I should be mad at. It's so hard to tell out here sometimes."

Larry lets out a long sigh. "I have to ask you something."

"What?"

"This is awkward. The sleeping arrangements. I tried to get a room in town but there's some convention. It was impossible." He crinkles his nose now, too.

"Sleep in my room with the cat, I don't care. I'll take Claudia's bed. Just remember to change her litter box."

"Thanks, Alley. And, look. For what it's worth, I'm sorry."

"It's not worth much."

"Wait a minute," I hear September say to Walker. "Are Aspen trees named after Aspen? That's the first time I ever really thought of that."

"Good luck with that," I say to Larry. I get up and head over to the cabin, and I can feel Walker's eyes on me, even as he's holding a firearm behind one of the hottest women in Hollywood.

CHAPTER 23

I wake up early the next morning and sit out on the porch with a cup of coffee and a worn copy of *Emma* that was in Claudia's room. Without my manuscript, my free time feels wasted, unformed. Without Claudia here I am feeling, for the first time, lonely and unmoored. What's worse is the closed door of my bedroom—I just don't want to be here when everyone wakes up. I don't want to have to play "single dorm friend" in the sex-and-drug haze Larry and September will inevitably be in. I head across the driveway, over to the bench by the range, where I put my feet up and drink in the cool Colorado morning. I'm wearing the pink tracksuit that has become my "comfy clothes" out here, and I've brought a notebook in which I start to jot thoughts about Walker's manuscript. I'm wondering how he intends to end the book, but I have ideas of my own. I start to sketch an outline.

"Fucking shit! Fucking shit!" I hear a crash from Walker's house and I freeze. I'm pretty sure Larry and September are over at the cabin, and I'm generally not supposed to go over to Walker's unless called. Under normal circumstances—rather, if it were anybody else—I'd immediately head in, thinking perhaps that something was wrong. But I'm not quite sure what to do until I hear a thin "Help . . ."

I race into the house and take quick stock of the situation: A broken plate. Walker huddled on the floor. A cigarette burning in the ashtray. A sink full of glasses. An empty tray of coke. A bag of opened tortilla chips. The place is surprisingly tidy otherwise. He looks up at me, and I realize a moment too late what this is—not at all a break-in or a health scare, but rather a private moment. A man in simple despair. At first I think he's going to kick me out, and I step backward as if retreating from a bear in the wilderness.

"What in the fuck are you doing over here?"

"You said, 'Help.' I thought something was wrong."

"So what if there was? What the fuck do you care?"

He pulls himself onto the circular couch and I start picking up pieces of broken plate.

"Do you buy special break-into-a-billion-pieces plates? Are these from a prop shop? Christ, who are you even throwing this at?"

"Get me a drink."

It's ten in the morning, so I'm not sure where we're at drinks-wise. He's wearing the khakis and button-down he was wearing last night. It doesn't appear that he's been to bed. "How about some Irish coffee?"

"Fine."

I put a filter in the coffeemaker and pour in some Maxwell House. I take out two large mugs and put two fingers of Bushmills in each and wait.

"Where were you?"

"On the range, reading."

"Why?" Walker looks like he's aged about ten years overnight.

His skin looks gray, and his eyes are rimmed red. His chest is slightly heaving.

"Why do you think?" The coffeemaker does its final sputter, and I fill our mugs. I grab a bottle of whipped cream from the fridge and squeeze two large dollops on top of the coffee. I sprinkle white sugar over that and place it in front of Walker, taking my own place on the circular couch. "Don't throw this."

"I don't know."

"Don't know what?"

"Why you were on the range." It's hard for me to have a bead on Walker in this moment. I can't tell if he's still drunk or high or on something else or just exhausted. He's acting confused, but not crazy. It's as if he's trying to figure out how he got here.

"I don't know. The guy I was kind of into is sleeping in my bed with a stupid, rich, beautiful dipshit that you invited out here."

Walker looks down at his hand, inspecting it, then takes a sip of his coffee. "This is really good. Thank you."

"Do you want me to go?"

"No."

"Do you want to work a little? I had a couple of ideas I wanted to run by you."

"No."

"What do you want to do?"

He waves his hand over by the rows of movies and lies down on the couch.

"How about *Shaft*?"

"Too black."

"*Caligula*?"

"Too depraved."

"*Smokey and the Bandit*?"

"Too pointless."

"*Scarface?*"

"Too loud."

"*The Godfather?*"

Walker considers this for a moment. "Fine."

"One or two?"

"One."

I put the movie in and try to remain as neutral as possible. I don't want to kick Walker when he's down, but I'm not about to let him off the hook either. Inviting September out here was nothing short of a "Fuck you." I don't have to pretend to like it.

"I love this part," Walker says ten minutes in. "You guineas really know how to make a movie." He's sprawled on the couch with his head on a pillow and an afghan over him. He's lying on his stomach, occasionally lifting himself up to sip his coffee.

"*Film*. This is definitely a *film*."

"Ha. She's *such* a dumb bitch."

"Yeah, well, you invited her."

"I know. You're mad."

"Damn straight." I stare at the TV and sip my coffee.

"Sweetheart, I might need you to go to Jim's again."

"Yeah, I'm not doing that again." While my drug run went off without a hitch, I want to make it clear that this is definitely not in my job description.

"You have to."

I glanced at the empty tray when I came in, but I figured that was perhaps only one envelope. "No, I don't."

"Don't tell me who's going to do what around here!" Walker snaps.

I give him my you-have-got-to-be-fucking-kidding-me face, and then the phone rings. Walker answers it on speakerphone.

"Yes, hello, Walker?" It's September calling from the cabin.

She seems to have developed a British accent overnight. "Hi, love, what're you doing? Are you up?"

If it were Claudia or me, Walker would tell us to go to hell, but he's different with celebrities—especially female celebrities—and the game face comes on. "Yeah, I'm up."

"Well, we retired so early . . . Can Larry and I come over? We're famished."

"Sure, come on over."

"Right. Thanks." She hangs up.

"Why does she sound like fucking Julie Andrews?" I ask.

"Actresses."

"When did they 'retire'?"

"Shortly after you abandoned me. I told them I needed to work. I think they were feeling frisky anyway."

"Ick." It occurs to me now that the empty tray of coke is Walker's doing. I think I'm catching him midbinge.

He sits up and puts on his aviators and Tilley hat, as if it's a uniform and he's about to go to work. He finishes the Irish coffee, then asks me to mix him a scotch and water as he lights a cigarette.

"What are we eating?" I ask.

"There's some spiral ham in there and eggs. Why don't you cook us up some omelets, sweetheart."

"Because I'm not a short-order cook, that's why."

"Alessandra. Please." I don't think I've ever heard Walker say *please*, nor has he ever called me Alessandra, and I'm inclined to just do what he says. I feel sorry for him. I pull out the ham and a dozen eggs, butter, bread, and American cheese. I imagine putting half a stick of butter in September's omelet and the other half on her toast, just so the cat suit will feel a little snug next week. As I set about preparing the omelets, Larry and

September bound into the house. I'm swirling butter around in a frying pan when I notice she's holding the three-ring binder that houses Walker's manuscript—the one that I've been editing. I start to feel slightly nauseated.

"Walker, we had an idea. I hope you don't mind this."

I catch Larry's eye and subtly shake my head to telegraph that the manuscript is not to be messed with. Then I start dicing ham, throwing it into the pan, as September asks me for a mimosa.

"Champagne and orange juice are in the fridge," I say. "Help yourself."

"Oh, that's all right. I'll wait till you're done with those." She motions to the ham crackling in the pan and the bowl of eggs I've whisked. "Larry tells me, Walker, that you read aloud," she says, now doing her best Margaret Thatcher. "I adore reading fiction out loud. It's just like acting."

"You know, omelets are almost done," I say, folding the first one over in the pan. "Let's eat. You said a mimosa?"

"Sounds good to me, honey," Walker says to September.

"Splendid," she says.

Larry has gone to the fridge and taken out the champagne and orange juice. I point to the cabinet where the champagne flutes are and shake my head, not liking where I think this moment is headed. Larry, slow on the uptake, cocks his head like a confused puppy dog.

September takes the manuscript, clears her throat, pauses a beat to get into some sort of non-British character, and starts reading the most recent chapter in a gruff, mumbly baritone that is a surprisingly impressive impersonation of Walker. As she plows doggedly through the first few pages, Walker's face first seems to register recognition, then pride, then confusion, and finally anger, as it appears to dawn on him that the words

September is reading are not entirely of his own making. Indeed, this most recent stuff is almost half me. My face, meanwhile, is a study in nonchalance. It's maybe not the best strategy, but I'm too paralyzed with fear to come up with a better plan on the fly. There's no sense in what I'm thinking—that perhaps he won't notice—but I keep frying and flipping, thinking maybe I'll luck out and a safe will fall on September or the ATF will come bursting through the door.

"This is good," Larry says, drumming on the table, genuinely excited. "Old-school Walker. Love it."

Walker's hands are on the counter in front of him, and his fingers start drumming, too. He's practically vibrating, rocking back and forth. The drumming hand is too close to a fist for my liking. I'm sure I'm about to be on the receiving end of an explosion, though I doubt Walker would do that in front of Larry and September. But as September continues to read, I'm not altogether certain Walker's even listening. I see him with the remainder of coke bag number two under the counter. From my perch I see him put a small spoon in the bag and then pretend to cough, snorting the lot of it. I get it. He's pissed, he's almost out, and he's not sharing.

It's then that I see it: a single bead of sweat that has formed at Walker's temple. As it slowly makes its way down the side of his face, slaloming from pore to pore, it's as conspicuous as a yacht in a puddle. I have never seen anything like it since I've been here, and it is telegraphing in no uncertain terms that something is very, very wrong. He clears his throat and I can see him blinking slowly through his aviators as September rambles on. Walker looks at me squarely, and I imagine he sees what he wishes he didn't: a face full of concern and questioning. A face that is asking, *Are you okay?* Imperceptibly he gives me his answer with a short shake of the head: *No. I'm not.* And that's when he goes down.

Seizures in real life are like nothing out of the movies. They are much more awkward and far less violent. What gets missed in the fictional staging is that stuff is usually in the way. Walker slumps on his typewriter, then off his barstool and onto the floor, where he knocks his head hard on the bottom of the counter. For a second September continues reading even after seeing this happen. I don't know if she's in shock or simply can't stand to silence the sound of her voice, but she looks expectantly over at Walker, as if he might pop up at any moment to applaud.

"Jesus, Larry. Nine one one. Now!" Larry can easily reach the phone from where he's sitting; he and September exchange a quick look. "Nine one one, Larry. Fuck!"

"He might come out of it, Alley," he says in his best TV-doctor voice. He might as well be shaking my shoulders and smacking me in the face. "Give it a second!"

For a minute I have to remind myself that Larry has no medical knowledge whatsoever—he's not a doctor, he doesn't even play one on TV. His tone has a faux urgency, but he's just sitting there spinning his wheels. If there's a reason to delay this call, it's a completely shitty one.

"What?" I grab the phone and dial 911 myself. I give the dispatcher Walker's address and tell her I think he's having a seizure. She tells me to time it, to make sure he's breathing and in a safe place, and to not shove anything in his mouth. I latch on to the last thing she says: "Someone's on the way." I get Walker totally on the floor and surround him with pillows from the circular couch.

The whole time I'm doing this, Larry and September are

huddled in a corner, screaming at each other—playing this scene out like they're auditioning for a stage version of *Sid and Nancy*. September is going on like some crazy harpy, but her focus is more in the "What is to become of us?" vein and has little to do with Walker's condition. Larry's role is to calm her down and be the godlike voice of reason. Meanwhile I'm getting the kitchen timer and focusing on the rise and fall of Walker's chest, praying to Christ it doesn't stop.

"Alley, we've gotta skate," Larry says.

"Skate?" The word is not registering. A pond comes to mind. "Skate where?"

"Go. We've got to go."

Again, I'm not comprehending. "Go where? The medics are on the way."

"September and I can't be here when they arrive. We can't risk this kind of publicity." And then this: "We're A-list."

I take in Larry and September, keeping my hand over Walker's heart, which is, thank God, still beating. His chest is still rising and falling. He's still writhing. The kitchen timer says only one minute, though it feels like twenty.

"Seriously? Larry, I need help."

"What are we going to do, Alley? The paramedics are coming, right? I'm sorry. We're out. We've gotta go. He's going to be fine."

"You're not A-list, you're . . . *shit*-list, you motherfuckers. Get out!" I yell.

But they're not waiting for my permission. Larry grabs what's left of coke bag number two and says, "You don't want them to find this. Trust me." He takes it, along with the bag of shake, thinking he's doing me a favor—or acting like it. I can't tell anymore. Then they're gone.

"Walker," I plead, hoping some part of his brain will hear

me. "Please come to. It's Alley. I'm all alone here. Please wake up." I hear an ambulance that sounds about a half mile away.

When Walker finally opens his eyes, the kitchen timer reads three minutes. "What the fuck?"

"Take it easy. You had a seizure or a heart attack. Something. Something happened to you. Doctors are almost here. Take it easy."

For a few seconds, it appears he's about to fight this—to reflexively fight it like everything else—but he doesn't have the strength. I take his hand, and he squeezes it. Then he exhales and stares at the ceiling, studying the blond wood as if he's never really noticed it before.

CHAPTER 24

"What did you do?" Claudia enters the cabin in a sweat. She's raced here from her home in Crested Butte, bolting for her car the second I called her. It's three in the afternoon. I can't tell what she's getting at—if she's wondering what I personally did or the collective *you* that was the four of us. She sounds like she's accusing me of something, but I can't imagine what.

"I didn't do anything, Claudia. He went on some sort of coke binge by himself."

"Impossible."

I look around to see if I've landed in some alternate universe. How that's "impossible" around here is beyond me. I'm surprised the paramedics aren't out here every day. "How is it impossible?"

"Do you know how many drugs Walker has done?"

"More than I ever could imagine."

"He knows how to get himself to the edge and back. Always has," Claudia says in a tone that I'm not liking.

"What are you implying?"

"You mix his drinks too strong. You mix his scotch and water like a real drink. I've seen you."

"I'm sorry, what am I *supposed* to do?"

"More water and less scotch. You've actually gotten him hungover."

"He has a full bottle of Chivas a day. How exactly is it me who's making him hungover? Besides, I'm not exactly shoving the coke up his nose."

"Not literally, no."

"What the fuck, Claude?"

"He was upset about you and Larry. I think it's making him act reckless."

"That's a relative term out here. And if you must know, Larry was out here with September McAvoy. Walker invited her." I leave out the part where Claudia didn't tell me about the magazine cover.

"He did?"

"Yes, and not only that, they stayed here. In my bed. I slept in yours."

"Oh."

"Oh, and on top of it, they hightailed it out of here when Walker went down. Some friends."

Finally, something approaching sympathy falls over Claudia's face. "Jesus."

"I wasn't even over there for most of the night. I came over here and went to bed. I was reading on the range when I heard him."

"Who?"

"Walker. In there. Freaking out. What about this is not making sense?"

"The whole thing, Alley. None of this is making sense to me."

I see Claudia's real problem is that she has been forced to traffic in denial for most of her tenure here—but she's been lucky. Walker's addictions in a person with a lesser constitution would have landed him in rehab or the hospital—or the morgue—many times over. That his addiction is so outsize, and that he somehow suffers it so well, coupled with its being intrinsically tied to the Walker Reade brand, has lent an almost cinematic glow to the proceedings. To the public, Walker is a character from a movie, except no one ever yells cut. I had assumed that Claudia knew better.

"How's Cody?"

"Oh, fine," Claudia says, lying. Her son has mono and Claudia left him on a dime to come here. "He'll survive."

"What do you need to know?"

"I just want to know what happened before I head over there. Tell me everything again."

"I told you. The paramedics came. It was around eleven this morning. He refused treatment and went right to bed. I came over here and called you. He's been asleep ever since. At least I hope so. I came over here and crashed myself." The phone rings, and we both sit for a second and stare at it.

Claudia picks up on the second ring. "Walker, it's me. I'm here." I can hear him barking something through the receiver about abandoning him in his time of need. "I'll be right over. . . . What? . . . Oh, okay. Yep. Okay." She puts the receiver down and says simply, "He wants *you*."

I look at her and shake my head. "I don't want to go over there. Not alone." I am happy to continue making my way through *Emma*, staring at peacocks, potting flowers, pretending like I'm not completely traumatized by what just happened. This is unmistakably in Claudia's job description: *Go over after coke-binge-induced, heart-stopping seizure and pretend everything is okay.* I didn't know exactly what I signed up for when I came out here, but I'm pretty sure it wasn't this.

"You have to go. That's what he wants. Remember, Alley, just be . . . be watchful." She's starting to sound like Jane Austen herself. "Just go."

I walk into our kitchen and look around for something distracting to bring over. I'm stalling. The pit that's typically in my stomach when I'm called over is more like a Florida sinkhole. I open and close the pantry door, then just sit at the kitchen table and put my head in my hands. I can barely breathe. But I can't wait much longer. Everything is worse if Walker has to call twice, so I grab a box of Russell Stover chocolates from the pantry and a six-pack of Heineken from the fridge.

As I make the long walk across the driveway, I take in the whole scene in the late-afternoon sun—the Caprice, the peacocks, the range, the flower flats, like so many props in this one-man show. What seemed like charming touchstones when I first arrived feel somewhat sinister to me now as I make my way to Walker's—or if not sinister, then like nothing more than work. I can feel, like a tangible weight, how exhausting it must be to keep up the appearance of being Walker Reade. I pause at the threshold of the breezeway. I literally have one foot in the door—I can't even see Walker—when he starts in on me.

"Wipe that look off your face, missy."

"What look is that?" I enter the kitchen, trying to appear nonchalant. "You can't even see me."

"Fear. Or maybe I'm just smelling it on you."

"Jeez, Walker. Can I get two feet in the door first?"

"No."

"What does fear even smell like?" I go to the bar and pour us two shots of tequila.

"Beer and gunpowder and lies."

"Jesus, write that down. That's good. I do have beer, if that's what you're getting at."

"Now, you tell me. Why on earth would I bother to write it down?"

"For the book, of course." The pause between us couldn't get any more pregnant. I hand him the shot and we both throw them back. "You wanted me over for something?" I sit on the barstool next to him and begin unwrapping the chocolates.

Walker looks better—rested, with color in his face. He's in one of his stolen hotel bathrobes, smoking a cigarette. He bites down on the filter. "You're my secretary. I'm ready to write," he says through gritted teeth.

"Your secretary? What is this, 1952? If anyone's your secretary, it's Claudia, remember?"

"What does that make you?"

"I don't know, I'm your assistant."

"Devaney was my assistant."

I roll my eyes toward him. "Is that what they're calling it these days?" Walker snickers a little at my joke. "So what *does* that make me?"

I remove the top from the chocolate box and wave the candies toward Walker. He chooses a caramel and a chocolate cream and places them next to the typewriter. I crack a beer and hand it to him. We sit in silence for a few minutes eating our chocolate-and-beer supper.

"Let's get to work."

"If you say so." I'm not exactly sure how this is going to go. We have effectively been working on two different manuscripts. That Walker is evading this newly confirmed reality, at least for the present, is puzzling. But I'm not about to call attention to it. I'll approach it the same way I've done everything else since the moment I arrived here: figure it out later.

"I say so. Get me my scotch." He puts a piece of paper in the typewriter while I mix the scotch and water according to Claudia's directions. "And do not water that shit down."

"How did you know I was going to do that?"

"Wild guess. Claudia's convinced I can't hold my liquor anymore."

"Oddly. Yes. Among other things."

"Just mix it."

"How are you feeling, by the way?" I ask offhandedly.

"Don't ever ask me that question again. I'm fine. Mix."

I get two highballs from the dish drain and fill them with ice. Then I pour in a three count of Chivas and fill the rest with water. "Walker, you know, I had some ideas—"

"Seems like you've had a lot of ideas about my work lately."

And there it is. I try to sound as casual as possible, placing the drink next to the typewriter. "Just a few. Nothing Lionel wouldn't do."

"Yeah, well, you're not Lionel fucking Gray. He's a legend. You're a bartender."

If I was on a tightrope before, now I'm also spinning a set of fine china on my fingertips while riding a ten-speed bike.

"You're right. I'm just the bartender," I say evenly. "Why don't we just get to work?"

"I have a better idea. Let's start with a little quiz. Trick question: Why don't you just finish this fucking book for me?"

"Because I'm not Walker Reade?"

"Well, I'm glad you finally remembered that. *Now* we can get to work." Then he does something so casually that for a moment I almost forget he shouldn't be doing it: He takes out a green envelope and pours some cocaine onto a tray. I'm mesmerized by the credit card, the word *VISA* coated in powder, as Walker deftly flicks it back and forth, cutting out four lines, all exactly the same size. A few things cross my mind, but I settle on the audacity—the solid brass ones—Walker has to lean over and snort two of the lines in front of me as casually as possible, as if he weren't just seizing on this very floor mere hours ago.

"Where did you get that?"

Walker is startled upright. "Safeway, you idiot. What do you mean, where did I get this?"

"I thought it was all gone." Visions of Larry taking the rest of bag number two are dancing in my head.

"The stuff you got is. Fucking Larry jacking my drugs. That leech."

In that moment I truly do feel like an idiot. When you're an addict of Walker Reade proportions, you have a stash. You always have a stash. He does two quick lines and hands the tray to me. I stare at him.

"Do not give me that wounded-deer look. What in the fuck are you looking at? Here."

"I don't know, Walker. Just . . . are you kidding me?"

"No, I am not kidding. Here."

"I'm not doing that. And I'm pretty sure you should lay off, too."

"Great, now I have a neophyte editor *and* a babysitter on my hands. Anything else you'd like to add to your job description? Peacock farmer? Director of ashtrays? I could use a good lawyer, actually."

"Don't forget bartender." Inexplicably, tears are welling in my eyes.

Walker is unmoved. "Stop working so hard, sweetheart. You're window dressing around here, and don't you forget it. Larry never did."

Even though I have learned in these moments to tune out Walker—the casual meanness, the cruelty—this one gets my Italian up. In a flash, I think of the worst thing I can do back, and that's taking the tray and flinging it clear across the room.

And then, astonishingly enough, I do it. The coke goes up in a trailing cloud that slowly descends to the floor like a miniature snowstorm. Out here, this is what they call a fireable offense.

"*What the fuck did you just do?*" Walker demands, even though his answer is all over the circular couch. "Just . . . Don't move."

Clearly this isn't the first time this has happened in Walker Reade's life. No doubt he's been witness to more party fouls than most, and he patiently waits for the coke to settle on the floor and the sofa, his hand up holding me in place by the counter. Then he kneels in front of the cushions and does his level best to scrape as much of the powder onto the tray as he can, even rubbing some on his teeth and nostrils as he goes.

"Are you crazy?" he asks, his voice rising.

"Fuck you, Walker."

"I repeat. Have you gone crazy?"

"You are nothing but a mean cokehead."

"What did you call me?" He turns his head toward me and takes his glasses off.

"You heard me. A mean cokehead. *Cokehead.* Stop the presses. Walker Reade is a *certifiable cokehead.* Look at you. On the floor."

"You can leave, little girl."

"We both know you don't want that."

"I said you can go home."

"Fine by me. I'm doing the same thing here as I was doing there." The tears are coming fast now.

"What's that, fucking off?"

"No. Tending bar to mean drunks. Except I actually used to make tips."

"*Get out.*"

"I'd already be gone if you weren't holding my manuscript hostage."

"Nothing but kindling, sweetheart."

"How in the hell are you going to finish this book without me? *Huh?* You can't even string two sentences together."

"You think I need you?" he says with a hint of desperation, and then does something with such purpose that it seems as if he's simply been waiting for the right time, like he's been practicing the move for years. Rising quickly from the floor, he grabs two objects from the cabinet next to him and, with two swift flicks—like a knife thrower at a state fair—sends them hurtling toward me. As I duck to miss the first, I realize the error I've made when the second one makes disconcertingly solid contact with my skull. I didn't calculate it correctly. Perhaps better to take a National Book Award to the temple than a Grammy. Those Grammys—I discover at the moment of impact—are nothing but brass and hard edges. The pain is immediate and intense. I crumple to the ground, and two small drops of blood fall on the floor in front of me. I either can't or don't want to get up, so I focus on those two drops, then three, and four, as they pool into one another. Walker's gone quiet—I can just hear him breathing—and we're both frozen in this moment, though I'm not sure who's more afraid. Peripherally I see the awards on the floor next to me, beautifully bronzed and serious.

"Who's the mean cokehead now?" he says.

I look up at Walker, whose face goes white.

"Fuck . . . Alley. Are you . . ." Then I see him dialing Claudia, can hear him telling her what happened, how I look. I wonder to myself why he's speaking so quietly—he sounds like he's in church or a library. The last thing I see before I lose consciousness is Walker mouthing, *I'm sorry*, but he's not really mouthing it. I just can't hear it for myself.

CHAPTER 25

"John Dante."

"Alley Cat. What's up? You okay?"

"No, are you alone?"

"Yeah, everyone's at Auntie's. What's up?"

"It's kind of awful. Do *not* tell Mom or Dad or anyone anything. Do you hear me?"

"Yeah, yeah. Calm down. What's going on?"

A butterfly bandage is over my right eyebrow, and I'm sitting at Claudia's desk; she's out grocery shopping. It's been two days since I was Grammied, and I haven't been over to Walker's since. I tell J.D. the whole sordid tale.

"Cat, it's pretty simple: just come home."

"My manuscript, J.D."

"It's not worth it."

"That's easy for you to say. I worked two years on that thing." There is a long pause on the other end. "What?"

"Nothing. I just bet you could get it back if you were leaving. Ask that chick Claudia to get it back. But . . . I don't know. I think if you're staying, it's for other reasons."

"What's that supposed to mean? You have no idea what it's

like out here." I've got to hand it to J.D. Even from two thousand miles away, he senses the compelling push-pull that drives each day. That for every dinner plate whizzing by my head there are pages and hot-tub romps and brushes with Larry Lucas.

"I think you don't really want to come home. I think we're all too boring for you. You think we're all stupid."

"No, I don't."

"Yeah, you do."

"Look . . . I'm just trying to make something of myself."

"Yeah, but look at you. What are you trying to make—the local news? Cat, just . . . come home."

"Then everyone is going to say I told you so. Everyone's going to think I'm a huge failure."

"Look, Cat, nobody really cares about what you're doing there. Everyone will be happy if you come home."

"And that's precisely the problem, J.D. Nobody really cares what I'm doing. Nobody cares what I become." The dam bursts. I break into hysterical sobs. "If I don't care, who will?"

"There are other ways to get to where you want to be, Cat. And . . . why in the hell are you crying?"

"Look, I don't feel like a very good person right now. I did a *drug run*, J.D. I'm doing more coke than John Belushi. All the things you warned me about, I'm doing them."

"Cat, just come home. We'll work it out." Buried in J.D.'s voice is an approximation of my dad's; it's almost creepy. I can practically hear my father's words: *Door's always open. When you come back. . . .*

"I don't know."

"Look, I'll buy your plane ticket. Just come home. We love you."

I hear Claudia pull into the driveway. "I've gotta run. I'll call you later."

"Okay . . . okay, Cat. Just . . . you know, just, like, hang in there."

Claudia comes into the cabin with four bags of groceries full of the things that have become our staples: frozen dinners, cigarettes, beer, wine, avocados, mushrooms, and coffee. I get up from the couch, where I have been passive-aggressively lounging for the past day and a half—nursing a headache and my ego—and in silence help her put everything away. I sit at the kitchen table and finger the butterfly bandage over my eye. Then she asks the million-dollar question. Or more to the point, the $25,000 question.

"So are you leaving?" she says with a heavy sigh. She clearly just wants to get this over with.

"I don't know." I take a pack of Dunhill blues out of the carton. "Do you think I should?"

"People have left for less. How are you feeling?"

"I'm fine." I pull the wrapper off the pack. I offer one to Claudia and take one for myself. She gets an ashtray from the dish rack and a Bic lighter from the kitchen table. "It's not a concussion, so . . ."

After the incident, Claudia had taken me down to the local clinic where she's friends with one of the nurses, while Walker stayed on the farm to sweat. By the time we got to the clinic, the dish towel pressed to my head was soaked through, affirmation of something my Mafia uncle had once mysteriously told me: Russos know how to bleed. The clinic visit resembled a bad made-for-TV movie about domestic violence, where the victim conjures stories of walking into walls (in this case, Claudia thought the corner of a cabinet was believable enough) while the bit actors, in their lab coats, stew silently in subtext and tension, not buying it. The nurse eyed the gash—her gaze moving from the cut to my studied veneer—and she deemed it CAT scan–worthy. The diagnosis: No concussion. No internal bleeding. The prescription: rest, ice, and aspirin.

Claudia lights both of our cigarettes and takes a seat at the kitchen table. "Walker's worried you're going to sue him."

"I'm sure he is. It's always about him."

"You knew that was the deal."

She's right. I had heard these very words from Claudia, but only now do I understand them. The deal is painfully clear: This is Walker's show. He's the star and the director. Claudia is the producer. And I'm not sure I want to be here for the final scene.

"Tell him to not worry. I'm not suing him. But can you see if you can get my manuscript back?"

"I'll see."

"Actually, Claude, I'm asking you. Please. Friend to friend. Can you just go get it sometime when he's out or sleeping or whatever? You know it's the right thing to do. It's mine. Then I can make a decision."

"Like I said, I'll see. Give me a couple of days. I have to head out on an errand. I'll be back in a bit."

After she leaves, I start cleaning out my drawers, folding all of the ridiculous clothing I've acquired over the months here: halter tops, miniskirts, high heels, bikinis, minidresses, cowgirl paraphernalia, leather pants, candy-colored tops, wigs, and one lime-green feather boa. I put everything into a garbage bag, tie it up, and set it at the foot of the bed. I pack up my family photos and the dull, monochromatic clothes I brought here, placing everything into my duffel. Then I realize that's it. Everything else out here—the bedding, the books, the computer, the furniture, the damn aspirin even—belongs to Walker. I lie down on the bed and take a book off the shelf—*The Great Gatsby*, one of Walker's favorites. I start reading when I hear a shuffling outside my door, which I presume is Claudia, back from her errand. But then, just as when I first arrived here, a note slides under my door.

I wait to hear the cabin door close and look at the single sheet of paper. *Please don't go. I'm sorry* is all it says. I fold it and put it in my duffel bag, lie back down on the bed, and resume reading.

The phone rings out in the living room and I ignore it, thinking it must be Walker. Five minutes later it rings again. I go out and take a seat at Claudia's desk and stare at it. I pick it up but don't say anything.

"Hello? Claudia?" It's Larry.

"No. It's Alley."

"Hey, good. You were the one I was trying to reach, actually." While Larry isn't exactly employing a full-on British accent, he has evidently acquired a spot of September's unmistakable Anglophile patois. Fucking actors. "Alley oxen free. How's it going, love?"

"Please don't call me that. Just . . . stop talking like that."

"Like what?"

"Like you're Rex Harrison. Like we're chums."

"Jeez. Sorry. How's Walker?"

"He's fine, I guess. Just as you said he would be. Didn't you read about it in the paper?" I reach for a cigarette on Claudia's desk.

"I did. That was some crazy shit, right?"

"Right. Crazy," I say as impassively as I can. There is a long pause that I refuse to fill with chitchat. If Larry called to talk to me, then he can do the talking.

"I'm actually calling to see how you're doing."

"Me? Awesome. I'm really awesome." I bite my bottom lip. My head is throbbing beneath the butterfly. "That was, like, totally my idea of a fun Saturday night."

"I'm sorry, Alley."

"I know, Larry. You're a sorry son of a bitch. How ironic you're playing a superhero."

"I would be pretty mad, too, if I were you." He says this like he's my therapist—like he's a dispassionate third party.

"Don't think that you're welcome out here anymore, by the way. You don't go taking drugs from Walker Reade and expect to be invited back to the party."

"Seriously, Alley. I was trying to help him. What if the cops had come and the drugs were still there? You think I can't get cocaine in LA?"

"Whatever. Look, just don't call over here again. Gotta go." I slam down the phone, and a minute later it rings again. "What about 'gotta go' don't you understand?"

"Christ. Please don't go." It's Walker. "Come over. Let's relax. Hot tub. Drinks. Whatever movie you want. Please." It's Good Walker. Fun Walker. Slightly Drunk Walker.

I look down at Claudia's desk calendar, which is empty save for a dentist appointment. I finger the word *dentist* and wait on the line.

"I need one of those margaritas you make."

"Fine," I say finally, feeling like a drink myself. "But just for one movie."

"Fine."

When I walk into the house, Walker is uncharacteristically bustling about the kitchen. The microwave is glowing, and something is rotating inside it. The whole room smells like burnt enchiladas. Walker has two plates out with silverware and cloth napkins, and the blender is set up. He's already juiced a bunch of limes, and the tequila and triple sec are arranged neatly on the counter. Two candles are burning, and Walker has a stack of movies by my plate—old comedies he knows I'm fond of: *Caddyshack*, *Airplane!*, *National Lampoon's Vacation*.

The microwave beeps, and Walker takes out a tray with an oven mitt. He looks nervous. As he slides the Mexican food onto our plates, I go to the freezer for ice and start mixing the margaritas.

"Are you nuking for me? You shouldn't have."

"I suppose it's the least I can do. I don't know how to do much else." Really nervous.

"You don't have to be so nice. I'm not suing you."

"Well, maybe I just feel like being nice."

"Okay."

"And I was thinking, if you're leaving, we should have some sort of exit interview."

"Right," I say, knowing he's fishing. "For HR purposes, of course."

"Right, HR." He chuckles. "Goddamn HR."

"And what if I'm staying?"

"Either way, we're gonna need a drink."

I start blending the ice and tequila, the limes and triple sec. I reach for the glasses to salt them, and I realize Walker is right beside me. He's so close I can feel the body heat from his arm, even though we're not touching. He's so close that I can feel how sorry he is.

"You taking notes? Because it's my secret recipe. I'm not writing it down."

"You mix a hell of a drink, sweetheart."

"Coming from you, I'll take that as a compliment." I salt the glass rims and pour the margaritas from the blender. "Let's eat."

"Do you want to watch something?" Walker motions to the stack of movies by my plate.

"Not really. Not if we're having an interview."

He motions for me to sit, and we start eating. The enchiladas are about a thousand degrees, entirely overnuked. I put a fork in mine, and an alarming cloud of steam rises to the ceiling. That's the thing about Walker: the man can ingest buckets of drugs and write Pulitzer Prize–winning books, but he can't microwave an enchilada.

"Are you trying to kill me again?" I ask, laughing.

"I followed the fucking directions. Oh, hell . . ."

"It'll cool down."

The phone rings, and Walker picks up. It's Claudia.

"She's over here. . . . Just leave it in the breezeway. . . . It's fine." Apparently the pig's ass is open for business again. He hangs up the phone and then stares at me for a long time. At first I think he might try to kiss me—but his demeanor changes from soft to steeled on a dime. "I just want you to know that there are about a million people who would trade places with you right now. They'd kill for this job."

"I'm sorry, is this an interview? An apology?"

"It's a fact. Do you know why they'd kill for this job?"

"I don't know, the promise of a nervous disorder . . . lung cancer . . . a traumatic brain injury?"

"Because out there, I still mean something. Maybe not here. Maybe not to you. You think I'm a joke. You think I'm a sorry, washed-up son of a bitch who needs help from you, a child. But trust me, my name in your life will get you places. You'll see."

I stare blankly at Walker, unsure of what to say.

"Wipe that look off your face. What did you expect here? Violins? Rose petals?"

"I don't know. I was under the impression that you were sorry and were going to apologize."

"I just did."

"I was expecting more."

"You aren't going to get it."

I hear Claudia come into the breezeway, and just as quickly the door closing. "You want to go get that?"

"You go get it. You're my assistant."

"Maybe I'm not."

"Well, then maybe you *should* leave. Did it ever occur to you that your approval and your opinion don't matter one goddamn bit out here? I made my name doing exactly what I'm doing."

"Or undoing. Seriously, Walker. It's like . . . I dunno . . ." I trail off before deciding that the truth will set me free. "It's like a . . . slow-motion suicide out here."

"Beg your pardon?" I half expect the dishes to start flying, but surprisingly, Walker just shakes his head. He's quiet for a minute, then reaches into the cabinet, pulls down a binder, and slides it across the counter to me. I open it and start thumbing through and realize it's the manuscript with my rewrites. A copy. I gulp down half of my margarita.

"What was your plan, little girl?"

"I didn't really have one. This place isn't exactly conducive to planning."

"Why do you think Claudia lives with my assistant? So you can paint your toes together? Talk about boys? She's not much more than a spy. I know what toothpaste you use. I know your brothers' names. Christ, I got your manuscript. You think she couldn't get my own?"

"How long have you known?"

"Since the first call to Lionel. Come on . . ."

"So why didn't you say anything?"

"Because it's . . . actually not all that awful." Walker says this more with surprise than admiration, but given the multitude of worst-case scenarios I've played out in my head these many months, it's as close to a compliment as I can possibly imagine in this moment. "I appreciate your naive enthusiasm, but at this point I am not much more than a cash cow for Lionel Gray and his enterprise. It doesn't have to be good, or even pretty good, anymore. It just has to get out there."

"I'm not sure what I'm even doing is all that great."

"Yeah, well, you work hard. That's what most writing is. Working hard for wild mediocrity. That's the bitch of it. Isn't it?"

"I guess so." I don't want this to be true. And a part of me refuses to have it be true about Walker.

"There's no free lunch, sweetheart. Comes with the territory. This is what this is. Now, please. Go get the envelope."

I head into the breezeway and pick up the yellow envelope on the floor. I might as well be putting the needle right into the junkie's arm.

"Thank you." Walker opens it. "I'm not going to beg you to stay. Maybe you keep this up, I don't want you to stay. Maybe I'll fire *you*. So watch yourself. You think you're indispensable, but trust me, you're not."

"It's not my editing that makes me indispensable." I don't exactly know what I'm trying to say when this comes out of my mouth, but it's met with enough silence to suggest that I might have, in fact, said something.

"What do you think?" Walker motions to the food.

"We can probably dig in now. It only looks about six hundred degrees." I pick the enchilada apart with my fork, but so much steam is still inside it, it's like a mini fog machine.

"Christ. Do you want to put one of those movies in now?"

"Sure." When I pick up *Caddyshack* and put it in the VCR, it's something of a relief. For months, our constant nighttime companions have been CNN, movies, vintage porn—our company and comfort, the background hum to our daily bacchanal. Saved from ourselves by the sublime idiocy of the movie, we drink and eat through the first half in almost total silence. Then, for dessert, Walker grabs the yellow envelope and fishes out the plastic bag inside. He does two lines but does not offer me any and motions to the couch. We climb over the back, then sit side by side before Walker puts his head in my lap and grabs an afghan for himself. His body makes a perfect fetal arc out of necessity. I have my hand on his chest, his hand draped over mine. We've sat like this a few times, Walker and me, in a pose best described as Mother and Sick Child. We watch the second half of the movie like this—there might as well be tomato soup and grilled cheese in front of us—and when it's over, we stay there. It wouldn't feel unnatural right now to shuffle down the hall and follow Walker into bed. Indeed, our intimacy is like that of a long-married couple, with its routines and slights, its complexity and codependence, even though I've been here less than five months.

Instead, Walker looks up at me from my lap and simply says, "Sleep on it."

"Sounds like a plan."

Walker gets up and grabs my rifle from behind the counter and hands it to me. "Get home safe."

"I will."

"I'll have my eye on you."

"I know."

We walk out to the threshold of the breezeway. The sky is holding a million stars, and the moon is holding court. When I face Walker, I lean in, eyes closed, almost as a reflex. The kiss comes like a sigh, with no urgency or desperation. Only tenderness. When I touch Walker's face, when my lips feel his, there is nothing but softness.

CHAPTER 26

The next morning at the cabin, Claudia puts on a pot of coffee and slides onto the table a blue Bic lighter, two unopened cigarette packs, and a large, clean glass ashtray straight out of *The Big Sleep*. "We need to talk."

"Looks like we're going to be here for a while. Should I eat first? Call a lawyer?" Cigarettes and coffee might be breakfast for Claudia, but I occasionally need real food.

"Well, definitely eat. I'll be back in a minute."

I pour myself a bowl of Raisin Bran and open both packs of cigarettes. Claudia comes back into the room with a brown paper bag and tosses it on the table. I can't see what's inside it, but it lands with a heavy thud.

"We'll get to that in a minute." She lights up a cigarette and crosses her legs. Claudia is decked out in her signature wardrobe: faded jeans, which she calls dungarees, and a loose-fitting top. Today her hair is in two braids, making her look like a hippie Heidi or a weathered Pippi Longstocking. I light up a cigarette for myself, which is Claudia's cue to begin.

"I need to know your plans."

"Right now?"

"Yes."

"Right this second?"

"Yes."

"Why? Why does everyone need to know what I'm doing right this second?"

"If you're leaving, we need to get another assistant."

"Just like that? Just hand the vat of aspirin to someone else?"

"We have to keep things moving. You know we're in trouble."

I take a long drag off the cigarette. Claudia's demeanor betrays the weight of the eight assistants who have come and gone with this book. Real worry passes over her face like a shadow.

"Okay. If you are asking me to answer you this second, I'm leaving."

"Why?"

"I don't know, I feel like I'm being pushed."

"Sorry, but there isn't a week here to spare while you get overly dramatic about a little cut." This is the first time Claudia has taken a tone with me. If familiarity breeds contempt, I am now officially familiar.

"Oh, really."

"Really."

"This isn't a good enough reason to leave?" I point to my eye.

"Around here? No. That's like a baptism." The coffeemaker starts sputtering, and Claudia gets up and pours two mugs full. She takes hers black but tosses the half-and-half on the table for me. "Do you know that Walker shot at me once? *Shot at me!* He wasn't trying to miss either. He grazed my leg."

"I'm sorry. Is that supposed to make me feel better about staying? Is this what I have to look forward to? Hoping for a superficial flesh wound?"

"Maybe."

"You told me when I got here that he would never really hurt me. That you never felt unsafe."

"That's still true. I repeat: you have a little cut over your eye."

It's amazing to me that these millimeters matter for Claudia—that there is a difference, in her mind, between a graze on her leg and a bullet hole through her thigh. She seems to view these near misses as precise and intentional rather than a product of dumb, drunken luck.

"With all due respect, Claudia, I think you're missing the big picture here. I'd start worrying about all of these guns if I were you."

"Please, Alley. Nothing is going to happen."

"It's not necessarily us I'm worried about."

Claudia inhales on her cigarette and lets out a short, sharp breath. She wraps her arms around herself so she looks either like a defiant child or like an old woman who's been left out in the cold. It's obviously not the first time this idea has crossed her mind, but Claudia has not survived this long out here by obsessing on what-ifs. What's in front of her is a mound of debt and an unfinished book.

"You're safe here," she says finally.

"Relatively speaking, I suppose you're right. It just doesn't feel that way."

"Don't you see: Walker only does stuff like this to the people he trusts—the people he thinks won't leave him. The people he likes. It's like the kid who gives shit to his parents because he knows they'll always love him."

"You think he'd really respect me if I stayed?"

"Trust me. He won't respect you if you go. He'll think you're chickenshit." Claudia punctuates this sentiment with a hard flick of her ash.

Claudia and I both hold our cigarettes the same way, with one arm folded over our midsection, supporting the elbow of the arm holding the cigarette. If we were both prettier, we'd look like models at a cocktail party, but in the confines of our spartan kitchen—the beige curtains yellowing on the inside, the cheap oak table and chairs—we're more like dormmates on a reluctant camping trip.

"Do you know that since you've been out here—almost five months—you've gotten one hundred and forty pages out of Walker? That's more than anyone has in the past two years . . . combined. Eight assistants."

"Yeah, I keep hearing about these eight assistants. What the hell happened to them? Are they buried under the range? Why did *they* leave?"

"Let's see: the first couldn't hang, second got engaged, third went a little crazy, fourth fell in love, fifth got another job, sixth was only out here to work on a tell-all, seventh was a whiner, and eighth was an idiot."

"Sounds like I'm in good company."

"You're at least getting pages."

"So what? They're not any good. He puts a piece of paper in the typewriter, starts pecking away. It's gibberish. I might as well be blindfolding him and turning him around three times with the state he's in when he tries to write."

"They're good enough. That's what Lionel says. And he'd tell me."

"Good enough—after I rewrite. I mean, now that I know that you know, let's cut the crap. Walker told me he knows about my edits. So you know I'm rewriting . . . a lot. But I'm still only rewriting to, like, a B-. I'm not even making it very good. He's shot, Claude."

"You rewrite to a B-. Lionel makes it an A. All good."

Claudia grinds the last of her cigarette into the ashtray. All of her smoking idiosyncrasies are violent: She inhales like it's her dying breath. She exhales like she's trying to exorcise something. She ashes like she's mad. And when the cigarette is done, she folds it in two and crushes it like a spider she's trying to kill.

"And look. If it weren't you rewriting him to a B-, it would be someone else along the line. That's how these things work, kiddo. A lot of mouths get fed by the Walker Reade brand—book publishers, agents, magazine editors, movie studios, audiobook producers. Christ, the man single-handedly keeps Tilley Hats and the Woody Creek Tavern in business. So what if the past ten years it's been a steady decline? What the hell do you expect? I mean, he's not living it anymore. There's no road trip anymore. He's holed up here being high and paranoid. Let's just say it. Do you really think he planned on living this long?"

"I honestly don't know how he has."

"So let's take this to its logical conclusion. You leave, and what are you going to do back East? Take some shitty job to make enough money to move back to the city and do what? Sling more drinks? Grind away at some magazine? Stay at your parents'? Help clean the house? Plumb?" This last word comes out of Claudia's mouth slathered in contempt.

"I can get a real job, you know. I have a degree. I have *this* under my belt now."

"Yeah, but how much is *this* really going to matter? No one wants a quitter."

"Is that what you tell yourself every day here, Claude, to get yourself through?"

"You bet," she says proudly, almost defiantly.

"So what's in the bag?"

"Open it."

I reach into the bag and am hardly surprised to pull out my manuscript. I figured it was in there. Still, deep reservoirs of relief wash over me as I feel its weight in my hands. I want to check for each page, as someone would the number of bills for a ransom. I want to make sure every word is there. But when I do so, flipping through the sheets, it appears the manuscript has been defiled, with red, blue, and green scratchings on every page. It's like Walker let a child get at it—or worse, Arlo. Then it dawns on me: this scrawl is in Walker's hand. He's edited my book.

Notes, line edits, structural suggestions, all are arranged and color-coded. The penmanship appears to be the work of a drowning man attempting to write underwater. But the edits are coherent. Professional. Incisive. Walker Fucking Reade has edited my book.

"This is what he's been spending his nights doing after you leave. He said it needs some work, but that he would hand this to Lionel in a second."

"If I stay?"

"If you stay."

"Where I come from, they call that bribery."

"That's what we call it around here, too. I'm not trying to sugarcoat it," she says, lighting up another cigarette. "He was impressed, by the way. That's not an easy thing to do."

It's all a bit much to process. "One more night to sleep on it?" I say, buying time. "I'll let you know tomorrow."

"Fair enough."

I excuse myself and head back to the bedroom, anxious to look through what Walker has done. As I leaf through, I can't help but imagine Walker's hands on these pages—my pages. Walker Reade has ripped apart my manuscript, which means Walker

Reade cared enough to rip apart my manuscript. His comments shed light on everything that is clearly missing. There are massive cuts. Some hilarious line edits. It's a revelation.

I sit there for hours, studying each comment as if it's encrypted—that it holds some truth I'm too young or dumb to understand. Which is just about the size of it. About halfway through, one comment in particular catches my eye. It says simply: "You're better than this." It's attached to a romantic passage—and I'm not sure if it is addressing the quality of the writing or the quality of the sentiments expressed. The phrase toggles around in my head until I've looked at it from all angles. From each angle it looks and feels different. It registers that I've never heard this from my family—indeed, it's almost always the opposite from them: you can't think you're too good where I come from. I never heard it from any professor, all of whom gingerly sleepwalked through my essays and short stories, doling out measured praise and A-minuses. It feels like the biggest thing that's ever been said to me. Maybe because it's the first time it's ever been said to me. I hug the manuscript to my chest like I'm taking in a lover. And in an instant, my decision becomes glaringly, comically, obvious.

CHAPTER 27

Nine years later I will hear about Walker—with New York still burning and me seven months pregnant, towels tucked into the window frames, worried about how that unforgettable stench might affect my unborn child. I'll sit there a long time staring online. There will be Walker's face, in signature Tilley hat and sunglasses, surrounded by stories about Al Qaeda and anthrax—anything unrelated to 9/11 buried deep within the news, even though it's been a month since the attacks. The obit headline will be simple: "Walker Reade, Author of *Biker*, *Liar's Dice*, Dead at 61." Before I even click on the link, I'll know, the image flashing to mind the one from the range. The night that could well have been this night, had there been one more bullet in the chamber.

Walker will have been on my mind, a political website having just published a piece of his about the attacks—a half-paranoid rant peppered with a litany of crazy-sounding predictions and insights that would ultimately bear fruit. I will have wished, as I read the piece, that Walker and I had stayed in touch after I left. But leaving the farm would be like leaving Mars. Unless you were there to help run the colony, you were out.

Before the e-mails start coming in, and the smattering of calls, my thoughts will turn to Claudia. I'll know—as sure as I know anything—that the story in the papers will not be the real story, but I'll click on the obit anyway. Among the ten works cited, there will be *Roadhouse*. Our baby. The one that ultimately took another year to finish. The one I stayed for—the only one I could handle before I left, for the sake of my sanity and my sobriety. In the Walker Reade oeuvre, it will have been deemed a minor trifle, but hardly an embarrassment. There would be the two more after that, which Walker did with another assistant, a twenty-six-year-old whom he later married. By then Hollywood would have gotten hip to Walker, one famously eccentric young character actor, Tommy Jagger, having claimed Larry Lucas's seat in the Colorado version of musical couch cushions—and parlayed that position into a starring role in the movie version of *Liar's Dice*. All of a sudden there would be plenty of money, and the legacy would be secured. But in the end, it was never about either of those things.

My husband will call. "Did you hear? Are you okay?"

"It was so long ago. Like a decade. I'm fine. Sad. It's just . . . sad."

It will be hard, in that moment, to conjure normal memories—the ones that come will be more tactile than abstract. Memories that I could more easily taste than re-create in my head: the bite of the Chivas, the bitterness of the cocaine, the sour-sweetness of the key lime pie. The feel of his lips, all of the uncertainty and fear that followed me like a shadow. I'll recall how Walker, when I declared it was time for me to go, set me free into the hands of Lionel Gray, letting me take my reward. And how my baby—my first one, I should say—*Pegasus*, took flight in Lionel's hands. My two subsequent babies would fare respectably, again, with Lionel steering the ship, and I'll be trying to finish my fourth novel before my actual baby is due in December. But on this day, I'll be expected to run a meeting at the women's magazine where I'm the managing editor. So I will ride up the elevator in my building in SoHo, carrying a dozen doughnuts for the troops.

Coworkers will greet me. Some will know about the time I spent out at Walker's. Some will not. Some will just not care. Some will rub my belly. Some will still be grieving. Some still won't have shown up, even though it will have been four weeks since the attacks. At the conference table, I will scan the faces. The anxiety on each will be different shades—but everyone will be wearing it. It will not be lost on me that Walker will have picked this time to bow out. *The bastards will rob the store blind.*

"Meeting's off," I'll say, before it has even started. "Let's just get to work."

I will make my way outside again—restless and, at seven months pregnant, hungry all the time. I'll head up toward Washington Square to a Vietnamese sandwich shop I've become obsessed with, even though it's only ten in the morning. They'll make me a *banh mi*, extra pork. The second I step outside, The Smell will get inside my nose—our offices being less than twenty blocks from where the unspeakable pile is still burning. Because I'm pregnant, I will be able to smell The Smell and categorize each note, like some diabolical perfumer: the computer, the paper, the leather and plastic and cloth, the awful smell of humanity. I will make my way up to Washington Square Park, grab the sandwich, and go look at the pictures of the missing plastered like wallpaper on the arch.

A month after the attack, there will still be so many of these pictures, even though the rains will have come and gone. All of these flyers will say these people are "missing," which will seem so odd to me. New Yorkers don't typically traffic in false hope—we live here for the reality that was perhaps so sorely missing in our young lives. For the smack in the face of truth. *These people are not just going to show up*, I will think to myself. *They're gone.* This thought will cling to me as I amble back downtown, my brown paper bag banging against my leg like a funeral drum, surrounded by chaos and sorrow and life—the thrill of it, the fear of it. It will feel like that first time I held the .44 on Walker's range, him behind me, holding me close, taking aim at the target we were going to blow up together. I will feel his breath, and I will hear him whisper, *You won't miss with this, sweetheart. You won't miss with this.*

ACKNOWLEDGMENTS

Thank you to my agent, Gary Morris, my editor, Lauren Spiegel, Sally Kim, and the team at Touchstone.

The following people either provided me a quiet place to write, read my book, took my picture, provided moral support, or did all of the above: Michael Callahan, Jen-Scott Mobley, Mark Ransom, Larry Smith, Piper Kerman, Helen Barnard, Will Freshwater, Barbara Gogan, Marla Garfield, Jenny Smith, and Dan Marano.

To my family: Jack and Joan Della Pietra, Lynn Della Pietra, Pat and Julia Grugan, Lynn Edwards and Peter Klein, and Dennis and Jenny Wenger.

To my brave, strong TJ: Thanks for showing Mom how it's done.

To my husband, Ty: Thank you for your steady hand, editorial guidance, patience, generosity, and humor. Thank you for not flinching during this best-worst year. Thank you for holding my hand through it all.

And to Hunter: Thank you for reminding me, as you often did, that "a day without fun is a day that eats shit."